Murder in the Bayou Boneyard

Also available by Ellen Byron

CAJUN COUNTRY MYSTERIES

Fatal Cajun Festival

Mardi Gras Murder

A Cajun Christmas Killing

Body on the Bayou

Plantation Shudders

Murder in the Bayou Boneyard

A CAJUN COUNTRY MYSTERY

Ellen Byron

CROOKED
LANE

NEW YORK

Copyright © 2020 by Ellen Byron

Published in the United States by Crooked Lane Books, an imprint of The Quick Brown Fox & Company LLC.

Crooked Lane Books and its logo are trademarks of The Quick Brown Fox & Company LLC.

Library of Congress Catalog-in-Publication data available upon request.

ISBN (hardcover): 978-1-64385-460-1
ISBN (ebook): 978-1-64385-461-8

Cover design by Stephen Gardner

Printed in the United States.

www.crookedlanebooks.com

Crooked Lane Books
34 West 27th St., 10th Floor
New York, NY 10001

First Edition: September 2020

10 9 8 7 6 5 4 3 2 1

*Dedicated to the man who sees
me more but talks to me less.
I couldn't do this without you.*

The People of Bayou Boneyard

The Family
Magnolia Marie—"Maggie"—Crozat, our heroine
Tug Crozat—her father
Ninette Crozat—her mother
Grand-mère—her grandmother on her dad's side

The Canadian Relatives
Susannah Crozat MacDowell—Tug's distant cousin
Doug MacDowell—her husband
Johnnie and Bonnie MacDowell—Doug's twenty-
   something twins from a previous marriage

Pelican PD Law Enforcement
Bo Durand—detective and Maggie's fiancé
Rufus Durand—Pelican PD police chief
Cal Vichet—officer
Artie Belloise—officer

Ville Blanc PD Law Enforcement
Zeke Griffith—detective
Rosalie Broussard—detective

Friends, Frenemies, and Locals

Lee Bertrand—service station owner and Gran's fiancé

Ione Savreau—friend and coworker

Mo Heedles—multi-tier marketing skin care maven

Vanessa Fleer MacIlhoney—frenemy turned friend . . . adjacent

Quentin MacIlhoney—defense attorney, Vanessa's fiancé

Helene Brevelle—the town voodoo priestess

Sandy Sechrest—Rufus Durand's girlfriend

Gavin Grody—tech entrepreneur CEO of Rent My Digs

Walter Breem—elderly hermit caretaker of Dupois Plantation

Xander Durand—Bo's eight-year-old son

Kaity Bertrand—teen Belle Vista employee; Lee Bertrand's great-granddaughter

Brianna Poche—high school student and helper at Crozat Plantation

JJ—proprietor of Junie's Oyster Bar and Dance Hall

Robert "Bob" Morrin—local bank president

Patria Heloise—local actress

Crozat Plantation B and B Guests

Emma Fine—stage manager

Barrymore Tuttle—actor

Lovie—parrot

DruCilla—Lovie's pet mom

Assorted others

Prologue

"It's a good thing we lay our departed to rest aboveground," Gran whispered to Maggie. "Because if I sunk any further, I'd be standing on a coffin."

A cold rain dripped down on the small group of mourners huddled under their umbrellas in the derelict Louisiana graveyard. They listened politely as Father Prit led prayers for Etienne Dupois, an octogenarian who had died during a randy romp with a fellow resident at the Camellia Park Senior Village. No one at the grave site was related to Etienne, a man whose only goal seemed to have been throwing an endless party while the Dupois home crumbled and its famed gardens were reclaimed by vines, weeds, and snakes. Still, Etienne was a Dupois, and his ancestry meant something in tiny Pelican, Louisiana, which is why the feet of a small portion of the town's citizenry—including Maggie, her parents, and her grand-mère—were sinking into the muddy ground of the Dupois family's centuries-old resting place.

As Father Prit continued the service in his thick Indian accent, Maggie snuck a few subtle glances at the cemetery's ornate tombs and mausoleums. A century and a half earlier, the Dupois family had been the richest in Cajun Country, and their famed ostentation didn't end with death. Every burial chamber in the graveyard featured ornate stone carvings or a life-size statue, some dignified, at least one not even close. The tomb next to the recently departed Etienne boasted the statue of a fan dancer, his great lost love. Not lost to death—bored with the country life, the fan dancer beat it weeks after tying the knot. Etienne, his heart broken, commissioned the tomb to memorialize the death of his one brief marriage, and segued into a life of mild debauchery.

Maggie shivered, but not from the early-September cold snap. She found the Dupois family plot disturbing. With no family members left to maintain it, the once-grand cemetery was now falling apart, its demise hastened by vandalism on the part of local miscreant teens. Statues were missing limbs, stained-glass windows in the fanciest crypt were broken, and anything of value had been stolen. In the gardens beyond the cemetery, the most famous in the country a hundred and fifty years ago, stone bridges and paths were slowly disintegrating into piles of pebbles and dust. The stately but run-down Dupois mansion loomed over the entire property, a ghost of its former self. In its day, it had been the region's grandest house, but no one had lived there since Etienne decamped to the senior village years earlier.

"*Place him in the region of peace and light,*" Father Prit read, "*And bid him be partaker with Thy Saints. Through Christ our Lord. Amen.*"

"Amen," the assemblage responded, and immediately began disbanding.

"I'm not the only one who finds this place creepy, am I?" Ninette, Maggie's mother, asked.

"No!" everyone chorused.

"We paid our respects," Gran said. "Now let's give Etienne the send-off he would have really wanted. A round, or two or three, of cocktails." This earned an even more fervent "Amen" from Maggie.

A loud cracking sound caught everyone's attention. "Is that thunder?" Maggie asked, looking at the glowering clouds crowding the late-afternoon sky.

"No. It's Lulu."

Tug, Maggie's father, pointed at the cemetery. The fan dancer had fallen from the top of her tomb, knocking over Etienne's statue and toppling both to the ground, where they were locked in a stone embrace.

"Etienne got in death what he couldn't get in life," Gran said. "Eternity in the arms of his sweetheart."

"Let's get out of here before the graveyard is swallowed up by some kind of paranormal sinkhole," Maggie said.

Her family, as eager to escape as she was, followed her to the Crozat bed-and-breakfast minivan. Tug hoisted himself into the driver's seat. He turned on the gas and accelerated. Soon the cemetery was in the rearview mirror. "At least with Etienne gone," Tug said as he drove, "we'll never have to set foot in that cursed place again."

It would only take a few weeks to prove him wrong.

Chapter 1

"You hate Halloween?" There was disbelief laced with amusement in Bo Durand's voice as he repeated what his fiancée Maggie had just confessed to him. "Who hates Halloween?"

The couple was putting the finishing touches on Crozat Plantation's brand-new spa, due to open in a few days. Once a lackluster 1920s-era garage, the building now also housed Bo and Maggie's future home, a spacious apartment above the spa facilities. Damage from a massive flood that inundated Pelican almost doomed the project, but the Crozats refused to give up on their dream of offering guests to their ancestral home—turned—B and B a pampering option.

Maggie focused on the fluffy white towel she was folding, embarrassed by her phobia. There wasn't a holiday Pelican didn't celebrate with massive gusto, but Halloween ranked at the top of the list, along with Christmas and Mardi Gras. Hating the holiday in a state that proudly billed itself as the most haunted in America was downright sacrilege. "I know it seems nuts, but I've always found it . . . I don't know . . . a little sinister and malevolent. Well, at least since I was nine. Some older kids dared me to sneak into the Dubois cemetery on Halloween night. I didn't want to look like a scaredy cat—"

"An expression I haven't heard since I was nine."

Maggie playfully swatted her handsome beau with a towel. "Anyway, I snuck in and was feeling all proud of myself when a rougarou jumped out from behind a tomb and roared at me," she said, referencing the Cajun version of a werewolf. "I thought I was gonna be the first Pelican nine-year-old to die of a heart attack. I screamed and ran home. After that, I trick-or-treated for a couple more years, but only with my mom and dad. I was terrified a rougarou would jump out from behind a tree or a car. When I was eleven, I stopped going out on Halloween at all."

"You do know that the rougarou is a mythical creature? There's no such thing, so it had to be some kid playing a trick on you."

"I'm not saying my fear is logical. It just left me with a bad feeling about Halloween." Maggie added the towel she'd folded to the stack on a freshly painted shelf behind the reception area. "I never should have told you."

Bo put down the towel he was folding and took Maggie in his arms. "I'm sorry—I shouldn't have teased you. I'm sad that you lost the fun of it. But I promise you will get it back when you come trick-or-treating with Xander and me this year."

Xander was Bo's eight-year-old son from his first marriage, and Maggie adored him. She gave Bo a warm smile. "If anything could make me rediscover how much fun Halloween can be, it's seeing it through Xander's eyes."

Bo released Maggie and went to put his folded towel on another shelf. Maggie stopped him. "That's where Mo's skin care line will go," she said, referring to friend who'd created her own line of products. Mo had also gotten an aesthetician's license and would be providing facials at the Crozat spa when she wasn't manning the reception area.

"That's my last towel," Bo said.

"Then we're done for now."

Maggie stepped back to survey the reception area. The walls were painted a soothing sage green with light-yellow trim. A couch and two lounge chairs upholstered in a soft violet were adorned with throw pillows covered in a fabric featuring all three of the room's signature Mardi Gras colors, but in muted shades. Across from the seating area, water gently cascaded over rocks in a fountain, providing the room with a soothing sound. A diffuser perfumed the air with the scent of camellia blossoms. Maggie breathed in the fragrance, loving it. "All we need is for our massage therapist to arrive, and we're set for the first weekend of Pelican's Spooky Past."

Bo squeezed Maggie's hand. "Another epic brainstorm from my brilliant—and gorgeous—fiancée."

Maggie laughed. "You flatter me on both counts. I just hope my idea works." A few months prior, she'd noticed that Crozat B and B's bookings were down. She'd traced the decline to a new app called Rent My Digs. Additional research revealed that Gavin Grody, the app's creator, was buying local housing and turning it into "owner" rentals. His venture was eating up a lot of affordable housing stock, as well as taking a toll on all the St. Pierre Parish hostelries. To combat this, Maggie joined forces with four other B and Bs to create a package she titled Pelican's Spooky Past, scheduled to run every weekend in October. Much as she disliked all things Halloween, she knew a great marketing opportunity when she saw one.

Each of the B and Bs was offering an event that capitalized on the Halloween traditions of the region—the emphasis being on the historical past, not the recent spate of murders that had bedeviled the small town. The Crozats chose the tamest themes possible for their events: food and crafts. Ninette planned on creating a meal featuring dishes that antebellum hosts might have served guests paying a condolence call during the Creole and Cajun cultures' extended period of mourning. Maggie and Grand-mère had put together a workshop that would teach their visitors how to construct *immortelles*—cemetery arrangements made from dried flowers, beads, and ceramics that were meant to be an "immortal" memorial to the dead. Maggie was thrilled by the enthusiasm generated by the Spooky Past packages. Several of the weekends had already sold out.

Bo checked the time on his cell phone. "I need to pick up Xander from school. We're going shopping for a costume."

"Does he know what he wants to be?"

"Either Aquaman, Captain America, the Hulk, a Transformer, an X-Man, a Guardian of the Galaxy . . . should I go on?"

Maggie laughed and held up her hands. "No need, I get it."

She and Bo walked to the front of the Crozat manor house. With a march of tall, square columns encircling the home, Crozat was the River Road's most iconic example of Greek Revival architecture. In keeping with the weekend packages' theme, skeletons currently occupied the Adirondack chairs on Crozat's wide veranda, and "cobwebs" hung over the Spanish moss dripping from the allée of centuries-old oak trees. Fake gravestones decorated the spacious front lawn, along with the remnants of a "witch" who had crashed into them. "Congrats on the decorations, by the way," Bo said.

"Ooh, wait until you hear this."

Maggie dashed up the plantation's front steps and pressed the doorbell. A loud shriek rang out, followed by a *bwaha-ha-ha* evil laugh. "Awesome, huh?"

"Uh-huh," Bo said, a little hesitant. "But I'm guessing after about the fifth time, that awesome's gonna turn into annoying."

Maggie grabbed a skeleton off an Adirondack chair and held it in front of her. "Just for that, the only kiss goodbye you're gonna get is from Bertha Bones here." She spoke in a breathy voice. "Hey, handsome, pucker up."

Bo shook his head, amused. "I'll leave you girls to yourselves. Call you later."

He got into his SUV and headed down the long drive from the manor house to the River Road. The home's front door opened, and Barrymore Tuttle poked his head out. Barrymore, a man of wide girth in his midsixties, was an insurance salesman–turned–actor in the mystery play Belle Vista Plantation Resort was offering as part of their Pelican's Spooky Past package. Each of the participating B and Bs had agreed to house a member of the show's cast and crew. When it came to pompous Barrymore, the Crozats had drawn the short straw.

"I was hoping that doorbell ring meant your massage therapist had arrived," the actor said in his carefully cultivated basso profundo theatre voice.

"Not yet," Maggie said, forcing a cheery tone. "She and her family will be here tomorrow."

"Hmm." Barrymore frowned, then cracked his neck. "My instrument is sore from the acrobatics of rehearsal."

"I didn't know you played an instrument." Maggie, sick of hearing the affected actor refer to his body as his *instrument*, couldn't resist baiting him.

Barrymore gestured to himself with both hands. "This. My body. The vessel for my craft."

A groan came from behind him. "Oh, please." Emma Fine, the production's young stage manager, who was also being housed at Crozat, appeared next to Barrymore in the doorway. "If I had a dollar for every time you said *instrument* or *vessel*, I could afford not to work with you anymore. And you do know you have to pay for that massage, right?"

"I assumed it was part of the services being offered to the performers," Barrymore said, over-articulating each word as if performing a Shakespearean soliloquy.

"It's not," Maggie said.

"Then, if you need me, I'll be running a warm bath." With this, Barrymore took a bow and disappeared into the house.

Maggie suppressed the urge to applaud his exit. "Thank you for that," she said to Emma.

She sat on the veranda swing and motioned for the stage manager to join her, which Emma did. "Twits like Barrymore give all actors a bad name," Emma said as the two women rocked back and forth. "I want to scream every time he tells someone"—Emma launched into a perfect imitation—"'With a name like Barrymore, how could I *not* be an actor?' I love pointing out that up until a month ago, he was selling insurance at a used-car lot. And he's a total mooch. I hate that."

"Well, to show my gratitude, I'm gifting *you* with a massage," Maggie said. "And making sure Barrymore knows yours *is* free."

"Excellent," Emma responded with a chortle. She pulled a pack of gum out of her pocket and unwrapped a piece, which she popped into her mouth. "Your grandmother told me the massage therapist is your cousin."

"Distant, but yes. She's from the side of the family that was in Louisiana for a while in the mid-1800s, then went back to Canada. Her husband got in touch with us for a genealogy project he was doing for her birthday. We started corresponding, and when I found out Susannah was a masseuse, I floated the idea of her working with us as part of our Halloween package."

"That was nice of you."

Maggie shrugged, embarrassed. "Maybe. Also a little self-serving. We don't have much family, so I was excited about meeting her. The spa where Susannah worked in Toronto went out of business, so the timing was perfect. She's coming with her husband Doug and his two adult kids from his first marriage. It'll give us all a chance to get to know each other."

"You're lucky." Emma spit her gum into a wrapper, replacing it with a fresh piece. "I don't talk to my family anymore. They cut me off after my last stint in rehab." She looked down at the ground.

Maggie wondered about the young woman. While only in her midtwenties, she seemed older, like she had already lived a hard life. Her tall body was too slim, her sandy-blonde hair appeared dry and lifeless, and her skin was more weathered and lined than it should have been at her age. "Alcohol?" Maggie asked.

Emma nodded. "And painkillers. I'm off everything now." She replaced the gum she was chewing with yet another piece, then held up the now-empty pack. "Except gum. Substituting one addiction for another. Here's hoping my teeth don't fall out from all the sugar." Her phone pinged a text. She read it and pumped a fist. "Yes!"

"What's up?"

Emma grinned and held up her phone. "Great news. Belle Vista got permission from Etienne Dupois's estate to move the play from their grounds to the Dupois cemetery."

Maggie felt her stomach knot up. "Oh. Okay. But . . . the Belle Vista grounds are so gorgeous. Wouldn't that be a better setting for the play? And you can light them at night. I don't know how you light that old cemetery."

Emma waved a hand dismissively. "We can figure that out. The cemetery is such a better environment for the play. It's all about how one of the Dupoises comes back from the dead. We were gonna have to use fake gravestones like those." Emma motioned to Crozat's Halloween lawn decorations.

"This will be so much better. It'll be environmental theatre, where there's no distinction between the performers' and audience's space. They're all in it together."

"Cool," Maggie said, her tone weak as she envisioned four weekends of shuttling Crozat's guests to the dreaded Dupois graveyard.

Emma jumped up, sending the swing flying back and forth. Maggie used her feet to slow it down. "I've got to go," the stage manager said. "There's a ton to do before rehearsal tonight."

She took off, leaving Maggie to stew over the play's change of venue. What Emma said made sense. Guests would love the cemetery's eerie atmosphere, and the point of all the B and B events was to give guests experiences that no home rental could match. *I'll have to get over my hatred of the place*, Maggie thought to herself.

The front door flew open, revealing Ninette Crozat. "There you are," she said. "I've been calling to you. You didn't hear me?"

Maggie shook her head. "No. Sorry." She noticed her mother looked harried. "Is everything okay?"

"Yes. Well, I guess so." Ninette gave her hands a nervous wipe on the apron she seemed to live in. "I got a call from the Canadians. They're on their way."

Maggie jumped up from the swing. "What? I thought they were coming tomorrow."

"They were, but Susannah said they were so anxious to meet us that they caught an earlier flight. It would have been nice if they told us sooner, but still, isn't this exciting?"

"Yes. Very exciting."

Maggie's strained smile matched her mother's. She followed Ninette into the house to help prepare a warm welcome for their newfound family, brushing aside an ominous sensation.

Chapter 2

Maggie and her father Tug navigated Crozat's cluttered attic in search of one last side chair for Maggie's art studio, which the family had turned into temporary housing for their Canadian guests. "If anything could convince me that ghosts exist, it's this place," Maggie said as she combed through antiques and detritus accumulated over the many decades since the historic home was first built.

She spoke through a dust mask—she and Tug wore them to protect themselves from whatever germs might live in the attic's dusty air. They also wore construction helmets with flashlights attached to guide their way. The only light in the space came from whatever sunlight snuck in through cracks in the old home's beams. A box almost as tall as Maggie stood sentry in the middle of the room. The box's plastic window allowed for a peek at what was carefully packed away inside— a centuries-old wedding gown. Maggie, like generations of women on Ninette's side of the family, would be married in the well-preserved gown stored in the manor house attic, first worn by a Doucet bride almost two hundred years earlier.

Maggie adored the gown, which was a stunning confection of silk taffeta and lace that had been carefully preserved by each bride who preceded her. She would have it fitted, wear it once, then preserve it for future generations of Doucet women.

Maggie walked past the gown to a cluster of furniture. She pulled sheets off a set of beautifully needle-pointed matching chairs. "These are gorgeous."

"Too nice for guests, family or not," Tug said. "Save them for your apartment." He pulled out a rocking chair carved from maple wood with a cane back and seat. "This is perfect. Let's go. We don't have much time."

He took the chair, and Maggie followed him out of the attic, locking the door behind her as well as she could. It was old, and the knob felt loose in her hand. They climbed down the narrow stairs to the second floor, where they were met by Gran. She held up two peach fabric swatches. "Which do you like better?" she asked Maggie.

Maggie took off her mask. "They look exactly the same to me."

"They're not." Gran held up one. "This is light peach." She held up the other. "And this is pale peach. Try to imagine each shade decorating every table at our wedding."

"I know an exit line when I hear one," Tug said. He escaped with the rocking chair.

Maggie eyed the samples her grandmother thrust in front of her. Having happily agreed to a joint wedding on New Year's Eve with Gran and her fiancé, service station owner Lee Bertrand, Maggie was just as happy that Gran had hijacked the wedding planning. Left to herself, Maggie would have eloped with Bo. But Grand-mère, who had married Maggie's late grandfather on a train platform before he shipped out to serve in the Korean War, had her heart set on a big shindig for her second time around. She even tried to paint it as an act of altruism. "The Crozat and Durand families coming together with you and Bo? We can't deprive Pelican of its version of a royal wedding." Maggie saw through the ruse but couldn't say no to her beloved grandmother. Given the go-ahead, Gran was all in on everything from table linens to favors. Watching her grandmother become an almost-bridezilla was proving to be entertaining.

"I trust your taste, Gran," Maggie said. "You pick. The Canadians will be here any minute. I need to focus on that. We all should."

"Yes, of course." Gran took turns holding each sample up to the light.

Maggie left her grandmother to the pale-peach-versus-light-peach dilemma and scurried downstairs. She dashed out the manor house's back door to the shotgun cottage she shared with Gran, where she took a quick shower to rid herself of attic grime. She put on a clean pair of jeans and an olive T-shirt that brought out the green in her hazel eyes, then brushed her thick thatch of wavy brown hair and headed back to the manor house. Maggie was about to go in when she heard a car coming up the old road that ran alongside the plantation grounds. A nondescript sedan made a left into the Crozat family's personal parking area. Maggie felt a flush of anxiety. *Stop feeling nervous*, she scolded herself. *They're family. It's going to be great!* She added the exclamation mark in her mind to really sell it, then pulled open the back screen door and called inside to her parents, "They're here."

Tug and Ninette hurried out the door. "Apron," Maggie reminded her mother.

"Yes, right." Ninette, who seemed as nervous as Maggie felt, untied her apron and tossed it behind her.

The sedan parked in the small graveled lot. A middle-aged man with gray-tinged strawberry-blond hair and a wide, toothy grin emerged from the driver's side of the car. "Hello there," he called to the Crozats. "Doug MacDowell and the gang here." He leaned into the car and yelled, "Susie, every-one, get the lead out."

Two twentysomethings, one male and one female, emerged from the back seat, each clutching a cell phone in one hand. Finally, a small, lithe, woman who appeared to be in her forties to Doug's late fifties, exited the car. This had to be Susannah Crozat MacDowell, the family's distant cousin. Maggie searched the woman's blonde coloring and delicate features for a family resemblance and found none.

"Hello, or should I say *bonjour*?" Susannah said with a small smile and wave.

"Either works with us," Tug said. "Welcome, cuz. Welcome."

The two families approached each other, meeting in the middle of the lot. After a round of awkward handshakes and hugs, Ninette said, "Come into the main house. We'll give you a tour and then celebrate with cocktails."

"If you don't mind, I'd rather rest first," Susannah said. "The flight here was a bit of a bear. We had to make two stops."

"I'm so sorry," was Ninette's automatic response to the hint of reproach in Susannah's tone. Maggie refrained from saying to her mother, *Why are* you *sorry?*

"No problem," Tug said. "We'll get you settled in, then rendezvous for dinner."

"Sounds like a plan," Doug said with geniality. "Johnnie, Bonnie, look alive. Say hello."

The twentysomethings reluctantly tore their attention away from their phones. "Hello," they said in unison.

"My twins," Doug explained.

"From his first marriage," Johnnie said. He exchanged a look with Bonnie, and both cast a baleful glance at their stepmother. The duo, who had inherited their father's strawberry-blond coloring, had matching pale-blue eyes that reminded Maggie of the terrifying children in *Village of the Damned*, an old horror movie an ex-boyfriend once made her watch. Maggie debated which she found more macabre: the film or the weird twins in front of her.

Tug, determined to dispel the tension, clapped his hands together and announced in a jovial tone, "Well, *suis-moi*. That means, follow me." Johnnie and Bonnie engaged in a conversation with each other in French, speaking too fast for Maggie to understand. "Right," her father said, embarrassed. "You speak French."

Doug popped the trunk. "Ignore the twins; they're a couple of a-holes." Ninette stifled a gasp at the man's description of his offspring. "Everyone grab a bag. Susiebell, I'll get yours."

"Thank you, my love." She held up her hands, which were thin to the point of bony. "I have to protect these. They're my livelihood."

One of Susie's stepchildren—Maggie wasn't sure which one—snorted. She did wonder how the woman's delicate hands could pummel muscles for hours on end, but Susannah had presented glowing references from two previous employers. Maggie shook off her doubts and pulled a suitcase out of the trunk. The group began their traipse through the woods to the plantation's schoolhouse–turned–Maggie's art studio–turned–MacDowell accommodations.

At six PM, the MacDowells joined their hosts in the mansion's front parlor. Maggie made sure to greet each MacDowell with a full glass of wine. She introduced the family to Bo, who was kitted out in a blazer and tie, which, given the number of times he'd tugged on his collar, he clearly hated. After a moment, Grand-mère wafted in, followed by a trail of gardenia perfume, and there was another round of introductions. "This couldn't be more exciting, could it?" She held the two peach fabric swatches up to Bonnie, who clutched a wineglass in one hand and her omnipresent cell phone in the other. "This or this?" Gran asked.

Bonnie pointed to one of the swatches with her wineglass. "This."

"I like her," Gran announced to all. She accepted a Sazerac from Tug, thanked her son, and took a seat.

Maggie passed a platter of Crawtatoes, an appetizer invention of her mother's consisting of new potatoes stuffed with a crawfish filling. There was a lull in the conversation. "How exactly are y'all related?" Bo asked, mostly to fill the silence. "Maggie told me, but I don't remember."

"My several-times-great-grandfather was the brother of Tug's several-times-great-grandfather," Susannah said. "He came to Louisiana from Canada in the early 1800s and bought land that abuts Crozat Plantation, then decided to return to Canada. He wasn't a fan of the humidity."

"Who is?" Gran said, sipping her Sazerac. "It's our cross to bear in this otherwise glorious state."

"Susie's family still owns the land," Doug piped in. "Thought we'd check it out for our senior years. Trade Celsius for Fahrenheit, eh?"

Gran giggled. "You said *eh*. That's adorable."

"How strong did you make her drink?" Maggie murmured to her father, who rolled his eyes.

"It'd be nice to have family as neighbors," Ninette said as she topped off Doug's wineglass. "Your business must be doing well if you're thinking about retirement."

"Can't complain. I own a couple of print shops."

Doug directed this to Bo, who nodded politely. "Ah." Bo turned to the twins. "What about you? Are you in the family business?"

"God, no," the twins said in unison.

Bonnie held up her phone. "I'm a lifestyle blogger. An influencer."

"Translation: unemployed," Doug said.

"*Daaaad*," Bonnie whined.

Johnnie held up his wineglass. "And I'm a poet."

"Translation: also unemployed." Doug drained his glass.

"You always belittle the simplicity of my life," Johnnie snapped at his father.

"Simple as it may be, your father is the one who pays the bills for it," Susannah said to her stepson, who responded with an ugly glare.

A timer in the kitchen dinged. "Dinner's ready," Ninette said.

She jumped up and practically ran out of the room. The others followed. Maggie pulled Bo back. "Tell me I didn't make a terrible mistake hiring Susannah," she said sotto voce.

Bo, uncomfortable emotionally as well as physically, tugged at his collar. "Whoever invented ties hated men."

"And whoever invented bras hated women. We've had this conversation before. Stop stalling. Back to Susannah."

Bo craned his neck, looking into the dining room, where the MacDowells had taken their seats. "You hired Susannah as a massage therapist. That's the make-or-break here. If she's good at her job—and you say she has great recs—you'll be okay."

"*Daaaad*," Bonnie whined again from the dining room.

Maggie downed the contents of her wineglass, then grabbed Bo's and knocked back his. "This could be a very long month."

* * *

Fortunately, Ninette's stellar meal, featuring Shrimp Remoulade, jambalaya, and Bourbon Pecan Bread Pudding, was such a hit with the MacDowells that the family shelved its squabbling. After dinner, Doug, pleading jet lag, retreated to the studio and the twins decided to explore Pelican's "nightlife."

"That's gonna be a real short trip," Bo warned them as they walked to their cars. "You got Junie's Oyster Bar and Dance Hall and . . . that's it."

Maggie gave Susannah a tour of the spa and was heartened by the woman's enthusiasm for the space. "The colors are exactly right, so soothing," the massage therapist said. She picked up a handful of decorative smooth stones from a bowl on the reception desk. "And these will be perfect for my hot-stone massage."

Preparations for the first weekend of Pelican's Spooky Past absorbed Maggie's time and attention for the two days after the MacDowells' arrival. In addition to making sure Crozat had everything the B and B would need for their guests' activities, she finished curating an exhibit of artwork inspired by the supernatural folklore of Doucet Plantation, once the home of Ninette's ancestors, now where Maggie worked as an art restoration specialist. Back at Crozat, Susannah offered Maggie a sample hot-stone massage that proved so rejuvenating it allayed any fears she had about the woman's expertise. The residual relaxation even made actor-slash-freeloader Barrymore Tuttle less annoying.

A jitney loaded with the weekend's first guests pulled up to Crozat midafternoon on Friday. Since Bon Ami Plantation's theme was "Late, Lamented Pets," plus a pet costume parade, some of Crozat's visitors were of the four-legged or feathered variety. Gopher and Jolie—the family's rescue basset hound and Chihuahua mix, respectively—barked greetings to the animals. In keeping with the Halloween theme,

Gopher was dressed as a doggy vampire and Jolie made an adorable canine ghost. "Love the costumes and decorations," Jennifer, a Rubenesque real estate agent from New Orleans, enthused. "Don't we, Benedict?" She directed this to Benedict Cumberpooch, the fluffy Pomeranian she held under her arm.

"Wait until you hear this," Maggie said. She ran up the manor house's front steps and rang the doorbell, which responded with a scream. Jennifer shrieked her joy while the guests laughed and clapped, much to Maggie's pleasure.

Gran was taste-testing wedding cakes at a variety of bakeries in Baton Rouge, so Tug and Maggie showed everyone to their rooms while Ninette prepared a treat of Scary Spicy Cajun Sugar Cookies decorated like bats and pumpkins. By the time the guests reconvened in the front parlor to receive a schedule of the weekend's events along with their cookies, night had fallen. "Tonight you'll have dinner here, and in keeping with the weekend's theme, it will be the kind of traditional meal our ancestors might have served to guests paying their respects to the family after someone passed away," Maggie said. "Tomorrow morning, my grand-mère and I will lead a workshop where you can make your own version of an immortelle, the beaded and dried flower arrangements used to decorate tombs in the old days. You can do any of the events at the other plantations, and we'll be happy to help with transportation. If you're interested, you can also book an appointment for a massage or facial at our brand-new spa."

"I'm up for both," Jennifer, who was fast becoming Maggie's favorite guest, said. "I also made an appointment with Helene Brevelle. I can't wait to hear what she has to say."

"Who's that?" another guest asked.

"Helene is the town voodoo priestess," Maggie said. "Which reminds me, we can also help you attend church services Sunday morning, if you'd like." It wasn't unusual for a Pelican resident to mention the voodoo priestess in the same breath as a priest or pastor. All were considered equal in the little Cajun village.

Dinner passed quickly, with the usual kudos for Ninette's cooking. "I'm so looking forward to this weekend," Jennifer told Maggie after the other guests said their good-nights. "I'm gonna take Benedict for a short poo walk, then hit the sack."

"If you or Benedict need anything, let me know," Maggie said.

She bussed the dining room table, bringing a tub of dirty dishes into the kitchen, where she found Gran and Lee. "I must've tasted over two dozen cakes," the octogenarian gas station owner said, patting his stomach. "Wedding planning's way more fun than in the old days, when we said *I do* and moved on with our lives." He kissed Gran on her cheek. "I think I'm crashing from all this sugar, so I'm gonna call it a night."

"Sleep well, dearest," Gran said, favoring Lee with a warm smile.

After Lee departed, Gran gestured to small slices of cake she had laid out on three separate plates. "It wasn't easy, but we managed to narrow down our choices. These are the top three from today's tasting. I'm thinking we could do one cake with three layers, each in a different flavor, like—" A loud scream came from the front of the house. "Someone's at the door."

The scream came again. "That's not a doorbell scream, Gran." Maggie said. "That's an actual scream."

Maggie and Gran rushed from the kitchen through the long front hallway and out the front door. Jennifer ran toward them, clutching Benedict in her arms. She stumbled, and Maggie hurried to catch her before she fell. "Jennifer, what's wrong? What happened?"

"I saw him," the woman gasped.

"Him who?" Maggie asked, bewildered.

"Him." Jennifer trembled. "The *rougarou*."

Chapter 3

Gran put her arm around the frightened woman's shoulders and led her toward the house. "Let's get you and Benedict inside and get you a nip of something. I don't know what you saw out there, but it was obviously terrifying."

"I saw a rougarou," Jennifer insisted. Her tiny dog barked as if to second what she said. "I was born and raised in this state. I know a rougarou when I see one. He had the body of a human but the head of a werewolf, and he was hairy all over, with horrible, sharp teeth. And he had sharp, ugly claws." Jennifer mimed claws with her hands. "His eyes were blood-red, and he snarled at me like this." She clenched her teeth and snarled, prompted teeth-baring growls from her pup.

"I'll go check the woods," Maggie said.

She started toward them, but Jennifer grabbed her arm. "No! It's not safe."

"Whatever it was is probably gone," Gran said.

"I'm telling you, it was a *rougarou*." Now Jennifer sounded angry.

"You know what, I bet you're right," Maggie said, eager to placate a guest who'd already booked two massages and a facial during her stay. "Some high school kid probably thought it would be funny to dress up like a rougarou and scare people."

"A prank?" Jennifer asked, slightly calmer.

"Yes, absolutely," Gran said, grabbing on to Maggie's theory. "Maggie, chère, when we get in, call Bo and report what happened to poor Jennifer. I will not have our guests terrorized."

The women guided Jennifer inside. "I think Benedict and I will go to bed," she said. "I feel better knowing it was probably someone's stupid idea of a joke, but still."

"Of course," Gran said. "You're staying in the Rose Room, correct? That is by far the best room in the house. Did you know the carved ceiling medallions are made of cypress and the design was imported from France by the original architect?"

Gran, extolling the wonders of Crozat, took Jennifer to her room. Maggie retreated to the front parlor, where Emma Fine was making notes on her tablet after a day of rehearsals. "Everything okay? That woman sounded upset."

Maggie poured a glass of wine and collapsed onto the sofa next to Emma. "A guest thought she saw a rougarou."

"A what-arou?" Emma, who hailed from the New York tristate area, asked.

"A kind of werewolf-meets-vampire creature. They're part human, part beast. Once someone's blood is sucked, they have to live a hundred and one days as a rougarou and then can transfer the curse to someone else by sucking *their* blood."

Emma shuddered. "Ugh, I hate that stuff. A hundred and one days seems arbitrary. Why isn't it a hundred days? Or a hundred and ten?"

Maggie shrugged. "Got me. Our ancestors were a superstitious lot. How did rehearsal in the cemetery go?" She asked this to force a change of subject. The last thing Maggie needed was the image of a rougarou emblazoned on her brain.

"Great," Emma said. "It's so atmospheric. The actors really responded to the whole aura of the place. All their performances improved, even that yutz Barrymore." She powered down her tablet. "I'll see you in the morning. Night-night. Don't let the rougarous bite."

The evening's misadventure left Maggie feeling jumpy, but she managed a chuckle for Emma's benefit. As soon as the stage manager departed, Maggie pulled out her cell and called Bo, who listened as she described what had happened. "I do think it was probably some jokester trying to be funny," she said, trying to convince herself of a harmless scenario. "But I don't like someone scaring our guests. It's bad for business."

"I'll let Rufus know," Bo said, referencing the Pelican PD chief who also happened to be his first cousin. "We'll definitely look into it. A stunt like that is bad for Pelican business in general. How are you holding up? You sound stressed."

"I am. The magic of Susannah's massage wore off. I kind of wish I hadn't had the whole Pelican's Spooky Past idea. The whole thing is starting to spook *me*."

"It's a fantastic promotion. Everyone in town is talking about it, especially about how the B and Bs are taking back a chunk of business from the home rentals. It's bad, Maggie.

We finally hired a couple of new officers today, but they can't find places to live in Pelican, so they'll either have to commute or take other jobs. That lowlife Gavin Grody, whoever he is, is buying up all the affordable housing stock. Pelican's finally gonna have to enact zoning laws, but it may be too late by then."

"Well, this conversation won't make me sleep better tonight."

"I'm sorry. Would it help if I said I love you?"

"That always helps. And right back at ya, cher."

She blew a kiss into the phone, which Bo returned, and the call ended.

Maggie's mood improved in the morning. Doug MacDowell joined the guests for breakfast. Susannah was at the spa tending to a client, and the MacDowell twins were mercifully asleep. Without the fractured family dynamics to drag him down, Doug was surprisingly entertaining. The Crozat guests roared when he described some of the printouts he'd found in copy machines his store repaired. "You wouldn't believe the body parts people copy," he said. "Friends, do yourselves a favor and always spray the screen with bleach before putting anything on it, because there's a good chance someone sat on it with their pants down."

The day went so smoothly that Maggie even found the courage to endure the debut performance of *Resurrection of a Spirit*, the loftily titled "theatrical experience" being staged in the Dupois cemetery, which had been written by none other than Pelican defense attorney Quentin MacIlhoney. He'd gotten an assist from his new wife, Vanessa Fleer MacIlhoney, who was Maggie's frenemy and police chief Rufus Durand's ex-fiancée. Vanessa also had a role in the show. "I'm way too young to be playing the mother of a teenager," she griped to Maggie, who had dropped by the cast's makeshift dressing room in the woods to wish her luck. The newly minted actress yanked down her antebellum costume to expose even more of her plentiful cleavage.

"There are women your age around here who are already grandmothers," Maggie pointed out.

Van pulled a shawl over her black gown and scowled at Maggie. "Go away. I need to prepare."

She joined the other actors in making a collection of strange sounds they described as vocal warm-ups. Maggie wended her way to the rows of folding chairs reserved for the audience. Luckily for the attendees, it was a warm night. But clouds covered the moon and the stars, preventing them from providing ambient light, so even with the jerry-rigged stage lighting, the grounds were dark. Maggie stumbled past decrepit old tombs until she reached the seating area. Suddenly she sensed someone watching her. She stopped and turned around. A pair of muddy brown eyes set in the ancient weathered face of an old man stared at her. Maggie gave a shriek, which didn't faze the man. He continued to stare while Maggie stood frozen. Then he disappeared among the theatergoers.

Maggie, adrenaline surging, searched the crowd. She saw Kaity Bertrand, Lee's great-granddaughter who worked as a concierge at Belle Vista, shepherding guests to their seats. The teen, always a fountain of bubbly energy, noticed her and gave an excited wave. She hurried over and threw her arms around Maggie. "The spooky weekend thing was such a good idea," Kaity enthused. "We're full up every weekend in October, and so are the other B and Bs."

"Glad to hear it, but not really focused on that right now. I just had a scary experience. Some strange old man was following me in the woods. I screamed and he went away."

"Was he dressed in kinda old, ratty clothes?"

"I'm not sure. I think so."

"It was probably Walter Breem, the caretaker of the Dupois place."

"Oh." Maggie relaxed. "I've heard about him but never seen him. He's a hermit."

"Yes, but harmless. He even lets the cast use the bathroom at his old cottage."

"Phew. That reminds me . . . this is going to sound weird, but have any of your guests reported seeing a rougarou or some kind of creature that scared them?"

"No. Why?"

Maggie explained what had happened the night before.

"Wow, that *is* weird. We had a kid say he saw a ghost, but I think he only said it to scare his little brother. The kid is seriously obnoxious."

Bo turned up as the show was about to begin and climbed over people to the seat Maggie had saved for him next to hers. Quentin took center stage—if standing between two tombs could be called that—and clapped his hands to get the audience's attention. "Hey, y'all, welcome. I'm Quentin MacIlhoney, playwright, director, and crack defense attorney if any of you get into trouble this weekend. You'll find my card on your seats." Quentin held up a business card, then pocketed it. "Our show takes place on All Hallows' Eve, many, many years ago." Spooky music played over a wireless speaker. "A yellow fever epidemic rages in New Orleans. Jean-Luc Dupois, founder of the Dupois dynasty in Pelican, fears for the health of his one son, Jean-Luc Junior, who's recently returned to the family plantation from a business trip to the Crescent City . . ."

The cast took their places. Barrymore Tuttle, playing the role of Jean-Luc, gesticulated and bemoaned as his wife, played by Vanessa, shared the news that their son was dying. The characters cycled through a dramatic display of fear, hope, and utter despair when the town doctor broke the news that their son had passed away. The audience watched, rapt, as a group of mourners moaned and keened during the funeral scene. "If only love had the power to bring someone back from the dead!" Barrymore cried to the heavens in a voice so booming the heavens might have heard him. The audience gasped when an angel materialized from behind a crypt. "I am here to answer your prayers," the angel said.

She waved her hands over Jean-Luc Junior's prostrate body. He slowly began to rise. "I live!" declared Rudy Ferrier, teen star of Pelican High School's somewhat controversial production of the Broadway musical *Urinetown*. "I am cured of the fever!"

"Son!" Barrymore and Vanessa cried out, Barrymore falling to his knees and stage-weeping for extra effect.

"Husband!" An actress swayed dramatically and then ran to Junior.

"Father!" Two petite twenty-year-olds cast as Junior's children threw their arms around the formerly dead character.

"Jean-Luc Junior has kids?" Bo whispered to Maggie. "I thought the guy was seventeen."

"I guess he started young," she whispered back.

Bo looked skeptical. "Those kids look older than their dad."

There was a flourish of happy music as the entire Dupois family embraced and then faced the audience, bowing to much applause. Bo took off after the curtain call, but Maggie stayed and congratulated the performers after she helped her father load Crozat's guests into the family van. "Best weekend ever," said guest Jennifer, who seemed to have forgotten about her rendezvous with a rougarou. So far, despite that blip, the Pelican's Spooky Past getaways were on track to be a success.

The following morning, there was another blip with Jennifer when she and Benedict Cumberpooch checked out. "How was your session with Helene?" Maggie asked while the woman paid her bill. Jennifer hesitated. "Oh, I ended up canceling. I figured I didn't need a voodoo priestess telling me I was having a great time." She punctuated the last comment with a loud laugh, but Maggie sensed something cagey in her response.

She's lying, Maggie thought to herself. *But why?*

Chapter 4

During the next two weeks, positive reviews on the travel website trippee.com confirmed that the Halloween vacation package was a hit. A red flag popped up during the second week when Kaity posted in the B and B owners' group chat that a child of a Belle Vista guest claimed he'd seen a "werewolf" in the woods. The staff searched and found nothing, but the little boy had nightmares that night and the family checked out the next morning, cutting their vacation short. Bon Ami posted a similar sighting; their guests who reported it also checked out. By the end of the weekend, several Crozat guests had reported rougarou run-ins. Fortunately, Gran managed to convince them it was all part of the Spooky Past weekend. "You can't celebrate Halloween in Cajun Country without a visit from our mythical monster friend," she declared, then muttered to Maggie that if she ever caught the prankster responsible for the sightings, whoever it was wouldn't survive a run-in with *her*.

Maggie focused on the positive. Crozat was sold out for the third and fourth weekends and weekday spa bookings were growing, with visitors and locals raving about Susannah's golden touch. Maggie occasionally saw Johnnie MacDowell wandering around with a pen and journal muttering to himself, while his twin Bonnie never missed a chance to complain about something, always ending with the refrain, "How do you live here? It's so *boring*." Maggie rarely caught a glimpse of Doug MacDowell, who she assumed was running his print shops from afar.

The third weekend arrived with a further assortment of pets, including Lovie, a chatty fifty-year-old parrot. Lovie's pet mom, DruCilla, was an amiable guest in her late fifties who smelled like patchouli oil and introduced herself as a Wiccan. Bo stopped by with Xander and the young boy's "girlfriend," eight-year-old fellow classmate Esme. The three had taken the St. Felice's Creole Mourning Tour on their way over to Crozat, and they shared the ghoulish customs they'd learned about on the tour with the B and B's enthralled visiting children. "Dead people were loaded into the hearse feet-first so they couldn't look back at the living people and doom them," Esme said, her tiny body bobbing up and down with excitement. "Everybody tried not to yawn, because a spirit could get inside you that way. And people in the olden days thought spirits could get inside you if you touched a coffin, which is why the guys carrying them—"

"Pallbearers," Bo said.

"Right, them—wore gloves. And just to make sure a person was really dead, nobody got buried for . . ." She turned to Xander. "How many hours?"

"Twenty-four to forty-eight," he said.

"Good memory, son," Bo said. He placed a hand on the boy's shoulder, and Xander responded with a shy smile. Maggie marveled at how much Bo's son, who had Asperger's syndrome, had blossomed during his year-plus living in Pelican. When they first met, he'd refused to speak or make eye contact. Now he did both, and so much more.

The front doorbell let out a shriek, startling the guests, who responded with more screams. "I'll get it," Ninette called from the kitchen.

"Tell us another story," a young boy from Shreveport on vacation with his parents begged.

"Everyone was super afraid of ghosts." Esme, with her white-blonde hair and alabaster skin, looked ghostlike herself. "They covered mirrors with cloth, because if you saw yourself after someone died, you'd die next. The ladies had to wear black way longer than the men, which I think is really mean. Even the *dolls* got put in black dresses. And—"

Ninette appeared in the front parlor doorway. "Maggie, chère, I'm so sorry to interrupt, but Helene is here, and she needs to talk to us."

"Is that the voodoo priestess?" asked a sleek Manhattanite visiting from New York with her boyfriend. "I was going to book an appointment with her, but something came up."

Helene Brevelle, a tiny black woman in her seventies, stepped out from behind Ninette. She crossed her arms and glared at the Crozats' guests. "And I know what that somethin' is."

Maggie jumped up from her chair. "Let's go to the office."

"I'll keep an eye on things here," Bo said.

Maggie threw Bo a grateful look, then followed her mother to the back parlor that served as the B and B's office. Helene stomped along with them. Tug and Grand-mère were already there. Maggie closed the door. "Helene, what's wrong? Why are you so upset?"

Helene adjusted the multicolored tignon wrapped around her dyed-black hair. It had come askew during her angry march down the hall. "Because I thought we were all friends and cared about each other."

"We are," Tug said, perplexed. "We do."

"Then why did you hire a psychic to steal my business?"

Every member of the Crozat family stared at Helene, dismayed. "I think I speak for all of us," Gran said, "when I say that we have absolutely no idea what you're talking about."

"Your masseuse," Helene said. "She's been spreading the word about how she's a psychic and offering readings for a cheap price, so people are canceling on me and going to her."

Four mouths dropped open. "Wha-wha-what?" Maggie stuttered.

"Yeah," Helene said, her anger replaced by surprise. "You didn't know?"

"No, we swear," Ninette said. "We'd never consent to anything like that."

"She's got a setup in the woods. Calls it 'The Tent of Telepathy.'" Helene snorted. "Talk about cheesy. She's probably selling snake oil from there too, or those magic pills that help old men do the nasty."

Maggie gathered her wits. "Helene, I'm so sorry about this. We'll take care of it, I promise."

Helene seemed mollified. "Well . . . I feel better knowing y'all weren't part of it. I'd appreciate it if you could make that tent go away."

"Oh, no worries," Tug said. "The last thing we want is some scam operation on our property, cousin or not."

Ninette steered Helene toward the door. "You know what would make you feel better? Some of my Scary Spicy Sugar Cookies and Chocolate Monster Milk."

"Skip the cookies and make the milk whiskey," Helene said.

The two left, Ninette pulling the door shut behind them. "*Psychic?*" Tug said. He searched for a reaction to the bizarre development and ended up with, "Susannah? What the *what*?"

Maggie paced the room. "Susannah never said a word about this. Not one word."

"She's obviously trying to squeeze more money out of her stay," Gran said. "I have half a mind to cross those MacDowells off our wedding list. Although I was hoping they were the kind of out-of-town guests who don't come but send a gift."

"We'll talk to her," Tug said.

Maggie stopped pacing. "No. I will. Hiring her was my idea. Laying down the law is my responsibility." She glanced at the antique walnut clock that sat on the room's marble fireplace mantel. "It's only six. I'll go up to the studio now. The sooner we end this, the better. Tell Bo what's going on and that I'll call him later."

Maggie left the manor house and traipsed through the woods to her studio. She rapped on the door. After a brief pause, Susannah opened it a crack. "Oh. Cousin Maggie. The twins are out. Doug and I were about to have dinner."

Maggie ignored the note of dismissal in Susannah's voice. "This won't take long." She pushed the door open and walked past the massage therapist, who was dressed in a chiffon-y black maxi dress. Doug sat at the carved oak table, a steaming bowl in front of him. The scent of vegetables wafted from it. "We have a small problem, but it should be easy to clear up," Maggie said.

Susannah seemed puzzled. "Has someone complained about my work?"

"No." Maggie decided to lead with a little flattery. "I've only heard raves, which is wonderful. The problem is that I've also heard you've set up a side business as a psychic."

"Oh, that." Susannah said. "For a minute I was worried. Yes, a few years ago, I realized that I'd developed a level of extrasensory perception through my ability to connect with a human body through massage. Since there's so much clairvoyant energy in Louisiana, I thought it offered a perfect chance to marry my two strengths."

Doug motioned to his wife with his spoon. "She's got a gift, that one."

"A gift you never mentioned before," Maggie said.

The woman shrugged. "You never asked."

"Susannah, we didn't bring you here to be a psychic," Maggie said, hating every word of the conversation. "I'm sorry, but you need to shelve that and focus on the strength we hired you for: massage."

"Wow," Doug said. He'd started eating and spoke with a mouth full of whatever vegetable mélange filled his bowl. "That's a pretty cold way to talk to family."

"I'm trying to keep this about business," Maggie said.

"I appreciate the amazing opportunity you've given me," the massage therapist said. "But I'm going to continue offering readings to my clients. I'm not going to deprive them because of a miscommunication."

Susannah turned her back on Maggie and went to join Doug at the table, her filmy dress floating as she walked. "I'm sorry, but that isn't going to work for us," Maggie said.

Susannah ignored her. She smiled at her husband. "Do you like the stew?"

"Yup. Who knew root vegetables could taste this good?" There was an edge to Doug's jovial tone.

Maggie watched the two for a minute. Then she said, "I'm an only child. When I was growing up, I envied friends who had extended families, so when you got in touch with me, I was thrilled. A long-lost cousin. Wow. But I never should have mixed family with business. That's on me." Maggie paused, dreading what she knew had to come next. "We're obviously not on the same page here. Much as I hate doing this, if you're not willing to stick to our original agreement, I have to let you go."

"You do you," Susannah said, using Maggie's least favorite expression. "I'll let my clients know that I'll be moving my massage appointments here." She gestured to the studio.

"No," Maggie said, now defiant. "First of all, you're not stealing clients who booked Crozat Spa's services. And if you're not employed here, you'll have to move out of my studio. If you want to stay in Pelican, that's your decision. We'll give you time to find a new place."

Doug ripped off a hunk of bread from a large loaf and swabbed his bowl. "Yeah, that won't be happening."

"*Excuse me?*" Maggie said, infuriated by the man's audacity.

Doug grinned at his wife. "Do you want to tell her or should I?"

"I should, since I'm the Crozat." Susannah turned away from her half-eaten root stew and faced Maggie. "You know how my family owns the land next to yours? Well, as it turns out, this old shack you like to call *your* studio is on *my* land. We're not going anywhere."

Chapter 5

Maggie's heart pulsed. Her face flushed. *I wonder if this is what a stroke feels like* was her sidebar thought. She found her voice. "This 'shack' was originally the Crozat schoolhouse, and it's on our land, not yours. It always has been, ever since it was built."

"Actually, that's not true. Here, I'll show you." Susannah got up. She and her dress floated to a set of shelves that had held Maggie's art supplies before the MacDowells commandeered the space. The massage therapist stood on her tippy-toes and removed a rolled-up document from the top shelf. "Doug, honey . . ."

"Oh. Sure."

Doug cleared the bowls from the table, placing them in the sink Maggie used to clean her paintbrushes. Susannah unrolled the document. It was a copy of an old map. "My late father ordered this from your town records before he passed on." Susannah pointed to a spot on the map. "There's your Crozat land. And here's mine. And there's the schoolhouse. On *my* land."

Maggie scrunched her eyes and bent over the map, studying it. She stood up. "What I see is an ink blot where the property line is."

"No, that's part of the property line." .

Maggie glared at her cousin. "I'll be at the Hall of Records first thing in the morning, which happens to be run by our town mayor, Eula Banks. I'll get my own copy of this map and show it to her, and we'll see who's right—and it'll be *me*."

Susannah rolled up the map. "I don't trust small-town cronyism. Doug and I will be there when your mayor takes a look at the map."

"Fine." Maggie strode over to the door and threw it open. "In the meantime, you're fired!"

Maggie slammed the door shut. She stormed through the woods to the manor house, where she found her mother in the kitchen. "You won't believe this."

Ninette put an index finger to her lips. "Shh. Calm down. Help serve our guests dessert, and then we'll talk."

Ninette handed her a tray of plates filled with slices of her famous rum raisin cake with rum frosting, then picked up a second tray. Maggie bumped the swinging door between the kitchen and dining room to open it. "Hey y'all, time for one of my mama's famous desserts," she said, plastering on a big smile.

"I can attest to our hostess's way with treats," Barrymore, who had availed himself of a free meal, told the guests. "If you happen to serve me the largest slice, I won't complain."

Maggie faked a laugh and distributed the plates, making sure Barrymore got the smallest slice. "Enjoy." She then retreated to the kitchen, where she texted her father and grandmother: *FAMILY MEETING. ASAP!*

Maggie waited impatiently for the guests to finish dinner. As soon as they departed for their lodgings, she pulled Ninette, Tug, and Grand-mère into the office. Lovie, the guest parrot, was spending the night in the room so that her occasional squawk didn't wake up nearby guests. Maggie relayed the upshot of her confrontation with the MacDowells. "That can't be right," Tug said when she broke the news about the schoolhouse.

"Acck! Can't be right," Lovie squawked.

"I agree, but we'll find out for sure tomorrow morning at the Hall of Records," Maggie said. She took a swig of the bourbon she'd poured to calm her nerves.

"You'd think *obnoxious Canadian* would be an oxymoron, but the MacDowells have proven that's not the case," Gran said. She held out her Old-Fashioned glass. "Another belt, please."

Ninette, who rarely drank, drained her glass and held it up to Maggie. "Me too."

"Acck! Belt, please. Acck! Me too!"

"She heard us, Lovie dear," Gran said to the bird. "No need to repeat."

Maggie refilled the women's glasses, as well as her own. "I am so Mac-done with the MacDowells. They are Mac-dead to me."

"Acck! MacDowells! MacDead!"

Gran pinched the bridge of her nose. "Lovie, my love, please give it a rest."

"MacDowells! MacDead!" Maggie could have sworn Lovie was taunting her grandmother.

"Uh-oh, sounds like I'm interrupting something." Emma Fine opened the door an inch.

"No worries, we can't solve our problem until the morning." Maggie drained her glass.

"I just wanted to let you know I noticed a little doggy business in the hallway," Emma said. "There might also be, um, a present from the parrot. Her owner was letting Lovie wander around the house this afternoon."

"It's come to this," Gran said. "We are literally running a zoo."

"Acck!" Lovie squawked. "A zoo!"

* * *

Eula Banks, Pelican's grandmotherly mayor, scoured the map with a magnifying class in the dusty room that served as Pelican's loftily named Hall of Records. The Crozats watched over one shoulder while Susannah and Doug hovered over the other. "Hmmm," Eula murmured, peering closely at the map.

"Hmmm what?" Maggie asked, trying not to sound as anxious as she felt.

Eula straightened up and adjusted her readers. "It does appear that the schoolhouse is on the other side of your property line," she informed the Crozats.

"Told ya." Doug said this with such glee that Maggie wanted to punch him. She noticed her father's clenched fists and realized he had the same idea.

Eula held up a hand. "Most of it." This earned her quizzical looks from both sides of the warring parties. "Not all."

She pointed to the ink blob on the map and addressed the Crozats. "This here runs through the schoolhouse, so about a quarter of it is on your side of the land."

The family examined the map. "You're right, Eula," Tug said. "The schoolhouse must've been built after they drew the property lines. I'm guessing it was meant for both families back then, so having a foot on either side of the land didn't much matter."

"We get the front door," Maggie to the MacDowells. "Which means you can't use it anymore." Despite the gravity of the situation, she enjoyed the small victory.

Susannah was unfazed. "We'll use the back door."

"The stove is on our side," Maggie shot back, "so it's off-limits to you."

"There's a grill in the back," Doug said. "On *our* side. The wife and kids'll tell you how much I love to grill a good hunk of meat. And vegetables, of course," he added, after a look from his vegetarian wife.

"We get the sink and fridge," Maggie said.

"We'll use the sink in the bathroom," Susannah instantly responded. "And that fridge barely works. We'll replace it with a nice new one. On *our* side of the schoolhouse."

Eula checked her watch. "Sounds like y'all are working this out," she said cheerfully. "I don't mean to be rude, but I got a meeting with the head of sanitation in a few minutes."

"Thanks, Eula," Ninette said, her tone despondent. "We'll get out of your way."

The MacDowells sailed out, followed by Maggie's much less cheerful family. Maggie hung back. She pleaded with the mayor. "Eula, we can't live like this. Did you hear how I sounded?" Maggie mocked herself. "'We get the front door; we get the sink.'" Embarrassed, she stopped. "I haven't been so petty since I fought over My Little Pony toys with my cousin Lia when I was five. Isn't there anything we can do? Claim squatter's rights or something? My family's been using that schoolhouse for years. It's my art studio. It's such a special place for us."

Eula shook her head. "I wish, chère. I looked into the situation before y'all came in this morning. When it comes to squatter's rights, we got a little bit of French law going on here, thanks to the state's Napoleonic Code." She directed Maggie to follow her to the H of R's wheezy old computer. Eula pressed a key and read from the screen: "'There must be a prescription for transfer of the property from one person to another. If a property owner has demonstrated that they have attempted to reclaim their land, then this action alone may be enough to resolve any squatter's rights to the property title or deed.'" Eula finished reading. "And from what I saw this morning," she said, "there was a whole lotta reclaiming on the part of your cousin."

Maggie swallowed to keep from crying. "Yeah. A whole lot. Well, I appreciate you trying. Thank you."

"I'm truly sorry for y'all." There was pity in Eula's voice. "If it makes you feel any better, I canceled my second massage with that terrible woman. And my reading." Eula looked guilty. "Well, I haven't canceled my reading yet. But I will. Promise."

Maggie left the Hall of Records. Feeling depressed and helpless, she called Bo on the drive home and vented about the MacDowells. "It's not only about my studio, which is bad enough. What if these horrible people do decide to retire here and build a house on the property? It's their right, but how could we ever be neighbors? It's already ugly. If Susannah follows through on her threat and sets up her own massage practice pretty much feet from our spa, it's only gonna get uglier."

"I wish there was something I could do to help." Bo sounded pained. "If they make any noise, I can get them on disturbing the peace."

"They're too smart for that." She slammed a fist on the steering wheel. "They planned this whole thing, Bo. They didn't care about meeting family. It was all about getting down here and stealing our business. Susannah's already had two weeks to build a client base. Of *our* customers." Maggie transferred her anger to her car horn, honking at the person in front of her. She rolled down the car window and yelled, "The sign says 'Stop,' not 'Stop, text, and take a selfie'!"

"Okay, you need to relax," Bo said. "For now, focus on your guests. Give them the kind of good time they can't stop talking about. You'll find another massage therapist. Until then, Mo will get word of mouth going about the spa being open and her fancy facials, which'll bring in new customers."

"You're right." Bo's sensible advice made Maggie feel calmer. "Thanks, cher. *Je t'aime tellement.*"

"I love you so much, too."

By the end of the conversation, Maggie had reached Crozat B and B. She pulled into the graveled lot next to the spa and parked. She found her friend Mo Heedles at work behind the spa's receptionist desk. "I canceled all the massage appointments," Mo said. "Word's out in town about how those MacDowells are trying to steal your art studio, so I can pretty much guarantee that the locals won't be paying Miss Susannah-Thinks-She's-All-That a visit. Of course, visitors still might."

Fatigued, Maggie rubbed her eyes. It was barely ten AM and the day already felt endless. "There's just so much we can do. I need to find a new massage therapist fast."

"I'm on it," Mo said. Maggie started to speak, but Mo held up a hand. "No arguments. I'm the one with connections in the beauty world. You handle your guests and your job. I'll handle the spa."

Maggie leaned over the desk and hugged her friend. "A gazillion thanks." She noticed the time on the reception desk clock. "Argh, I'm late. I better get to Doucet or I won't have a job to handle."

Chapter 6

Long as the morning felt, the rest of the day flew by. Ione, Maggie's boss at Doucet and close friend, agreed to allow the historic plantation to host Helene Brevelle, which would help her make up for any business she lost to Susannah. She and Maggie set up a room in the annex for the voodoo priestess, who would explain the history and rituals of the practice to visitors. Grateful for the gig, Helene gifted Maggie with a beautifully crafted voodoo doll painted in vibrant colors. "I love it," Maggie said. She sorted through a box of stray art supplies and pulled out a bag of straight pins topped with round black balls. "I even have a black pin to send some pain Susannah's way."

"No, no, no, no." Helene shook her head. "No using the black pin on that doll—it's for evil. I know your cousin is bad, but don't go to the dark place. Don't even joke about it."

Ione poked her head in the room. "Quittin' time, ladies. Maggie, see you at Junie's?"

"Oh, you know it," Maggie said. "Gran and Lee are going to listen to bands for our wedding, so Mom and Dad are keeping an eye on the guests to give me the night off." Maggie's cell phone rang. She checked the number. "Ugh, a spam call. Third one today. Blocking."

The women locked up Doucet, and Maggie headed home to the shotgun cottage. She lay the voodoo doll on the antique desk where she kept her laptop and changed from her work clothes into jeans and a stretchy T-shirt decorated with the logo of a recent po'boy festival. Then she drove to Junie's and parked in front of the old establishment, located in the heart of Pelican's historic town square. As always, local merchants had gone all in with the holiday theme. Fake spider webs hung from the ornate iron balconies, which played host to blow-up ghosts, vampires, and monsters. The village green gazebo featured a band made up of animated ghouls playing spooky music. Normally the creepy decorations would have unnerved Maggie, but she was too distracted by the clash with the Mac-Dowells to even notice them.

Junie's was packed with locals and visitors. "Hey, gorgeous," JJ, the proprietor of the restaurant, having inherited it from his late mother Junie, called to Maggie. "Where's your Halloween duds?" JJ himself was clad in a pumpkin-and ghost-decorated orange caftan, which he'd also inherited from his mother.

"Wasn't feeling the holiday today, JJ."

"Boo," JJ said, giving her a thumbs-down. "Or should I say, boo!" He mimed scaring her, and Maggie had to laugh.

Bo had arrived early to save a large table for their group, which included Ione, Quentin, Vanessa, Rufus, and Ru's girl-friend Sandy Sechrest, along with Maggie's cousin Lia and her husband Kyle, enjoying a rare night away from their infant triplets. Bo waved Maggie over. They exchanged a kiss, and he pulled out a seat for her. "I filled everyone in on what all's going on with your newfound 'family.'"

"I'm trying to figure out ways I can arrest them for something," Rufus said. He tossed a popcorn crawfish in the air and caught it in his mouth.

"We're all helping with that." This came from Vanessa, wife to Quentin but formerly betrothed to Rufus and the mother of his child, Charlotte. Life could be complicated in Pelican.

"I pointed out that since they're not American citizens, they can only stay in the country for six months," Quentin said. "They gotta scoot back to Canada after that."

"With what all's going on, that could be a very long six months," a gloomy Maggie said. "And it doesn't stop them from owning the land. Lia, count yourself lucky the MacDowells aren't on your side of the family."

Lia started. "Huh? Sorry, I think I dozed off for a minute."

Kyle rubbed his wife's back. "To be honest, we're too tired to process much of this. We're just happy to hear adult voices and conversation."

Emma Fine came into the restaurant, followed by Johnnie MacDowell. "That's an odd combination," Maggie murmured to Bo. The duo saw her and approached the table. "I don't mean to interrupt," Johnnie said after greetings were exchanged. "Emma and I had a meeting at the church across the street."

"We're both in recovery," Emma said. "Alcohol."

"And drugs in my case," Johnnie said. "*Lots* of drugs. Anyway, Maggie, I wanted to apologize for my family. They're horrible people, obsessed with money and materialism. Look at my sister over there. She's all over that Rent My Digs trillionaire or whatever he is." Maggie glanced at the table Johnnie was referencing. Bonnie MacDowell, made up and dressed in a skintight black minidress, appeared to be fawning over a good-looking hipster in his late twenties who wore jeans and a black T-shirt.

Vanessa craned her neck to see who Maggie was looking at. "Ooh, he's hot."

"That's Gavin Grody, the guy buying up all the places around here and turning them into day rentals," Sandy admonished her. "He's the enemy."

"They disgust me." Johnnie mimed gagging. "As do my father and stepmonster."

Maggie turned her attention back to Johnnie. She was about to respond to him when her cell rang. She checked it and grimaced. "Great, more spam."

"Have you been getting a lot of that lately?" Johnnie asked. Maggie nodded. "You can thank Susannah. It's a thing she does to get back at people. She sends their phone numbers to telemarketers. The best thing to do is block the calls and don't let her know it's ticking you off. She'll get bored and stop. I'm telling you, she is the *worst*. When I think of the sideshow tableau that is the people I'm forced to cohabitate with, I could—ooh, Bonnie and her boyfriend are leaving. Let's grab their table."

Johnnie and Emma hurried off. Maggie's phone trumpeted another call, and she glared at it. "Anyone have a permanent marker on them? I'm thinking about writing Susannah's telephone number on all the stalls in the men's bathroom."

* * *

The MacDowell nightmare gave Maggie a restless night. At dawn, she dragged herself into the kitchen to make coffee. Gran was already there, thumbing through a stack of wedding magazines. "Coffee's made, chère," she said to her granddaughter.

"Thanks." Maggie poured herself a cup and sat down at the kitchen's café table across from her grandmother. "You couldn't sleep either?"

Gran shook her head. "Too energized by my anger at those awful Canadians." She put a finger under Maggie's chin and raised her face into the light. "You look exhausted, beloved. Go back to bed. Your father can take guests to the pet parade. I'll lead the immortelle workshop. You can manage the caravan to the cemetery show tonight. How does that sound?"

"Wonderful," Maggie said. "Brianna Poche and some of her high school friends wanted to help out, so I asked her to do a nature walk and pick up any interesting plant life she found for the immortelles. She dropped off a box yesterday, so you're good on supplies for the workshop. I'll make it up to y'all by handling everything next weekend."

Maggie put her coffee cup in the dishwasher and returned to bed, where she passed out for hours. By the time she woke up, the sun was low in the sky. She grabbed a quick bite and then shepherded Crozat's playgoers into the van for the trip to the Dupois cemetery. They disembarked into a darkness lit only by the torches that director Quentin thought would enhance the location's otherworldly atmosphere. A few guests clutched their immortelles in their arms. "We thought it would be a way of showing respect to the family," explained Julie Mulhern, a teenager visiting with her parents.

Maggie admired the girl's glass-covered wooden box filled with an arrangement of dried flowers shaped like a heart. "It's beautiful," she said. "If there were any Dupois descendants, I'm sure they'd appreciate it."

"Oh, they do." DruCilla—Lovie's pet parent—closed her eyes and inhaled. She opened her eyes and graced the others with a beatific smile. "They send their regards."

I buy her psychic powers more than I buy Susannah's, Maggie thought. She forced herself to banish all thoughts of the MacDowells and concentrate on her guests. "Julie, why don't you put your immortelle on top of Etienne Dupois's tomb? He only passed away a few weeks ago, so his is bare."

Maggie led Julie to Etienne's tomb. Julie crossed herself and laid her immortelle on top of the tomb. Maggie was reaching for Julie's arm to lead her to their seats when the teen let out a scream so ear-piercing it triggered sympathy screams from pretty much everyone in the cemetery, including Maggie. "In the woods!" Julie pointed, shaking. "I saw eyes. He was staring at me."

DruCilla gasped and put her hand on her heart. "The rougarou. I heard one of those was terrorizing the town."

"No, not at all," Maggie responded quickly, eager to shut down the rumor before it spread and scared guests. "I'm sure it's Walter, the caretaker of the property. He's not social, but he sometimes looks through the trees to see what all's going on. He's harmless."

Maggie's explanation helped the panic subside. She led her group to seats, which soon filled with guests from all the plantations.

"Excuse me, ma'am, is this seat open?"

She looked up to see Bo grinning at her. She patted the chair, and he sat down. "You're a brave man to sit through this show again," she said.

"How else am I gonna see my girl on a Saturday night in October?"

He put an arm around her shoulder, and she snuggled up to him. "I'm so glad you're here," she said. "You missed the hysteria a few minutes ago." Maggie relayed Julie's sighting. "I'm pretty sure it was Walter, but there's something hinky about all these rougarou sightings."

"Yeah, there is," Bo said, lips pursed. "Pelican PD is taking a look into it."

While the audience waited for the play to begin, Maggie craned her neck and searched the dense growth behind the cemetery for any sign of the strange caretaker. She thought she saw a branch move, but local high school students serving as stagehands extinguished the torches and the night went black as coal. There was a moment of tension; then floodlights borrowed from Pelican PD illuminated the cemetery, where the actors had taken their places. The play began.

Barrymore Tuttle emoted while Vanessa Fleer MacIlhoney overacted. For some reason known only to her, Patria Heloise, the voluptuous young actress playing their daughter, delivered her lines in the voice of a Marilyn Monroe impersonator. Maggie's attention strayed to the outskirts of the acting area, where she saw playwright-director Quentin mouthing the words of his script along with the actors. He was dressed in his version of how a theatre professional should dress—black slacks, an expensive black cashmere turtleneck, and a black beret, giving him the look of an aging 1950s beatnik.

After forty-five minutes that felt like four hours to Maggie, who was on her third go-round with the play, the performers launched into the final scene. Rudy Ferrier slowly began to rise from his deathbed. "I live!" he cried out.

"Son!"

"Husband!"

"Father!"

"Grgh-agh!" The groan came from the offstage area. Suddenly someone dressed like a rougarou stumbled out of the woods into the scene. The audience gasped—as did the actors, who froze in place, stunned.

"When did Quentin add that character?" Bo whispered to Maggie.

"I don't think he did." Maggie pointed to Quentin, who looked as stunned by the unexpected appearance as his actors.

Vanessa was the first to recover. "It's a miracle, a miracle sent from heaven above," she ad-libbed. "The curse of the rougarou has been lifted. We are free!"

"Gagh-ahhh!"

The rougarou tried pulling off the head of its costume and failed. Distraught, it twirled around and let out another groan. Its entire body spasmed. The creature let out a yell, arched its back, and collapsed to the ground. The actors exchanged nervous looks. They grabbed each other's hands, stepped over the rougarou, and bowed to thunderous applause. Bo and Maggie ran to the prostrate rougarou as the audience dispersed. The actors, joined by Quentin and Emma, huddled around them. "What on earth happened?" asked Quentin, in shock. "What was that? What *is* that?"

"*That*," said Barrymore with gusto, "is theatre at its best. Impromptu. Invigorating. Electrifying."

"If you don't shut up, the only thing electrified around here will be you," Emma hissed at him.

"Whoever or whatever it is, it's sick," Bo said. He carefully lifted the head off the still body. Cast members screamed and stepped back. Maggie clutched Vanessa and willed herself not to pass out.

Staring up at her with wide and very dead eyes was Susannah Crozat MacDowell.

Chapter 7

Bo switched into police officer mode. "Clear the area, but no cast members can leave."

Kaity Bertrand raced over. "I saw what happened and called Pelican PD. They're on the way."

"Good. Keep your guests calm. For all we know, this was a prank gone bad," Bo replied.

"Susannah wasn't the prankster kind," Maggie said. Her instincts were sounding the alarm that the massage therapist's death was no accident, and the thought nauseated her.

"Oh no," Patria said, her voice shaky as she stared at Susannah's prostrate body. "That's the psychic I saw last week. She said I was gonna meet my husband this year. Now what's gonna happen?"

Emma stared at her. "You're kidding, right? Tell me you're kidding."

"She was trying to get the mask off," Vanessa said. She bit her lower lip. "Do you think there was something in there?"

"No idea, but we don't want rumors to start flying around," Bo said. He looked up at Maggie, his face grim.

"Get your guests back to Crozat. *Now.* If anyone asks what happened, tell them one of the actors took sick. That goes for everyone here, got it?"

Intimidated by Bo's harsh tone, the others gave nervous nods.

Maggie hurried to the Crozat van, where the B and B's guests were waiting for her. "Sorry about the delay."

"Is everything all right?" Julie's mother asked.

"Oh, yeah." Maggie forced herself to sound casual. "The actress playing the rougarou wasn't feeling well, that's all." She herded the guests into the van.

"What an inspired ending," DruCilla said as she buckled a seat belt around her waist. "I did not see that rougarou twist coming. It really added an element of surprise."

You have no idea how right you are, Maggie thought.

She turned the key in the ignition and drove as fast as she could without endangering the lives of her guests. "Man, I thought we put pedal to the metal in California," Julie's dad said as everyone tumbled out of the van. "But I surrender the speeding crown to you."

"I don't usually drive this fast, but it's late and I'm sure everyone's tired." Maggie faked a yawn. "I know I am. 'Night, all."

She watched the guests make their way to their various lodgings, then sprinted to the manor house, where she found her parents eating a late dinner. "Terrible news," she blurted. "Susannah's dead."

"*What?*" Tug said, dumbfounded.

"Oh my Lord." Ninette crossed herself. "That poor woman. Her poor family. How did it happen?"

"We don't know." She relayed Susannah's surprise appearance in the play. A pained expression colored Maggie's face as she recalled the massage therapist desperately trying to pull off the head of her costume. "There was something wrong with her mask. And whatever it was may be what killed her."

Ninette put a hand to her head, trying to puzzle out the evening's bizarre chain of events. "What was she doing there? And why on earth was she dressed like a rougarou?"

"All questions I'm sure Bo and Pelican PD will find answers to." Tug's tone was somber. "We need to think about Doug and the twins. I'm sure the police will want to tell them what happened, but we should offer support. I know things have been bad between our two families, but at the end of the day, that's what we are to each other. Family."

Ninette scraped their plates into the trash. "I'll put together a basket of cinnamon-sugar muffins." Baking was Ninette's way of coping with stress.

"I can't go to bed," Maggie said. "I'll never fall asleep. I'm going back to the cemetery."

"Be careful," her father said. "I got a bad feeling about all this."

Maggie pursed her lips. "You and me both, Dad."

* * *

Maggie jumped in her Falcon and drove back to the scene of what she had to assume was a crime. As she parked and headed toward the cemetery, she walked past a phalanx of patrol cars from Ville Blanc, the town next to Pelican. Once a charming village like Pelican, Ville Blanc was now a sprawl of subdivisions and commercial development, its inadequate streets choked with traffic. While its citizens might grumble, its leadership touted the town as a "beacon of the future, not a relic of the past," a dig at its quaint neighbor, Pelican.

The cemetery was swarming with law enforcement, many of whom looked unfamiliar to her, which meant they were members of Ville Blanc's law enforcement agency. Maggie knew the whole small department at Pelican PD and was proud to call the officers her friends. She saw Bo talking to a man about his own age who was clad in a suit that looked expensive even from twenty feet away. Maggie gave a small wave to let him know she was there. Bo didn't make eye contact, restricting acknowledgment of her presence to the slightest of nods. After a minute, he finished his conversation and headed to Maggie.

"What's going on?" she asked. "Why is Ville Blanc PD here?"

"Half the cemetery's in their town, half is in ours."

"Seriously?" Maggie shook her head in disbelief. "What is it with property lines in this parish?"

"They go back hundreds of years and nobody pays much attention to them until they have to."

"Like with us at Crozat," Maggie murmured. She watched Ville Blanc and Pelican investigators scour the area around the now-covered body of her late cousin Susannah, occasionally bumping into each other. "So, it's officially a crime scene."

"Not until the cause of death has been determined, but it's pretty dang suspicious."

The man Bo had been talking to a few minutes earlier sauntered over. "It's a little crowded over there," he said, gesturing to the collection of tombs. "You can call off your guys. Mine know what they're doing."

"So do mine." Bo's tone was measured, but Maggie knew him well enough to pick up his dislike of the man. "Maggie, this is Ville Blanc detective Zeke Griffith."

"Hey there." The detective cast an appraising glance at Maggie. "Crozat, right? You knew the deceased. I have a few questions for you."

"Oh. I . . . I'm . . ."

Maggie looked to Bo for help. Before he could respond, Griffith said, "Just trying to dodge any hint of impropriety, seeing as how you two are a couple."

Maggie saw Bo clench his teeth, a visceral response to the underlying threat in Griffith's pseudo-casual comment. But Bo simply responded, "Good idea." He hesitated a minute, then stepped away.

Griffith motioned to a row of folding chairs. Maggie sat down, clasping her hands together in her lap like a nervous schoolgirl. "This may be for nothing," Griffith began. "For all we know, the deceased died of natural causes. But in case that's *not* the case, I like to talk to people when an event is fresh in their minds."

"I don't know how much help I can be," Maggie said, silently cursing the perspiration beading up on her forehead. Something about the Ville Blanc detective's attitude was pushing her insecurity buttons. "I was watching from the audience like everyone else."

"Must have been a shock to you, seeing Mrs. MacDowell appear all of a sudden like that."

"Only because I'd seen the show before and knew there was no rougarou in it." *Good answer*, Maggie congratulated herself. "There was an incident before the show started that I should share with you. One of our guests made eye contact with something in the woods. The experience terrified her. Another guest insisted it was a rougarou. I thought it might be Walter Breem, the Dupois caretaker. But maybe it was Susannah, in her costume."

"Ms. MacDowell is staying with you, right?"

"Yes. She's a distant cousin. We only recently connected. We hired her to be the massage therapist for our new spa facility." *Just the facts, ma'am, just the facts.*

"But the relationship went south in a fight over property, and you fired her."

Griffith shot this comment at her like it was attached to an arrow and Maggie was the bull's-eye in his target. How had he dug all this up already? He was certainly on top of his job. Maybe a little too on top of it, which concerned her. Maggie's heart fluttered, but she forced a calm response. "Susannah was fired because she secretly established a side business we hadn't approved. We hired her to be a massage therapist, not a psychic, so she was let go for breach of contract. The property dispute had nothing to do with her dismissal." Maggie's cell rang, startling her. It was another spam call. She gritted her teeth and blocked the number.

"Okay. I guess that's it for now." Zeke stood up. "You know what, you and Bo and me and my girlfriend should have a double date someday. Play cards or something."

"Cards?" Maggie was thrown by the detective's abrupt change of subject. "Why cards?"

Griffith grinned. "Because you have a terrible poker face."

Maggie stood up and faced him. "Everything I've told you is the truth. And you might want to rethink that double date because I happen to be a *great* poker player."

She marched off before Griffith could respond with a comeback and found Bo, who was on his cell. He held up his index finger, and she waited for him to finish. "Right . . . okay. I'll be there." Bo ended the call. "Rufus. He's on his way. Sandy dragged him to a yoga retreat this weekend, and he can't downward dog his way out of there fast enough. We're gonna meet at Crozat and inform the MacDowells of the death."

"After you leave, we'll check in with them to make sure they're okay."

Bo nodded. "Sounds good. How'd it go with Dirty Harry?"

He made a dismissive gesture toward Zeke Griffith, who appeared to be in the middle of an interview with Little Earlie Waddell, the editor, publisher, and delivery boy of the *Pelican Penny Clipper*. The *Penny Clipper* was a freebie handout that Little Earlie was determined to upgrade to a legitimate source of news despite his predilection for penning tabloid-style headlines and articles. The sight of the pugnacious journalist made Maggie groan. "I'm getting out of here before Little E sees me. He'll be all over this, whether there's a story here or not. Text me after you break the news to the

MacDowells." Maggie started for her car, then stopped. "Oh, and cher . . ."

"Yeah?"

"You need to teach me how to play poker."

* * *

Despite the late hour, Maggie, her parents, and Grand-mère trooped over to the schoolhouse to pay their condolences as soon as Bo notified Maggie that Pelican PD had broken the news of Susannah's death. Doug MacDowell, now a widower, opened the door to them. "Thank you. We're all in shock," Doug's bleary-eyed, unkempt appearance confirmed his statement.

"I'll take that," his daughter Bonnie said, reaching for the basket of fruit and baked goods offered by Ninette. She inhaled the butter and cinnamon scent wafting from the muffins. "These smell so good. Please tell me they're made with real butter and flour. Everything with Susannah was dairy and gluten-free."

"Bonnie, show your late stepmother some respect," Doug barked, then collapsed onto the room's couch and dropped his head in his hands.

Bonnie, contrite, put down the basket and sat next to her father. She put an arm around his shoulder. "I'm so sorry, Daddy. I didn't mean to be disrespectful. I'm just hungry."

"OMG, you're a *monster*." This came from Johnnie, who emerged from the bathroom. The aspiring poet's skin was clammy and pale, and Maggie noticed his hands were shaking. "How can you even think of food right now? I'm so nauseous I think I may need to be hospitalized."

"Stop being such a drama queen," his sister said with an eye roll.

Johnnie threw his hands in the air. "If by drama queen, you mean a human being with actual feelings and emotions, then I'm proud to be called a drama queen."

"Shut up, both of you!" Doug roused himself from grief long enough to yell at his children, then sagged again.

Maggie's cell rang. She quickly turned it off. "Sorry, spam."

Bonnie cast a knowing look at her brother. "Susannah?" He gave a slight nod. "She was such a *b-i-t-c*—"

"I can spell!" Doug roared.

The Crozats exchanged uncomfortable glances; then Maggie spoke for her family. "We feel terrible about your loss. We can't imagine what you're going through right now, but if there's anything we can do to help, we're here for you."

Doug lifted his head. He looked lost. "I don't understand. Why was Susannah at that show? Why was she wearing that costume? What happened to her? None of this makes any sense."

"Dad, you need to lie down. Let the police answer all those questions." Johnnie helped his father to his feet, then addressed the Crozats. "Thank you for your kindness. It's comforting to know some people around here have hearts."

"Oh, shut up," Bonnie said, with another eye roll.

"You shut up!"

"Both of you shut up!"

The three MacDowells devolved into quarreling among themselves. "We'll leave you to your grief," Gran said as the Crozats backed out of the schoolhouse.

Tug pulled the schoolhouse door shut. "Wow. How old are those two again?"

Maggie made a face. "Chronologically or emotionally?"

"I'm a little worried about Johnnie," Ninette said as the family made their way through the thick brush back to the manor house. "He seems fragile."

"Agreed," Maggie said. "I think he and Emma have become friends. I'll ask her to keep an eye on him." The family walked in silence. "Poor Doug. Those questions he asked, they're baffling. Why *was* Susannah at the play? And why was she dressed up like a rougarou? Is she the one who's been scaring the B and B guests? It doesn't make sense. Or does it make sense in a way we haven't figured out yet?"

"Oh my, this is giving me a headache," Gran said. "I feel like we've fallen down a rabbit hole of confusion, or rather a rougarou hole."

The family reached Gran and Maggie's shotgun cottage. "We better pull ourselves out of that hole and get a decent night's sleep, so we're chipper for our guests in the AM," Tug said. "We want them to go home with fun memories, not disturbing ones."

The family chorused agreement and said their goodnights. But Maggie knew a good night's sleep would be out of reach for all of them.

Chapter 8

Despite a communal exhaustion, the Crozats found the energy to send their guests off in the morning with a smile, along with a bag of Ninette's sugar cookies as an added gesture of goodwill. With the help of their part-time employees, Marie and Bud Shexnayder, they spent the next few hours cleaning and prepping the rooms for the next batch of guests. Only DruCilla and her wing-baby Lovie were booked for the entire week, which allowed the Crozats some respite. Ninette and Tug delivered lunch to the MacDowells, reporting back that the family was in the middle of an interview with a couple of Ville Blanc detectives. This news made Maggie lose her appetite in the middle of a sugar cookie.

"I don't know why you're so jumpy," Gran said when Maggie confessed her concern. "You've done nothing wrong."

"It's a feeling, Gran. Like we Doucets and Crozats sometimes get. A premonition."

"The best thing to do is distract yourself." Gran, who was thumbing through yet another bridal magazine, held up an ad for a poufy, frilly gown decorated with excessive lace and beading. "Do you think I could pull this off?"

"God, no," Maggie instantly responded.

"Ouch." Gran made a show of closing the magazine. "I'm sad to see that your nerves have made you tactless."

"Sorry, Gran. I didn't mean to hurt your feelings. You know what, I'm going to text Bo." Maggie pulled her cell phone from her jeans pocket. "Oh, he just texted me. He's here. With Rufus. And wants to meet us at the manor house. All of us. Come on, let's go."

Maggie and Gran found the Pelican law enforcement agents in the kitchen with Ninette and Tug. Rufus was inhaling a large bowl of Ninette's jambalaya. "Soon as I finish this, I won't say no to seconds. Sandy's got me on this health kick. There should be a state law against making jambalaya with quinoa, whatever the heck that is."

"There's plenty more food, Rufus, although we're not sure how long you'll be staying?" Maggie knew Ninette's posing this statement as a question was her mother's indirect attempt at extracting the reason for the Pelican PD visit.

"We'll be here for a while, most probably," Rufus said through a mouthful of Ninette's dish. "Bo, you wanna break it to them?"

"I, uh . . ." Bo stammered and looked down at the floor. Maggie tried recalling a time she'd seen her unflappable fiancé at a loss for words. None came to mind. After a minute, he looked up. "Ville Blanc's crime lab has the budget to work fast. They already came back to us with a report on Susannah

MacDowell's rougarou mask. It was laced with strychnine. Her death is officially a murder investigation."

Rufus scraped his bowl with his fork. "Your honey is tiptoeing around the reason we're delivering this news in person."

Maggie picked up Ru's bowl, put it in the sink, and faced him. "Which is?"

Rufus held her glance. "Y'all are suspects. *All* of you."

The Crozats digested this development. Gran was the first to respond. "I believe it's score one for your instincts, Magnolia dear."

"Why all of us?" Tug asked. "Make that, why any of us?"

"Two reasons, Dad," Maggie said, recalling her unpleasant conversation with Ville Blanc detective Zeke Griffith. "I fired Susannah. I, not we, on that one. But we were all in on the property dispute."

Ninette looked stricken. "Oh my, y'all can't possibly think we'd resort to murder over a property line."

Rufus shrugged. "There's been people killed over a pair of sneakers, so yeah. I can think that. Although let me be clear here. Knowing your family as I've come to know you, I have trouble imagining a Crozat going to that dark place."

"Unfortunately," Bo said, "Ville Blanc's lead detective on the case doesn't."

"Wait, alibis." Maggie grabbed at this as a possible out. "I told Griffith I was watching the play. Do you all have alibis for last night?"

"Lee and I were taste-testing a wedding menu at Big Mama Catering," Gran said. "I took notes for us, Maggie. There were some tasty choices."

"Your mama went to bed early and I was poking around on the computer," Tug said. "I ordered a couple of albums. Nothing beats vinyl for sound."

"So there," Maggie said. "We all have alibis, unless you can picture my mother sneaking out the bedroom window and shimmying down the gutter with a mind to murder."

"Chère . . ." The expression on Bo's face reflected his discomfort. "I don't have to tell you where Rufus and I stand on this—"

"Although there was a time," Rufus said, "when I did dream of jailing one or all of you for years. Or forever."

Bo shot his cousin a look, then continued. "But we've got two problems. One, this case isn't about the time of death, it's about when the poison was placed in the mask. I'm not sure even Ville Blanc's brilliance"—Bo's tone was heavy with sarcasm—"can determine that. And speaking of Ville Blanc, they're problem number two."

"Bunch a dang neck-breathers," Rufus muttered. "Think they're so great with their brand-new SUVs and state-of-the-art facilities and stupid awards for their stupid-high rate of collars. I know, I know, hashtag *jealous much?*"

Crozat's front doorbell screamed, and everyone jumped. "I'll get it," Tug said, heading out of the kitchen.

"Good thing I had that stent put in last year, or I'd be having a heart attack right now," Rufus said.

"I feel like I'm a step away from one myself," Maggie said. "So, what happens next?"

Bo's cell pinged a text. He checked it and glowered. "What happens next is walking down the hallway with your father. And they will be here in—"

Tug pushed open the swinging door between the kitchen and dining room and led Zeke Griffith into the kitchen. A woman dressed in gray slacks and a black blazer followed the two men into the room. Maggie recognized her from the group working the cemetery scene the night before. Given that the woman had the same air of nonchalant arrogance as Griffith, Maggie assumed she was also a Ville Blanc detective.

Rufus stood up and positioned himself next to Bo as if creating a blue wall. "Griffith," he said, curt.

"Durand One," the detective responded, his way of noting that Rufus was both Bo's boss and Bo's cousin. He motioned to Bo with a sly grin. "And Durand Two."

Bo worked his jaw. Maggie feared he might blow up at his Ville Blanc counterpart, but when he spoke, his voice was calm. "I've explained the situation to the Crozats."

"Thanks for saving me the trouble," Griffith said. "My partner and I'll divvy up the family for interviews. You can hang out with them to make sure they don't try to line up their stories."

"A big old no on that," Rufus said. "If you got any problems with my detective here conducting interviews, seeing as how he's soon to be related to the family in question, we got the newest addition to our force, Detective Rogert, on his way over."

"Or we can go with my plan and save time."

"Or not."

The tone in the Pelican police chief's voice went from jocular to menacing. Rufus folded his arms across his chest and widened his stance, reminding Maggie of the years when he'd been a formidable enemy of the Crozats. She took some pleasure at seeing Ville Blanc's finest at the receiving end of Rufus Durand's enmity for a change.

Griffith hesitated, then turned to his yet-to-be-identified partner. "I'll take them one at a time until Pelican's guy gets here. You stay in here with the others."

"I believe I'll hang around too, just for giggles and grins." Rufus, his voice softened, addressed Bo. "Go back to the station. I got this."

Bo responded with the slightest of nods, then walked out of the room. Maggie ached for the love of her life, sidelined in an investigation he'd be helming under other circumstances.

Griffith crooked a finger at her. "Let's pick up where we left off last night."

"We can talk in our office," Maggie said.

She led Griffith to the B and B office. "Nice," he said, glancing around the room after taking a seat in a carved walnut side chair upholstered in a rich burgundy velvet. "I admire the way you upper-cruster Pelican families live. The antiques in here must be worth a fortune."

"Which removes financial gain as a motive for murder," Maggie said. "And trust me, we *wish* we were 'upper-crusters.'"

Griffith acknowledged her comeback with a slight smile. "I'm an MCM guy myself. That stands for—"

"Midcentury modern. I lived in a Brooklyn loft before I moved back to Pelican. My ex-boyfriend and I decorated the place with a fantastic collection of MCM."

"Acck! MCM!" Lovie squawked.

Startled, Griffith looked in Lovie's direction. "Interesting choice of pet."

"Not ours. Lovie belongs to one of our guests. You wanted to ask me some questions?"

Griffith removed a pen and small notebook from the inside pocket of his jacket. "Walk me through your day yesterday."

"All right. I was feeling stressed about . . . life in general . . . and was pretty much up all night Friday. I had coffee with my grandmother early in the morning. She said I looked terrible and insisted I go back to bed, which I did. I woke up around four PM."

"You were asleep that entire time?"

"Yes."

"Alone."

That single word deflated Maggie's last shred of confidence. *Alone.* Meaning there was no one to alibi where she'd been all day. The detective had only her word that she'd been sleeping during the crucial period prior to Susannah's death. "Yes," Maggie admitted. "Alone."

MacDowell wrote in his notepad. "Okay. Tell me about your relationship with the deceased."

"I explained all that to you yesterday."

"But yesterday this wasn't a murder investigation. Today it is. So, explain it to me again."

75

Maggie repeated the details of her relationship with Susannah, from hiring to firing. "You make it sound so rational," Griffith said. "But there were—are—those spam calls." Maggie's cheeks colored. She opened her mouth to speak, then closed it. Griffith leaned into her. "One of Susannah's stepkids informed me about them. A vindictive modus operandi, I have to say. I wouldn't blame you one bit if that nasty trick of hers got to you."

Maggie inhaled, then exhaled. When she spoke, her voice was calm. "The calls were annoying for sure, but nothing more. And there were less and less of them. At the risk of sounding repetitive, Susannah was fired for breaking the terms of our original agreement. In a separate issue, our families argued over a property line. That's all it was—an argument. I never would have wanted her dead over it."

"Acck! Mac-done with the MacDowells! They are Mac-dead!" Maggie and Griffith simultaneously turned to Lovie. "MacDead!" Lovie squawked. "MacDowells MacDead."

Griffith stared down Maggie. For the second time in the detective's presence, she felt herself perspiring, and tamped down the urge to blot her forehead. She affected a casual attitude. "We all say things we don't mean when we're angry. And if Lovie was being accurate, she'd squawk 'Mac-dead to *me*.' Those were my exact words. Which are completely different from wanting someone dead. Which I didn't. And don't."

Except for that parrot right now.

* * *

To Maggie's relief, Griffith wrapped up the interview shortly after Lovie's potentially incriminating statement. As soon as the detective moved on to interviewing other members of her family, Maggie typed *Is a parrot's testimony admissible as evidence?* into the office computer's search engine. "Great," she muttered at the long list of cases featuring chatty parrots. It seemed that no parrot had ever been called to the stand, but their testimony had proved useful in some cases. *While prosecutors may not be able to put parrots on the stand during a trial*, Maggie read, *their utterances to law enforcement and owners can have an effect on who is charged with a crime.*

"Acck! Peach and gold! Peach and gold!"

Maggie faced Lovie. "Oh, *now* you parrot Gran and her wedding plans. Why couldn't you do that an hour ago?" Lovie made more noise and pecked at her empty food bowl. Maggie sighed and got up to replenish it. The parrot devoured her meal and made purring noises. Maggie petted the bird's soft feathered head. "It was my fault. I shouldn't have used this room for the interview."

Lovie nuzzled Maggie's hand with her head. "Acck! Lovie is a love! Lovie is a love!"

"You kind of are," Maggie had to admit.

She rewarded the parrot's affection with a little extra bird chow, then left the office for the kitchen to see how her family was faring with their police interviews. The kitchen was empty, so she retreated to the cottage, where she found Gran pouring a cup of coffee. "I'm making myself a café brûlot."

Maggie watched her grandmother add a shot of brandy to her cup. "Unless you add a strip of orange peel and light that drink on fire, I'd say you're just spiking a cup of coffee."

"I prefer to think of it as my own recipe. Want one?"

Maggie shook her head. "I'm going with straight black coffee. I can't afford a booze brain fog with what all's going on around here."

"Detective Rogert showed up. He's interviewing your mother. That Griffith character, who positively reeks of attitude, is taking on your father." Gran sat down at the kitchen's small café table. Maggie poured herself a cup of coffee and sat opposite her grand-mère. "I had a lovely chat with the lady detective," Gran said, sipping her drink. "Her name is Rosalie Broussard. From the Ville Blanc Broussards."

Maggie curled her upper lip. "I don't know if you can call a police interview a 'lovely chat.'"

"They're simply crossing their *t*'s and dotting their *i*'s, chère. We didn't spend much time talking about Susannah's unseemly passing at all. After we got through with that, I showed Miss Broussard the ad for the wedding dress I liked that earned a thumbs-down from you, and do you know what she said?"

"That the dress would work if you wore it with glass slippers and pulled up to your wedding in a pumpkin turned into a coach?"

"No, Snarkarella. She said it's my day—"

"*Our* day," Maggie reminded Gran.

"And I should wear whatever I want. So there."

Maggie reached over, took her grandmother's hand, and squeezed it. "Much as I hate saying this, Detective Rosalie

Broussard from the Ville Blanc Broussards is right. Do what makes you happy, Gran. You'll look beautiful in anything you wear."

Gran placed a hand over her granddaughter's. "The truth is, chère, it doesn't matter what I wear, because all eyes will be on you," she said with affection. "You will be an absolute vision in that spectacular Doucet heirloom gown."

"I love you so much." Maggie leaned over the table and kissed Gran's soft cheek. She caught a glimpse of her reflection in the kitchen window and pulled a face. "Ugh, I'm breaking out. That hasn't happened in forever. It must be from stress." She drained her coffee cup and stood up. "Mo has a miracle zit-zapper product she's selling at the spa. I'm going to run over and buy a tube."

"You reminded me—I must book a facial with Mo." Gran patted her face. "If I'm going to be a jailbird, which seems to be Detective Griffith's intention for all of us, at least I'll be one with a flawless complexion."

Maggie put her cup in the sink, then made her way to the Crozat spa. The air was damp and cold and the sky a collection of angry clouds, indicating an approaching storm. Maggie loved the rain but prayed it would contain itself to midweek. Life was complicated enough without a soggy Pelican's Spooky Past weekend. A few fat wet drops fell on her head as she unlocked the door to the spa, which wasn't due to open for another hour. She flipped on the reception area lights and stepped behind the desk to scan Mo's display of skin care products. Maggie picked up a tube of Mo' Better Buh-Bye Breakouts and went to swipe her credit card on the spa's computer. She noticed the booking calendar was open and couldn't resist checking. What Maggie saw worried her. There were far too many empty slots where massages should be. But she was relieved to see that Mo had an interview with a potential massage therapist scheduled for later that afternoon.

Maggie stepped into the spa bathroom and applied the cream to the area around her chin. Buh-Bye Breakout's potent tea tree oil scent provided the added benefit of clearing her sinuses. The spa phone rang, and she dashed out to get it. *Let it be a booking, let it be a booking.* Maggie grabbed the phone. "Crozat Spa and Wellness Retreat." The Wellness Retreat was more of a wish than an actuality, but Maggie liked how it sounded.

"Hi, um, this is Kelly Brandt. I had an interview scheduled for the massage therapist position."

"Hi, Kelly. It's *have*, not *had*. You're on the books. Mo and I are looking forward to meeting you."

"Um . . ." The girl on the other end of the call paused. "I'm sorry, but I have to cancel."

"Oh. No worries, things come up. When would you like to reschedule the interview?" Maggie checked the wide-open schedule. "We might be able to squeeze it in tomorrow."

"Um . . . I'm not going to reschedule."

"No?" Maggie couldn't hide her disappointment. "Why not?"

"Uh, I've got a lot going on, and—"

Maggie cut the girl off. "Kelly, it's okay. It would be really helpful if you were honest with me."

"You sure?"

"Positive." Maggie steeled herself for what Kelly might share.

"Okay, well, my friends here in Ville Blanc are saying there's weird stuff happening in Pelican. Like, werewolves and freaky stuff. At first I was all, 'Really? You people believe that BS?' But then that woman dressed as a rougarou died, and she was a massage therapist like me, and I was like, wow. There's definitely some bad mojo going down."

Maggie's instincts had warned her this would be Kelly's response. She knew bucking local superstition was futile but tried anyway. "I think people are overreacting to all of that. It's almost Halloween, which brings out the pranksters in town. As to Susannah's death, that has nothing to do with werewolves *or* her being a massage therapist."

"Then what does it have to do with?" Kelly didn't wait for Maggie to come up with a response. "I'm sorry, it's all too creepy for me. And for my massage therapist friends. Good luck."

"Thanks."

A dial tone indicated Kelly had hung up. The barren booking schedule taunted Maggie from the computer. In an act of desperation, she Googled *massage therapy license Louisiana*. A list of options came up. She clicked on one after the other, and all told the same story. Earning a license required five hundred hours of training from an approved program and passing a national massage licensing examination. Even if Maggie dropped everything else in her life to pursue a new career, Crozat's spa wouldn't survive the time she'd need to complete the training.

The door opened, and Mo Heedles came in. The attractive black woman held an umbrella over her head. She took off her jacket as she spoke, revealing a white lab coat over a beige knit dress. "It's coming down out there, but better today than the weekend, huh?" She closed her umbrella and mimed walking a runway to show off her lab coat. "You like this? I figure it makes me look like a medical professional."

Maggie tried to muster up a smile. "You look like there should be a *doctor* before your name. But I have bad news. The massage therapist we were going to interview canceled."

Mo opened the spa door and shook out her umbrella. "Her loss. We'll find someone else."

"After the conversation I just had, I'm not sure we will." Maggie had pinned so much of Crozat's future on the spa expanding the B and B's guest base. She'd convinced her family that the facility was an investment that would quickly pay for itself. Instead, her grand plan was devolving into a disaster. "I feel terrible, Mo, because I dragged you into this whole thing, but we can't sustain the spa on a cut of your facials." Maggie's voice quavered. "I'm making an executive decision. We're closing it down."

Chapter 9

Mo wrinkled her brow. She tapped an index finger against her lips. "Or—"

"We can't afford an *or*, Mo," Maggie said. "We've already sunk so much money into this place. We've been operating at a loss, but I expected that in the beginning. What I didn't expect was a murder."

Mo's mouth dropped open. "*Whaaaa . . . ?*"

"Yup, Susannah didn't die a natural death. Add her to the list of murders that somehow always seem to involve Crozat. The bottom line is that we can't keep going the way we're going right now, and I don't know when things will change." Maggie chose not to mention that Zeke Griffith considered every member of her family a suspect. She was determined to direct his investigation in another, less ludicrous direction.

The skin care maven pondered this. Then she spoke. "Or . . . I take over the space, rent it from you, and run it as my own place. Mo' Better Beauty and Day Spa. No stink of Crozat on it—if I can be blunt—but your guests still get first dibs at appointments."

Maggie took this in. She searched for a downside to Mo's plan and came up empty. "I love it," she declared, a sense of relief flooding over her. "I'll present the idea to my family, but I can't imagine they'll be anything but enthusiastic about it."

"Woo-hoo." Mo pumped the air with her fist. "First stop, Pelican; next stop, Mo' Better franchises around the country. Around the *world*."

Maggie laughed. "Dream big, my friend, dream big."

Mo threw open her arms. "Let's hug on it."

The two women shared a hug. Maggie broke free and stepped out from behind the reception desk. "I'm going to run this by my family right now."

"And I'm gonna put out feelers to the Baton Rouge massage therapy community," Mo said, replacing Maggie behind the desk. "I've got a friend who wanted to partner on a makeup line. I'm putting in a call to her, too."

Maggie left a busy Mo and hurried through the rain to the manor house kitchen. The Ville Blanc team of detectives was gone, but Rufus was once again seated at the room's large wooden trestle table, a half-empty bowl of Ninette's gumbo in front of him. Gran was also at the table, but instead of gumbo, she was enjoying a cocktail. Maggie pulled a tea towel from a drawer and used it to dry her hair. "I have good news about the spa," Maggie said.

"I'm looking forward to hearing it," Ninette said, "but Rufus was about to share what might be happening next with the investigation into Susannah's death."

Ninette ladled more gumbo into Ru's bowl, then added a dollop of potato salad. Rufus helped himself to a large spoonful. "No wonder my officers always fight about who gets to respond to a call at Crozat. With cooking like this, it's a wonder they don't fake an incident just to come over here."

"You were saying . . ." Tug prompted.

"I wasn't saying nothing, but I understand your anxiety about this whole situation." Rufus alternated speaking with shoveling in spoonfuls of gumbo. "What happens next is that Griffith will try and get a warrant that'll allow him to search whatever premises a judge agrees to. But after how the ADA railroaded Gaynell last spring, I can pretty much gar-on-tee you he won't be bringing charges unless Ville Blanc PD offers him a rock-solid case. He's still recovering from a bad case of humiliation."

"Good, he deserves it." After a sketchy music producer was murdered during Pelican's inaugural *Cajun Country Live!* music festival, Jace Jerierre, St. Pierre Parish's assistant district attorney, had arrested Maggie's close friend, musician Gaynell Bourgeois, on a trumped-up murder charge. Gaynell's story had a happy ending—she and her band, Gaynell and the Gator Girls, were on tour after a smashing debut at the New Orleans Jazz & Heritage Festival—but Maggie would never forgive the ambitious ADA for almost ruining her friend's life.

Rufus pushed his bowl away. "Anyhoo, while Griffith is getting all up in your business, know that me and Pelican PD'll be hunting down genuine suspects. Your beau Bo is already on it, Miss Magnolia. There's no such thing as a conjugal visit in the Louisiana penal system, and that's all your future mister needs to hup-to on this."

"Thank you for everything, Rufus," Ninette said. "Can I get you a slice of my Bananas Foster Coffee Cake?"

"I'd love to say yes, but I better save room for a coupla forkfuls of whatever healthy nightmare Sandy's cooked up for me." Rufus stood up. A pained expression crossed his face. "My stomach's already not too happy about the thought of that."

Rufus departed, leaving a glum collection of Crozats. "I wouldn't mind a piece of that coffee cake," Tug said. "I could use some comfort food."

"Me too," Maggie said. "Anyone else?" Ninette and Gran raised their hands. "That's four orders of coffee cake, coming up."

Maggie helped her mother cut four large pieces and warmed them up in the B and B's oven. She heard singing in the distance. Someone was crooning a Nat King Cole standard.

Gran crooked her head. "Is that Lovie?"

"Acck!"

"I guess so," Maggie said. "Which reminds me, be careful what you say around that bird. She's got a big mouth. Thanks to her, I'm Griffith's number-one suspect."

"He can't be serious," Ninette said. "I'm sure he'll get over it and focus on a genuine suspect." She took the coffee cakes out of the oven and scooped a large helping of homemade whipped cream onto one.

"That boatload of whipped cream you loaded onto your coffee cake tells me you're nervous," Maggie said.

"No, no, I'm . . . in a whipped cream mood." Ninette distributed the desserts to her family. She held up the bowl. "Anyone else want some?"

"Me," Tug and Gran said simultaneously.

"Me too," Maggie said with a sigh. She took the bowl and piled cream high on top of her cake.

"As long as we're on the subject of being nervous, we got cancellations for the weekend," Tug said. "We went from sold out to fifty percent capacity. I hope they solve the case fast enough to fill those spots. We're already heading into a slow month."

"Maybe we can advertise them as a last-minute reduced rate," Ninette said.

"We run the risk of ticking off the guests who paid full freight, and some of them are repeat visitors. We don't want to chase anyone off to those dang Rent My Digs."

The phone rang. Gran picked it up off its stand and answered the call. "Crozat Plantation B and B. Celebrate Halloween with a Pelican's Spooky Past weekend." Gran listened as the person on the other end of the call spoke. "Yes, you did hear that. There have been several rougarou sightings and a mysterious death . . . Yes, a reported ghost sighting as well . . . No vampires, I'm afraid. Yet."

"*Shh.*" Maggie, trying to shut up Grand-mère, made a cutting motion with her hand to her neck.

Gran put a hand over the phone's mouthpiece. "It's a group of paranormal aficionados." She returned to the call. "We have a few rooms available, but they're going fast. The Spooky Past weekends are already legendary."

"More like infamous," Tug muttered.

"Uh-huh . . . uh-huh . . . Yes, the ten percent discount is only available if you book online. . . . Wonderful. We'll see you tonight." Gran ended the call. "That was a woman who's with a group that calls themselves the Paranormals. They heard about the goings-on in Pelican and can't wait to visit. They're booking our empty rooms, bless their supernatural-loving hearts. I thought we were going to lose them when I said there hadn't been a vampire sighting. You might have to buy fangs, put on a tux, and come out only at night, Tug cher."

Ninette toyed with her half-eaten slice of coffee cake. "I hate that we're pulling in the kind of people who are looking for a ghoulish thrill."

"I think we need to let go of that, Mom," Maggie said, "and be grateful we're pulling in anyone at all."

"True dat," Ninette said.

"Maggie, chère, you had news about the spa?" Gran prompted.

Maggie slapped her forehead. "Right. I was so distracted by what Ru said, I almost forgot. If y'all approve this, our spa will be operating under a new name and new management." She detailed Mo's offer. "I think it's the best shot we have at keep the spa going right now. The only shot, really."

Maggie waited anxiously for her family's reaction. A wide smile creased her father's weathered face. "It's a great plan. Takes the pressure off us."

"I like it too," Ninette said. "But I want to make sure we charge Mo a fair rental rate. I don't want any issues between us. There's been enough ugliness around that spa already."

"Agreed," Maggie said with a vigorous nod. "Gran?"

"As long as I get my day of beauty before our wedding, I am all in," Gran said. She fluffed her shiny silver pageboy. "I might even dye the tips of my hair peach to match our color scheme."

"Show of hands," Tug said. "All in favor?" Everyone raised a hand. Maggie raised two. "It's a done deal. Let Mo know."

"Fantastic," Maggie said. "I'll tell her on my way to Doucet. I'm doing a special Halloween-themed painting workshop for the kids I teach. They were so excited I couldn't say no."

She polished off her cake and left the manor house. The day's rain, now over, had been followed by a blast of cool autumn air. Maggie, who loved fall weather, took a deep breath and let the air fill her lungs. She stopped by the spa to deliver her family's decision to Mo, who was elated. "I've been sketching a logo," she said. "Look."

She handed Maggie a piece of paper. Under the words *Mo' Better Beauty and Spa*, Mo had drawn the outline of a voluptuous woman in a sexy pose. "She looks a little like a mud-flap girl," Maggie said.

"The universal symbol of hot."

"To monster-truck drivers," Maggie said with a laugh.

"*And* their girlfriends," Mo pointed out.

Maggie handed the paper back to her friend. "The spa's your baby now. May your bookings be filled with mud-flap wannabes and their credit cards."

Mo held her hands up in a *raise the roof* gesture. "Amen, sistah."

Maggie left Mo to her sketching and drove to Doucet. Sunday was a busy day for the popular historical site, but she found a parking spot near the annex that housed her on-site studio. She opened a large folding table and laid out canvases and paint for her eight students. She also put out juice boxes and a container of her mother's sugar cookies, this time decorated as witches and pumpkins.

Ione knocked, then came into the room. "Just me. I've got messages for you." She passed them to Maggie.

"This is from Brandon's mother," Maggie said. "Canceling for today." She quickly read the others. "Cancellations. Seven of them. Everyone but Xander." Humiliated, Maggie sank into a chair. "Word must have gotten out that I'm a suspect in Susannah's murder."

"You don't know that." After Maggie shot Ione a look, she said, "Okay, it's probably what happened." Ione, angry, crossed her arms in front of her chest. "I swear, I do *not* understand people. Your family helped found Pelican. The Crozats and Doucets have been here longer than America's been a country. How can anyone think y'all had anything to do with what happened?"

"I blame Halloween."

"Huh?" Ione said, bewildered. "How can you blame Halloween?"

"All the emphasis on the supernatural—it puts a weird aura in the air. People get jittery, especially when they think they see ghosts and werewolves and rougarous, and boy, would I love to get my hands on whoever's doing that to scare our guests. Anyway, I think Halloween brings out the paranoia in people."

"Huh," Ione said, unfolding her arms. "I never thought about it like that. You're not entirely wrong."

"Thank you for not telling me I'm nuts," Maggie said. She pressed the heels of her hands against her eyes to hold back tears. She released her hands and noticed a small head peeking into the room. "Xander, honey. Hi, come on in."

Bo's son took a tentative step into the room. His mother Whitney followed, pushing a baby carriage. "I heard class might be canceled," she said, "but Xander insisted we come and find out for ourselves."

Maggie and Ione stood up. "Xander lucked out," Maggie said. "He's getting a private lesson today."

"I'll leave you to it," Ione said. She headed for the door, stopping to coo over Bella, the baby Whitney and her second husband Zach had recently adopted.

"You don't have to teach him, Maggie," Whitney said. "I'm sure you have lots to do."

"No, I want to. It'll be the best part of my day." Maggie gave Xander an affectionate smile. "I'll drop him off when we're done."

"That's okay, I'll wait."

Whitney pulled a folding chair to the side of the room. She sat down and jiggled the baby carriage, eliciting happy gurgles from her infant daughter. "What's the matter, you don't trust me?" Maggie, aiming for a jocular tone, failed. She found it impossible to hide how strained she felt.

"Of course I trust you." Whitney's forced laugh also failed dismally. "I just never get the chance to be around one of Xander's classes, so I thought, why not now?"

"Why not," Maggie said flatly. She stepped over to a cabinet above the room's sink and took down a container of paintbrushes. "Xander, do you have any ideas about what you want to paint today?"

"Yeah. I made a drawing." Xander took off his Batman backpack and unzipped it. He took out a sketchpad Maggie had given him for his birthday. "I wanna make a rougarou. Like this."

Xander showed Maggie his drawing. The boy, a preternaturally talented artist, had drawn a rougarou lying on the ground in a cemetery, surrounded by crypts. Maggie recognized the haunting image. "Wow, this is really good," Maggie said, forcing herself to sound enthusiastic. "Did you copy it from something?"

The boy nodded. He reached into his backpack and pulled out a copy of the *Pelican Penny Clipper*. The cover photo showed Susannah's body, clad in the rougarou costume, splayed out in the Dupois graveyard. A headline screamed, "Masseuse Death Ruled a Homicide."

But it was the subtitle that made Maggie feel ill.

"Suspects Include Local Family."

Chapter 10

"If I ever do murder someone, it's gonna be Little Earlie," Maggie fumed to Bo through her Bluetooth as she drove home. "Can't I sue him for libel or something?"

"I wish you could, except . . ."

"It's not libelous because it's true." Bo's silence confirmed this. "I guess it does look bad, with us firing Susannah and the whole property line thing. At least it looks that way to people who don't know us, like Zeke Griffith. But you'd think the locals had a little more faith in my family." She shared the list of art class cancellations with Bo.

"That's insane." Bo's anger made Maggie feel a touch better. "Forget those numbnuts. You got Pelican PD on your side."

"That's a true godsend." Maggie made a right turn onto the side road by Crozat. Night had already fallen, so she put on the Falcon's bright lights. "Can you come by tonight? I could use a hug. And maybe more."

"I better not."

"Right," Maggie said, deflated. "The appearance of impropriety. Can't have you consorting with suspects."

"Ugh, I hate this," Bo said with a growl.

"Me too. I'll call you tomorrow. If Griffith isn't tapping our phones."

Maggie ended the call. She turned off her car's brights and parked. Her phone pinged a text from her mother: *Paranormals here. Come join us. PLEASE.*

Maggie dragged herself to the manor house, where she found her parents entertaining the B and B guests with wine and cheese in the front parlor. Barrymore and Emma were mixed in with a half-dozen unfamiliar faces. Barrymore was holding court, while Emma, ignoring him, read one of the magazines the Crozats made available to their guests. DruCilla was there as well, Lovie perched on her shoulder. As soon as Maggie came into the room, Ninette jumped up. "There you are, chère. Everyone, this is our daughter Maggie. Maggie, these are our new guests, the Paranormals. Oh my, look at the time. I best get dinner going."

Tug leapt to his feet. "I'll help, dearest."

Maggie's parents made a quick exit, leaving her with the group. "I was in the middle of reliving the deadly twist to *Resurrection of a Spirit* for our newcomers," Barrymore said, leading Maggie to understand why her parents had disappeared so fast. The actor had positioned his wingback chair to face the others as if he were performing a one-man show, which it turned out he was. He leaned toward his listeners, who responded in kind. "There we were, in the final moments of our evening's production," he shared in a sonorous voice. "The climax, as it were. Suddenly, a costumed creature appeared from nowhere—"

"A rougarou," DruCilla explained to the group.

"Whatever you want to call it." Barrymore didn't look happy about his performance being interrupted. He resumed his story. "We were aghast, but being the professionals that we are—well, at least *I* am—we seamlessly improvised around the unexpected intrusion."

"It's true," DruCilla told the others. "They did."

The actor cleared his throat and shot her a look. "To finish my story, the audience was thrilled by our tale. Applause, applause, and then . . . the creature . . . *died*."

Barrymore somehow made the final word reverberate, and his audience gasped. Maggie caught Emma's attention, and the two shared an eye roll. "I'm so disappointed I missed it," groused one of the Paranormals, an attractive older woman named Cindy.

"It *was* the death of another human being, so there's that," Maggie said. From the kitchen came the sound of the china bell Ninette used to announce a meal. "Dinner's ready, everyone."

Maggie motioned for the guests to follow her, which they did. The Beckers, a young couple from New Orleans who had booked the B and B's last available room on impulse, joined them. "We did some shopping in town," Ashley Becker said. She held up a bag from Bon Bon Sweets and a box from its sister store, Fais Dough Dough Pastries. "Everything is decorated for Halloween. Look, they even used strands of string cheese to wrap the croissant like a mummy."

Maggie admired the croissant Ashley showed her. "I'm so glad you liked the stores. My cousin Lia owns them."

Will Becker pulled a mug decorated with a vibrant illustration of Crozat from another bag. "We got souvenirs, too. Not often that we get to say, 'Hey, we know the artist.'"

Maggie, the artist in question, blushed. She'd put her talent to use creating a line of souvenir items featuring her designs of local landmarks. "Thank you so much. A percentage of sales goes to our local historical society, so they thank you, too."

"I love your style," Ashley said. "Are you working on anything new?"

Maggie flashed on her beloved art studio, currently commandeered by the MacDowells. The moment of anger subsided, replaced by guilt and then fear. The MacDowells had suffered a loss—a loss Ville Blanc detective Griffith seemed determined to pin on her. "No, I'm not working on anything new right now," Maggie said, keeping her response judicious. "I've been busy with our Spooky Past weekends. But I'll get back to my art eventually." *If I'm not jailed for a murder I didn't commit.*

Dinner was refreshingly uneventful. Even Barrymore was low-key—worn out, Maggie assumed, from his impromptu performance. When the meal was over, Maggie decided that a visit to her future home with Bo would help take her mind off murder. She unlocked the entryway door and climbed a flight of stairs to the apartment above the spa. She flipped on the lights to reveal the apartment's spacious interior. The main living area featured an open floor plan, with no separation between the kitchen, living, and dining spaces. A hallway led past a bathroom to three bedrooms: Xander's room, a master with an en suite bathroom, and a third bedroom that Maggie hoped would someday be a baby nursery. The hallway ended at a bonus room, which would serve as the couple's shared office.

Maggie noticed that her father had transferred the beautiful needlepoint chairs from the attic to the apartment's living area. Their soft palette of golds and greens blended perfectly with the room's pale-yellow walls. She wandered through the space from one end to the other, imagining it fully furnished and humming with life. The antique chairs would face the sage-colored couch she and Bo had picked out together—their first joint purchase for their new home. One corner of the large room would be dedicated to Xander's needs: a desk and computer for schoolwork, an easel for his artwork, right next to a window that flooded the room with natural light. Maggie was overcome with emotion. *Nuh-uh, no crying,* she admonished herself, and shook off the moment of vulnerability. "Instead of crying," she declared to the empty room. "Action."

* * *

Maggie strode into the cottage, where Gran was sorting through a box of wedding favor samples. She put a blunt question to her grandmother. "Who do you think killed Susannah?"

Gran, taken aback, put down the box. She held up a magnet decorated with a photo of a bride and groom. "I was going to ask what you thought about this as a possible favor, but that question feels rather lightweight right now."

Maggie plopped down on the sofa next to Gran. "I can't sit around waiting for Pelican PD to clear me. They're doing their best—I know Bo is all over it—but I can't live with the threat of being carted off to jail hanging over me."

"It does put a damper on our wedding-planning efforts," Gran acknowledged.

"The only way for me to clear my name—for all of us to—is to find the real killer."

"Then let's talk about suspects," Gran said.

"Good idea."

The women furrowed their brows and thought. "The only people in town who knew Susannah were us and her family," Maggie finally said.

"Helene Brevelle certainly had a bone to pick with her," Gran pointed out. "Plus, Susannah had clients, both as a masseuse and as a psychic. She might have seriously offended one of them."

Maggie nodded. "Good point. She could have given a client a bad reading, one that pushed them over the edge for some reason."

"Unfortunately, *our* motive is crystal clear," Gran said. "Susannah's departure from the earthly plane rids us of both a spa competitor and a property dispute. No wonder Detective Griffith likes all of us for the crime. Ooh, listen to me, I sound so *Law and Order*. I cannot stop watching those reruns."

"You're assuming Susannah's death means the end of our fight over the property line, but what if Doug inherits her property?"

"Well, *duh*, as the kids say. Which means the grieving widower might really be a manipulative murderer." Gran got a crafty look on her face. "What time is it?"

Maggie glanced at the antique brass clock decorating the room's fireplace mantel. "Eight thirty."

"It's not too late to pay a call on the MacDowells. Checking in, worried about them and all that. We can gather a little intel before they leave town, which I assume they will, now that their one connection to Pelican is gone."

"That's good and bad news," Maggie said. "Good news if I get my art studio back, bad because three suspects will be gone. It's too bad the police can't say 'don't leave town' anymore."

"I think that was mostly a trope of mystery novels. A convenient way to keep all your suspects in one place. What are you doing?"

"Confirming we have an extradition agreement with Canada." Maggie held up her cell phone. "We do."

Gran stood up. "Go to the manor kitchen and put together a meal we can bring to the MacDowells. You know Bonnie will welcome us. She's a chowhound, that girl."

"I'm on it."

Maggie darted over to the manor kitchen. She assembled a healthy collection of to-go dishes that included her mother's shrimp Creole, fried okra, and corn maque choux. She found half a chocolate Doberge cake in the refrigerator and wrapped it up, along with several biscuits. Arms full, she met her grandmother outside their cottage, and they tramped through the woods to the old schoolhouse.

Doug answered their knock on the door. He looked no better than when they'd seen him the day before. In fact, he looked worse. His eyes were sunken, the bags under them pronounced and puffy. "The kids are out," he said, motioning for them to come in. "We spent the day making arrangements for Susie. It was pretty draining, so they went to grab a drink in town."

Maggie suddenly remembered the *Pelican Penny Clipper* and its lurid story casting suspicion on her family. She searched the room with her eyes and was relieved to there wasn't a copy of the paper lying around. It didn't seem like the MacDowells had been alerted to the Crozats' status as suspects, although there was no preventing them from coming to that conclusion on their own. The faster she and Gran extracted information from Doug, the better.

Gran, who Maggie guessed was thinking the same thing, had already helped herself to a seat. "Magnolia, dear, put the goodies away in the fridge." Doug sat down opposite the octogenarian. "Can we heat you up a plate, Doug?"

"No thanks. I don't have much of an appetite right now."

"Of course you don't. I imagine that's true of the twins, too. Although their relationship with your wife seemed, I don't know . . . a bit contentious."

Doug snorted. "Pretty much every relationship with those two is contentious. They've been giving me grief ever since me and their mom broke up, which was ten years ago by now. Never mind that she's remarried and happy as a pig in you-know-what." His lower lip quivered. "Susie and I had that. I was happy as a fat little piggy. But I didn't deserve her. She was too good for me. I did some things I feel real bad about now."

Doug began to blubber. Gran helplessly patted his leg. "There, there. Let it out."

Maggie found a beer in the refrigerator. She twisted off the bottle top and brought it over to Doug. "Here." Grateful, the widower took the bottle and chugged its contents. "I think being here makes it harder on you. In Pelican, I mean, not in the studio," she added hastily. "Once you get back to Toronto, you'll be able to start the healing process."

"Oh, we're not going back."

This revelation took Maggie by surprise. "You're not?"

"Nope. This was Susannah's ancestral home."

"Technically, that would be Acadia," Maggie felt compelled to say. "In Canada. Your homeland."

"This is where Susie's heart and soul were." Doug made an expansive gesture with his arms.

"My goodness, after only living here several weeks?" Gran said. "That's quite a commitment."

"Yes," Doug said, taking her brittle comment at face value. His lower lip quivered again. "We're getting Susie's ashes back tomorrow. We're going to scatter them here. On her land."

At a loss for words, Maggie simply responded, "Huh."

Gran took the lead. "What a lovely gesture. I'm sure she'd appreciate it. Have you thought what you'll do with the land after you've . . . immortalized her?"

"No. We're each other's beneficiaries, so I'll have to figure that out at some point. Might be best to keep the ashes in one place. Do a memorial garden or something."

"Another lovely gesture." Gran stood up. "If you need anything, do let us know. Maggie?"

Gran took her granddaughter's arm and gently pulled her out the door. "Close your mouth, chère—you'll swallow flies.

Or worse, mosquitoes. I wouldn't put it past those critters to bite from the inside."

"I couldn't stand hearing him say *her land*," Maggie said, tromping through the woods with large, angry steps.

"*Was* her land. Now it's his. Which gives him motive. Although I have to say, I found Doug's grief sincere. I could be wrong."

"No," Maggie said. "My instinct says he's genuinely devastated. But I'm guessing mostly about being left to handle his obnoxious children without Susannah as a buffer."

"Maybe Susannah really did fall in love with the area," Gran mused. "She wouldn't be the first person to find Cajun Country irresistible."

"No." Maggie gave her head a vehement shake. "There's more to it than that. I know it. Susannah was an operator. I'd even call her a grifter. She was one of those people who could fake sincerity so well people believed it. Even me." Maggie kicked a branch blocking her path out of the way.

The two women reached the cottage. "We're done for the evening," Gran said to her granddaughter, "so get a good night's rest, chère. You need it."

"Sleep isn't my friend these days."

Gran eyed her granddaughter with concern. "Yes, and it's starting to show."

"Ouch," Maggie said with asperity. "Thanks for that."

"I mean in terms of your anxiety level and the physical toll it's taking on you. You're too thin, your eyes are shadowed, and you're all-around jittery. Do whatever it is young people do these days to relax. Well, whatever's legal in this state." Gran put her arms around Maggie and held her in a tight hug. "I don't want you wheeled down the wedding aisle on a gurney."

Maggie did her best to follow her grandmother's advice. Before going to bed, she contorted herself into a few yoga positions and did deep-breathing exercises. Once under the covers, she tried lulling herself to sleep with meditation. But a list of potential murder suspects replaced images of flowering fields and waterfalls, and Maggie gave up trying to turn off her brain. Instead, she ran through the list, beginning with bereaved widower Doug MacDowell. *Killers have been known to grieve for their victims*, she mused, *and he was Susannah's beneficiary.* This train of thought led Maggie to wonder if the twins were in Susannah's will. Considering their fractious relationship, she assumed not. But the removal of their stepmother from the pictured offered the aggravating duo a chance to further whatever slim bond they might have with their father. *I wonder if they're in* his *will.*

Walter Breem, Dupois Plantation's loner caretaker, was up next on Maggie's list of suspects. She resented Zeke Griffith's lack of interest in the strange man. Breem certainly had opportunity. But did he have means and motive?

Maggie checked the clock on her wicker nightstand. Its digital display read two AM. She fluffed her pillow and rolled onto her right side toward the bedroom wall, grateful that her days in the narrow twin bed were numbered. She and Bo had ordered a luxe king-size mattress for their matrimonial bed. *Then again, my bed here is probably twice the size of what you get in prison*, she thought glumly. Restless, Maggie rolled onto her left side, facing the bedroom window. *There have to be more suspects.* She revisited the possibility that Susannah had made an enemy out of one of her clients. Patria, the gullible young actress in Quentin's play, had readily admitted to a psychic reading. Maggie knew performers were generally an insecure lot, which made them susceptible to the hocus-pocus of someone like Susannah. Maybe one of Patria's castmates received a reading he or she didn't like and decided to punish the messenger.

Tomorrow I'll put Gran to work finding out if the twins benefit in any way from Susannah's death. Pelican PD can take a closer look at Walter Breem. And I'll poke around the play's cast to see if anyone besides Patria availed themselves of Susannah's psychic "powers."

A plan in place, Maggie finally began to relax. She was about to doze off when she noticed a flash of light coming from the manor house. *Or was I dreaming?* she wondered. She threw off her bed's vintage quilt, padded to the window, and peered across the graveled parking lot.

It was no dream. Nor was it a ghost. Someone was in Crozat Plantation's attic . . . at two o'clock in the morning.

Chapter 11

The light went out a moment after she spotted it, but Maggie wasn't taking any chances. She threw on clothes and raced over to the manor house, heading up the back stairs with light footsteps so she didn't disturb the B and B guests. She almost collided with her father, who was coming down the stairs. He wore slippers and a bathrobe over his pajamas. "You saw the light too?" she asked.

"No," Tug said. "The Beckers, that young couple from New Orleans, woke me. They're staying in the Damask Room and heard footsteps above them in the attic. Freaked them out. They were about ready to jump in their car and head back to the city. I convinced them it was just this old place creaking."

"It wasn't."

"You and I know that, but let's not mention it to our guests. We got enough trouble going on right now as it is." Tug motioned for Maggie to follow him. "Walk quiet. I told the Beckers I might be poking around for a minute or two, but I don't want to set them off again."

A sign reading *Employees Only* hung from a rope, blocking access to Crozat's attic. The two tiptoed upstairs to the attic door. As Tug opened it, the knob came off in his hand. "This wasn't much protection to begin with, but someone loosened it." He used his flashlight to point out loose screws in the doorknob plate.

Tug and Maggie walked up the handful of steps into the attic. He let his flashlight circle the room. Maggie had spent enough time riffling through the century and a half's accumulation of Crozat personal belongings to recognize that someone else had also been pawing through it. Furniture had been rearranged. A trunk lid was thrown open. "Do you know if anything's missing?"

Tug shook his head. "Not offhand. I'll have to check in the morning. Nothing more we can do tonight. Except for this." He used his flashlight to indicate a Victorian mahogany davenport writing desk. "We'll use the old desk to block off the attic door. Help me carry it."

Maggie took one end of the desk and Tug the other. Solid and beautifully made, it was also heavy. The two managed to carry it out of the attic without making noise. They closed the door and placed the desk in front of it. "If anyone tries to move this, we'll be sure to hear it," Maggie said. "I'll call Pelican PD first thing and have them send someone over."

"I want you here with me," Tug said. "We can go over the place together with the police and see if we can find footprints or other clues about who was up there."

"It has to be a guest, right? Someone who has access to the house."

Tug looked embarrassed. "To be honest, I've gotten a little lazy about keys over the years. If guests forget to turn them in, I don't hound them about mailing them back. I just make new ones."

"So what you're saying is, there are a whole lotta keys to this place floating around and pretty much anyone in the universe could be our intruder."

"Pretty much," Tug said sheepishly.

Bemused, Maggie shook her head. "I'm thinking it's time to research the cost of programmable key cards." She ran a hand over the writing desk's smooth finish. "One upside to tonight. I found my perfect desk for the apartment."

Tug used the back of his hand to wipe sweat from his neck. "Nothing else to be done now, chère. Go back to bed. Something tells me tomorrow's gonna be a busy day."

To Maggie's surprise, given the evening's concerning events, she had no trouble falling asleep. She didn't wake up until eight the next morning, when she was greeted by the aroma of coffee and baked goods wafting through the air. Sleepy-eyed, she stumbled out of bed and into the kitchen. She found Bo, not Gran, brewing coffee and setting out an assortment of fresh pastries. Instead of his detective attire, he was clad in jeans and one of the T-shirts Maggie had designed for Pelican's *Cajun Country Live!* festival. "You're the most welcome sight ever," Maggie said. She threw her arms around him, and they kissed.

"I'm looking forward to future morning greetings like that," he said with a sexy grin.

Maggie picked up a croissant and tore it in half. The delicious breakfast treat was still warm, and laden with an aromatic almond filling. "With all that's been going on since Susannah was killed, I didn't know when I'd see you next."

Bo poured them each a cup of coffee and sat down at the café table. "I took the week off. Said I needed to be with my kid to do all the Halloween stuff, like buying candy and baking cupcakes for school."

Maggie threw her beau a skeptical look. "You're baking cupcakes?"

"Someone is," he said with a wink. "And that someone is whoever's doing the baking this week at Fais Dough Dough."

"Aside from the fact that the sight of you makes my heart go pitty-pat, we had an incident here last night."

Bo's expression grew serious. "Talk to me."

Maggie's cell rang. She checked the number. "Tell you in a minute. It's Kaity at Belle Vista." Maggie answered the call. "Hey, Kaity. What's up?"

"Sorry to call this early." Kaity sounded tense, a contrast to her usual boundless supply of upbeat energy. "Have y'all had any rougarou sightings last night or this morning?"

"No. I haven't seen any since poor Susannah passed away in that strange costume. Have you had one?"

"Yeah, and it almost gave one of our guests a heart attack. She was gonna check out, but I bribed her into staying with a free massage."

"No rougarous, ghosts, or vampires here, but we did have a prowler in our attic last night." Bo raised his eyebrows. Maggie mouthed to him, "I'll explain."

"I thought maybe the lady was seeing things," Kaity said, "but she described it pretty clear. Whether it was real or in her mind, it's bad for business."

"True dat. I'll keep an eye out over here and let you know if we have any sightings. As long as I've got you on the phone, any chance you could share your massage therapist? Mo Heedles is taking over our spa. She's looking for a full-time masseuse, but we could use someone part-time until then."

"I wish I could help y'all out, but our masseuse has been booked solid since your gal got offed. It's like they say, one man's trash is another man's treasure."

"Yikes," Maggie said. "Not sure that's the best analogy for the situation, but I get what you mean." She ended the call.

"You were saying about a prowler," Bo prompted.

"Right. Let's move on from murder and monster sightings to *that*." Maggie shared the previous evening's mystery with him. "I don't know if someone was trying to scare us or steal something."

"As soon as you're done with breakfast, we'll have a look."

"Okay." Maggie took a bite of her pastry. "I'm eating slowly. This feels so nice and normal compared to everything else that's going on. I don't want it to end."

"It's gonna be our forever, chère," Bo said.

"If I don't end up in the hoosegow, the big house. If they don't send me up the river. When I lived in New York, I found out what that meant. Sing Sing prison is up the river from the city. In Westchester County. On the Hudson River. Probably the prettiest setting for any prison in America. Except for Alcatraz. What a view of San Francisco!"

"You're stalling."

"I know." Maggie willed herself not to cry but couldn't contain the quiver of her lower lip.

Bo reached across the table. He took Maggie's hands in his. "You going to prison will happen over my dead body."

"Please don't say that. Given what's happened around here, that expression is literal, not figurative."

"Stop worrying." Bo leaned forward and gave Maggie a gentle kiss on her lips. "I've got your back, and so does the entire Pelican police force. Trust me, as much as everyone likes you and the rest of your family, they resent Ville Blanc PD a hundred times more. So that's a whole lotta motivation for our local boys in blue."

"I know Ville Blanc's got a job to do, but does it have to come with so much attitude?"

"It doesn't, but unfortunately, it does." Bo let go of Maggie's hands and tapped a text on his cell phone. "Since technically I'm off today, I'm gonna get one of our boys over here ASAP to take a look at your attic." Bo's phone pinged. "Artie Belloise's on his way."

Maggie couldn't help laughing. Belloise, a self-proclaimed chowhound, never passed up the chance for an investigation at Crozat, knowing it always came with snacks or even a meal from Maggie's mother. "Of course he is. I'll tell Mom to put out a spread."

"Knowing Artie, he'll probably put on the cruiser siren to get here fast, so we better head over or there'll be more eating than investigating on Artie's part."

Maggie and Bo managed to beat Artie to the manor house, which the police officer didn't look happy about when he showed up fifteen minutes later, siren blaring as predicted. "I smell Mama Crozat's fine seafood gumbo, so let's get the show on the road here. Durand, my friend, I hear you're on vacay this week, so I'm gonna pretend you're not even here."

Tug and Maggie led the officers to the attic. With Bo and Artie's help, they pushed aside the antique writing desk. "I had a locksmith come by to change the lock on the door," Tug said, "but it turns out we need a whole new door. I'm ordering it today, but it won't be here for at least a week." He handed them each a dust mask. "Best to wear these if we're gonna be up there for any length of time."

The four donned the masks and entered the attic. Artie circled the space with a torch flashlight. He used it to point toward footprints in the attic floor's dust. "Those either of yours?" he asked Maggie and Tug. Both shook their heads.

"Too big for mine, too small for my dad," Maggie said. "Can I borrow that?" She took Artie's flashlight and shone it on two sets of footprints closer to where the four stood. "Those are ours."

She handed the flashlight back to Artie, who circled the room with it a second time. "Notice anything missing?"

"There's so much stuff up here, it's hard to tell." Tug held up a brass candlestick. "I'm pretty sure we had two of these. Other one might be around here, might be lost. Or might be stolen."

"Given that extra set of footprints, I'd go with stolen." Artie turned to Bo. "In your off-duty opinion, Detective?"

"Agreed, Officer." Bo addressed Maggie and Tug. "Keep an eye out for a guest who seems flusher than they were before. And whoever's doing housekeeping should look out for something that either suddenly appears or doesn't seem to go with the guest's belongings."

"Marie and Bud Shexnayder are helping us clean the rooms," Maggie said. "I'll tell them."

"All righty then, we're done here," Artie said.

The four trooped down the attic stairs. At the bottom, they pushed the writing desk back in place. "My new desk for the apartment," Maggie said to Bo with pride.

"I like it," he responded, planting a light kiss on her lips. Artie *ahem*ed. "I'm off duty, remember?"

Artie ignored him. He rubbed his stomach. "Man, investigations work up an appetite."

"Ninette's ready for you with double servings of everything," Tug said.

"Your missus knows me so well. *Allons-y*. Let's go."

Tug and Artie left for the kitchen while Maggie walked Bo back to his car. "Murders, burglaries, ghosts, rougarous," she said. "I was safer in Brooklyn. The bad parts."

"They still have bad parts? I thought every inch of it was gentrified."

"There might be a sketchy block or two left in the borough. Gentrification makes me think of Rent My Digs. We wouldn't be in this whole mess if pressure from that stupid app hadn't made me think up the spooky weekends, which made me think of opening the spa to time with them, which made me think of hiring Susannah as our masseuse." Maggie paused to take a breath. "If you can nail that slimeball techie Gavin Grody for any crime besides generally ruining Pelican, go for it."

"I wish. But sadly, being an SOB isn't a crime. Much as I wish it were." The couple reached Bo's car. "Be safe, chère."

Bo kissed Maggie, this time lingering on her lips. Then he hopped into his SUV and took off. Maggie scampered up the steps into the cottage. Gran was there, dressed in navy pants and a gray silk top that brought out the shine in her silver hair. "Morning, darlin' girl," Gran said. "Lee took me to a wedding supply store outside Baton Rouge that just opened."

"Already?" Maggie couldn't help being amused by her grand-mere's passion for wedding paraphernalia. "It's only a little after nine o'clock."

"We had to go first thing. Lee needed to get to work because the service station is swamped with cars having all sorts of troubles. He swears the Halloween season has brought out spirits that are making mischief with people's engines. Anyhoo, the wedding shop owners were a bit surprised to see us knocking on their door at dawn's early light. But because we were their very first customers, we earned ourselves a few freebies." Gran held up two small bride and groom statues. "Look at these. Senior citizen cake toppers. I love how custom-ized everything is these days. The bride has hair my color and the groom's got a cane. How cute is that? And I thought this was *so* you." Gran held up a small statue of a bride in jeans and a wedding veil flashing a peace sign. "And this is for Bo."

Gran displayed the figure of a man with a pipe wearing a caped coat and deerstalker hat. He clutched a magnifying glass in his extended hand.

"Gran, that's Sherlock Holmes."

"Exactly. Because Bo is a detective. What? Too on the nose?"

Before Maggie could yell "Yes!" at her grandmother, her cell rang. "Hi, Mom. Has Artie eaten us out of business yet?"

"He left. I made him a to-go bag. A big one. Honey, we have a problem." Hearing the anxiety in her mother's voice, Maggie tensed. "Those detectives from Ville Blanc are here," Ninette continued. "They're asking for our consent to do a search. Your dad left to finalize the order for the new attic door and he forgot his phone, so I can't reach him. I don't know what to tell the detectives, so I'm stalling."

Gran, worried, put down her collection of wedding cake toppers. "I don't like the look on your face. What's wrong?"

Maggie put a hand over her phone. "Ville Blanc detectives are asking to do a search."

The octogenarian planted both hands on her hips. "Tell them no, *non*, ix-nay, nada, forget it," she said, defiant. "And as they say in all the mobster movies and series, fuhgeddaboudit."

"I don't want to make things worse," Maggie said. She returned to her mother. "Keep stalling. Tell them I'm in the shower so you can't reach me either."

Maggie ended the call and punched in a different number. "Are you calling Bo?" Gran asked.

"No. Ville Blanc is looking for an excuse to cite him for impropriety. I don't want to give them any ammunition." The cell on the other end rang only once before someone picked up. "Rufus, hi. We have a situation and need your help."

Maggie filled Rufus in. He responded with a barrage of profanity that made Maggie, no slouch in the scatological department herself, blush. "Those nimrods have to come begging to do a search because they're having trouble getting a warrant. Let me handle 'em. I'll be there in five," Rufus said, before hanging up.

Maggie decided to give truth to Ninette's lie and jump into the shower. She rinsed off attic grime from her body, then stood under the soothing flow of water until she heard the scream of a police siren growing closer. She reluctantly turned off the water and got dressed, opting for a staid look of black pants and a cotton polo shirt decorated with the Doucet Plantation logo.

She found Rufus, her mother, grandmother, and Ville Blanc detectives Griffith and Broussard in the B and B's office. Maggie got great pleasure from seeing that Rufus was already on a tear. "Next time, y'all better think long and hard before you try sneaking around our department and the law," Rufus railed.

"Acck!" Lovie screeched. "Long and hard, long and hard."

Gran raised an eyebrow. "Oh my, that sounds *wildly* inappropriate."

"We're not the Mayberry RFD buffoons you think we are, Griffith." Rufus glared at the VBPD lead detective. "Not one of the Crozat family members has a motive for murder. Susannah MacDowell's death doesn't benefit anyone but her widder husband, Doug. He's the beneficiary of her will, so the land and all that comes with it goes to him. That's a big old motive in my book."

Griffith didn't seem the least bit ruffled by Ru's hostility. This frustrated Maggie. But his response terrified her. "Anger," he said. "Vengeance. Humiliation. I see a property dispute gone bad. Turned ugly. Deadly ugly."

"Acck, ugly! Deadly! Ugly!"

"Will someone please shut that bird up?" Griffith snapped, his equanimity finally disturbed. "And I don't wanna hear from you anymore either, Durand. You're obviously in cahoots with the Crozats, just like your cousin."

Rufus turned bright red with rage. Sweat poured off his forehead. "If you're saying we let our personal lives blind us to criminal activity, that's about as insulting as it gets, Griffith. If evidence pointed to anyone in this family as the killer, I'd be the first to march them out the door and into a patrol car, even Granny here."

"Excuse me!" Gran, ire raised, barked. "Nobody ever calls me *Granny*. Do I look like I sit on a rockin' chair on the ol' front porch smokin' a corncob pipe? I don't *think* so."

"My apologies, ma'am," Rufus said, abashed. He resumed his tirade. "And who uses *cahoots* anymore? Are we solving crimes in the 1940s? But you know what, if being sure the citizens of my town get the fair treatment they deserve is being 'in cahoots,' then I am cahooting away. And let me tell you something else, Detective I'm-So-Cool-I-Should-Be-on-a-TV-Show, I—ah—I—agh—"

Rufus cried out in pain. He clutched his stomach, doubled over, and collapsed to the floor, unconscious.

"Acck!" Lovie squawked. "Oh my! Oh my, oh my, oh my!"

Chapter 12

Maggie might not have been a fan of the Ville Blanc detectives, but she was impressed by how quickly they jumped into action. Griffith provided emergency medical assistance to Rufus while Detective Broussard summoned an ambulance. Rufus came to and groaned. "Lord, my stomach. Who took a knife to me?"

Ninette dropped to her knees and dabbed his forehead with a moistened kitchen towel. "No one, Rufus. Nothing murderous here for a change. You got something bad going on inside you."

"The ambulance is here," Broussard said.

"I'll fetch them," Maggie said.

She ran down the hallway and threw open the heavy, centuries-old front door. EMTs Regine Armitage and Cody Pugh pushed a gurney through the doorway. "Where's the body?" Cody asked as they raced the gurney down the hall.

"Back parlor, our office. It's Rufus, and he's alive."

"That's a nice change of pace with y'all," Regine said.

"Yeah, thanks, my mother mentioned that, too," Maggie tossed the acerbic response to the EMT's back. Regine and Cody were already strapping a moaning Rufus onto the gurney.

"Call Sandy," the police chief, his voice weak, said to Maggie as he was wheeled out of the room.

"I will," Maggie promised. "We'll meet you at the hospital."

Within minutes, a siren announced that the ambulance was on the way to St. Pierre Parish Medical Center, leaving Maggie to face Detectives Griffith and Broussard. "Thank you for helping Rufus."

"Just doing our job," Griffith said. "Which started with our coming here to ask for permission to do a targeted search of the premises."

"Right." Maggie assumed a thoughtful position, then said, "*Fuhgeddaboudit*. I'd walk you to the door, but I have calls to make. Enjoy the rest of your day."

She left the room for her car, tapping in Sandy's cell number as she walked. Before she could finish entering it, her phone exploded with a flurry of texts from various friends in a group thread.

Heard about Ru going to hospital. Is he okay? What's going on?

OMG, Ru Durand's stomach exploded.

Heard Ru was poisoned.

Whaaa??? Noooo!

Maggie typed a response to quell the rumors, which were spiraling out of control: *Ru had stomach pain. Maybe appendix.*

No exploding, no poison!!! Calm down, all! Then she jumped into her vintage convertible and took off for the hospital.

Maggie found Bo in the ER waiting room. The two embraced, then released each other. "Any updates?" Maggie asked.

"Not yet. Sandy is with him. What happened?"

Maggie shared the details of the Ville Blanc detectives' visit and Ru's sudden illness. Bo was more upset by the former than the latter, which would have amused Maggie if the situation hadn't been so dire. "I can't stand that Griffith," Bo fumed. "He's an ambitious operator who's just trying to make some career noise. Tell your family, don't give him anything."

Bo's dark tone concerned Maggie. "Do you think we should hire Quentin?"

"No. You don't pull that trigger until you have to. If you hire a defense attorney now, it could give the appearance of guilt to someone as hungry for an arrest, any arrest, as Griffith." Bo's cell rang. "Sorry. With Ru out of commission, I'm the go-to guy. Which means it's also the end of my week off."

Maggie waved him off. "Go. Protect our fair city, Commissioner Gordon."

Bo grinned. "Maybe that should be my costume for Halloween. The commissioner to Xander's Batman."

Bo stepped away. Maggie took a seat on one of the room's unwelcoming hard plastic chairs, only to jump up when she saw Sandy Sechrest, Ru's girlfriend, running down the hall toward the waiting room. She met Sandy halfway and enveloped the lithe exotic dancer–turned–exercise instructor in a hug. "What's going on?" Maggie asked. "Is Ru going to be all right?"

Sandy nodded. "Yes, thank goodness. He had a gallbladder attack, which isn't life-threatening. But the doctors have to remove it. They'll prep Ru today and do the surgery tomorrow."

The women walked into the waiting room. Maggie bought them each a bottle of water from the vending machine. "I've always thought they should sell booze instead of water in the ER," she said, handing Sandy her bottle. "If there's any place you need a drink, it's here."

"Agreed." Sandy opened her bottle, drank half of it, then collapsed into a chair. "Ow, these are hard."

"I know." Maggie sat down next to her. "Another strike against the ER."

Sandy placed her elbow on the chair's arm and rested her head in the palm of her hand. She was dressed in purple leggings, a sports bra, and a tank top decorated with the logo of her exercise studio, DanceBod. "When you called me, I was terrified. All I could think was, don't you die on me, Rufus Durand. He can be smug, overbearing, opinionated, lazy, a total slob—"

"And you're with him why?"

Sandy teared up. "Because he's smart and funny and loves me more than anybody I've ever known."

"All good reasons." Maggie pulled a clean tissue from her purse and gave it to Sandy. "Do you want me to stay with you?"

"It's okay. But could you do me a favor and take King Cake for a walk?"

"Absolutely. I'll do that right now." Maggie stood up. She saw Bo end a call, then answer another one. "Let Bo know what's going on with Ru, and where I went. I'll touch base with you later."

After Sandy gave her the key, Maggie departed for the dance studio. As she drove, she contemplated the recent developments. With Rufus immobilized and Bo forced to step back from the investigation into Susannah's death—plus having to take on Ru's Pelican PD duties—the Crozats' two most powerful allies were sidelined. *I'm pretty much on my own*, Maggie thought to herself as she drove past fields of sugarcane into Pelican's scenic town center. She parked behind the studio and let herself in. King Cake, Sandy's corgi-Chihuahua mix who served as the instructor's beloved companion and therapy dog, barked a sleepy hello and wagged his tail. "You're a terrible guard dog," Maggie chided him with affection.

She put on King Cake's harness and leash and took him out the front door. DanceBod was only a few doors down from Junie's Oyster Bar and Dance Hall. Maggie watched as a brand-new Tesla did a sleight-of-hand parallel-parking job in front of Junie's. Bonnie MacDowell exited the car from the passenger's side. A moment later, Rent My Digs mogul Gavin Grody emerged from the driver's side. The two, each glued to their cell phones, managed to make their way into Junie's without tripping or colliding with someone or something. When Maggie was sure they were out of sight, she walked King Cake to the Tesla, and he promptly peed on one of the tires. "That's my boy," Maggie said, reaching down to pet him. He ran in circles, then crouched on his back haunches and took a poo next to the driver's door. "Well done," Maggie congratulated him. "I so wish we could leave it there for a certain jerk to step in when he gets in his car. But we can't."

Maggie cleaned up after King Cake, then walked him back home. He devoured the treat she gave him, then sacked out in his deluxe doggy bed. She left the studio, but instead of heading home, she headed for Junie's. It was time to do some investigating of her own.

JJ greeted her with a kiss on each cheek. Instead of wearing one of his late mother's caftans, he was outfitted like a Valkyrie, complete with horned helmet. "What's with the costume?" Maggie asked.

"You like?" JJ struck a pose. "It's from when Mama was a supernumerary in *The Ring Cycle* up in Baton Rouge." He blasted out a few shrill notes from the opera. The patrons, most of whom were used to JJ, ignored him. "Make yourself at home. I'll have Old Shari mix you something." He waved at the restaurant's nonagenarian bartender, who was busy with a martini shaker.

"No drinking for me right now," Maggie said.

"I know what that means, Nancy Drew-cette." JJ gave her a theatrical wink. "If you need a Watson to your Holmes, lemme know."

"That's a whole lotta mystery references mashed up into one, JJ," Maggie said, amused.

JJ sauntered off and Maggie scanned the room. It was lunchtime, so the bar was half empty, but the tables were full. Her goal was to finagle useful information out of Bonnie. She saw Patria, the ingenue actress from the cemetery play, at a table with a few castmates. *Someone who was at the scene of the crime*, Maggie thought, *which sounds ridiculously dramatic but is true.* She noted that Bonnie and Gavin had just placed their order with JJ. They'd be there a while, so Maggie decided to home in on Patria first. She watched the actress get up and disappear into the restroom. Maggie waited a beat, then negotiated her way around a few tables and pushed the door to the restroom open. Patria was at the sink washing her hands.

"Hi," Maggie said, affecting surprise at seeing the actress. "Patria, right? From the play?"

"Yes, hi." The ingenue preened, assuming she'd been recognized for her bravura performance. "I'm sorry, I don't remember your name."

"Maggie. Maggie Crozat. My family owns Crozat B and B. We've been bringing our guests to the play. You're amazing." Maggie cringed at how unctuous she sounded, but it had the desired effect.

"Oh my, thank you," Patria fluted. Maggie half expected her to take a bow. Patria's face darkened. "It sucks, because pretty much all people remember about the show now is that lady dying."

Maggie marveled at the actress's self-absorption. "I know. She was the massage therapist at our B and B." This didn't seem to spark with the actress, but Maggie didn't care. It was a segue into a more useful topic. "And a psychic. Oh, now I remember. You saw her and she said you were gonna meet your husband, and you were worried that it might not happen because she died." *I sound like a total bimbo, but if it works, who cares.*

"Right." Patria gave her head of blonde-highlighted hair a vigorous nod, which she followed with a Cheshire cat grin. "No worries there no more. I got someone who's *very* interested."

Maggie didn't doubt that Patria's combination of shallow personality, blandly pretty looks, and knockout figure had nabbed a guy—or girl, depending on Patria's sexual orientation—who found those qualities irresistible. It was time to move off the topic of Patria, which Maggie hoped was possible. She dropped a line in the water to see if the actress would bite. "I wonder if all of Susannah's readings were as on-target as yours."

Patria bit. Her eyes lit up with the delight of sharing dirt. "They wish. Barrymore saw her a couple of times. He wanted her to tell him if he'd get hired as the spokesguy for Crawdaddy's, that fast-food chain outa Lafayette. She told him there was a curse on him and she could remove it, but it would take several visits. He paid her, like, over a hundred dollars, and he didn't even get an audition for the commercial. He was *so* mad."

"I bet."

"They had a big fight. I stopped by to get him at your place once last week when his car was in the shop, and he was getting all up in her business about the money." Patria gasped. "Do you think he killed her?"

Maggie shrugged. "Who knows? Maybe."

Patria looked genuinely worried. "I'd best be careful around him. Stay on his good side."

Maggie dropped another line. "I wonder if Susannah ticked off anyone else."

"I know Emma and that poet guy Johnnie saw her."

"Johnnie was her stepson," Maggie explained. "I doubt he got a reading from her."

"He talked Emma into it as joke. She told me she was mad at him at first and was gonna report Susannah for being a fraud, but he convinced her not to. Said it was all a big goof and not to take it so seriously." Patria scrunched up her face. "Although when you think about it, that makes it sound like Emma should've been the one killed, if she was gonna report Susannah."

"Good point," Maggie had to acknowledge.

"I better get back to my friends," Patria said. "I'll see you at the show. Tell your guests I'm happy to sign autographs."

Patria flashed a sunny smile enhanced by perfect teeth and flounced out of the bathroom. Maggie reflected on their conversation. The actress had inadvertently added a twist to the mystery. What if Susannah hadn't been the mask's intended victim?

A group of giggly teenagers came into the tight quarters of the restroom. One girl caught a glimpse of herself in the mirror and cried out, "OMG, I need some blush. I look like a dead person!"

Honey, if you only knew, Maggie thought as she squeezed past them back into the dining room. Bonnie and Gavin had begun eating. Maggie walked by them and did a double take. "Hey, y'all. You mind?" She directed this to another table and, without waiting for a reply, pulled the empty seat from that table over to where Bonnie and Gavin sat.

"Have a seat," Gavin said, amused.

Bonnie glared at Maggie. "We're eating."

"I know, and it looks great," Maggie said, then called out, "JJ, chère, would you fix me a bowl of this shrimp Creole?" JJ blew her a kiss and flashed a thumbs-up. "My fiancé loves JJ's Creole," she said to Gavin and Bonnie.

"That's right, you're engaged." Bonnie seemed to relax a bit and dug into her dish.

"So," Maggie said, "Whatcha all up to?"

Her stomach growled, and it occurred to her she hadn't eaten in hours. She swiped the last piece of French bread from the table's basket, slathered it with butter, and took a big bite as Grody watched. "Not eating any more bread, for one thing," the techie said.

Bonnie flipped her stick-straight orangy gold hair over her shoulder and made a flirty gesture toward him. "Gavin's taken me on a tour of his Digs. They're so awesome. No creepy, moldy old furniture that make the places around here look like before pictures in some TV fixer-upper real estate show. Rent My Digs have all brand-new furniture, and decoration from places like Ikea." She spoke the name of the chain that introduced the Allen wrench to the world with reverence.

"That moldy old furniture has lasted hundreds of years because it's so well built," Maggie felt compelled to point out. "I doubt a box store bookcase will stand the test of time."

"Who cares?" Bonnie said with a dismissive shrug. "It's not like we'll be around that long. Gavin's Digs have flat-screen TVs, microwaves, coffeemakers—"

"All of which we have," Maggie said, "plus a pool."

"Yeah, but this is different."

"How so?"

Maggie tried her best to sound ingenuous and not pros-
ecutorial, but she'd put Bonnie on the spot. Gavin spooned
his gumbo and watched the two women with amusement. "It
just . . ." Bonnie said, flailing. "It just is."

Sullen, she picked at her Cajun chicken salad. Maggie,
regretting that she'd let her ego control the conversation, tried
a different tack. "I've been wanting to ask, how are you holding up since Susannah's death?"

"Oh," Bonnie said, thrown by Maggie's change of topic.
"I'm doing okay. We weren't close. I mean, we didn't hate
each other or anything and I'm sad and stuff. Working with
Gavin is helping me a lot." She gazed at the techie with such
a besotted look that Maggie half expected cartoon hearts to
pop up in the young woman's eyes. Gavin, who was swiping
on his cell phone, didn't notice. "We're talking about using
my position as an influencer to attract investors so Gavin can
take Rent My Digs worldwide. It's such a relief that I get to
stay here now."

This offhand comment got Maggie's attention. "What do
you mean, now? I thought Susannah's plan was to stay here
as long as she could."

"That was her plan when we got here. But then she got
a job offer from a spa she always wanted to work at. One of
their massage therapists got carpal tunnel and had to quit.
It's, like, the most high-end place in the city. We were supposed to leave the day after she was . . . she died."

"You were?" The revelation caught Maggie by surprise.
She paused to consider the ramifications.

"My salad's getting cold," Bonnie said.

It was a ham-fisted way to get rid of her, but Maggie took the hint. "I'll get my lunch to-go. If you need me, you know where to find me. Somewhere among the creepy, moldy old furniture at Crozat."

While Maggie waited for JJ to pack up her shrimp Creole, she dissected what she'd learned from Bonnie. Despite Doug's emotional pronouncement about Pelican being Susannah's town soul mate and his declaration that he planned to plant himself in Pelican, the MacDowells had been only a day away from bailing on Cajun Country when Susannah was killed. That made two MacDowells happy to stay put.

It was time to find out where Johnnie, the third MacDowell, Mac-stood on the subject.

Chapter 13

A plea from Ione for Maggie to fill in for a sick Doucet tour guide delayed her hunting down Johnnie. She eventually found him at twilight, perched on a fallen tree overlooking the bayou behind Crozat B and B with his ubiquitous pen and journal. "Hey," he said. "How're the spam calls?"

"I'm down to one, maybe two a day."

"Progress." Johnnie gazed upward to where the combination of clouds and a setting sun created an early-evening palette of orange, pink, and gold. "The sky gives poets so much to work with." He stood up. "It's time for my Zen walk. Want to come?"

"Sure," Maggie said, grabbing the chance to extract clues from him. "How does it work?"

"We walk in silence. Absolutely no talking."

Silence was exactly the opposite of what Maggie needed from Johnnie. "What if we need to say something?"

Johnnie held up his journal. "We write it. But all verbal communication has to be kept to a minimum. Come. Let's start."

Maggie held up a hand. "It's getting dark. Before we go, do you have a flashlight?"

Johnnie held up both hands. "Nuh-uh. No flashlights on a Zen walk. Our senses are our guide."

He began trekking through the thick Louisiana brush. Maggie followed, hoping the bond of a Zen walk would lead to Johnnie sharing whether his future plans jived with those of his father and sister.

The two hiked for what felt like forever in no specific direction. The color-streaked sky disappeared, replaced by inky black clouds that blocked the moon. The air was damp, as was the ground. Maggie and Johnnie negotiated their way around swampy puddles, shoving errant branches out of their way. Maggie began to perspire. A mosquito buzzed, then stung. Another dive-bombed her. She stumbled as she swatted it away. "Ow."

"Shh," Johnnie admonished.

Maggie glared at his back but kept walking. Her mind drifted. Doug was Susannah's beneficiary, which made him a prime suspect. But he and Susannah seemed to have been on the same page with their life choices. Her desire to take a new job in Toronto didn't negate a future in Louisiana, if that's what he dreamed of. So why kill her? Then again, only a psychopath found logic in murder, and affable, slightly dim Doug didn't fit any profile Maggie knew of.

A fallen branch crunched under her feet. Her eyes had yet to adjust to the pitch-black night, and she just missed stepping into a marshy patch of land.

Maggie's attention pivoted to the Crozats' mysterious attic burglar. How long had he or she been at it? Hopefully not long enough to make a dent in the collection of antiques handed down over centuries. She vowed to corral her family into doing an inventory of the B and B's belongings and ratchet up security, which might be pricey. *We'll have to sell an heirloom or two to pay for protecting the others. Ironic.* She thought so, anyway—she was never sure if she was getting the definition of irony right.

"We're done," Johnnie announced.

Maggie saw that they'd reached the old schoolhouse. "I have to say, I enjoyed the Zen walk."

"It's rejuvenating, isn't it?" Johnnie closed his eyes and inhaled a deep breath. He slowly released it, then opened his eyes. "I feel cleansed."

"Me too." Maggie saw a chance to bring up the question she'd originally wanted to ask Johnnie and went for it. "I'd love to do another one sometime. Are you planning on staying here or going back to Toronto?"

"Either or," he said with a shrug. "I'll see you tomorrow at Susannah's memorial."

"I didn't know that was happening." Maggie hesitated. "Are you sure you and your family want us there? We're all doing an excellent job of being civil to each other, but I don't know if that carries over to a memorial service invitation."

"Are you worried because you're all suspects?" Johnnie chortled. "Oh honey, it's *Susannah*. She was a *horror*. Who *didn't* want her dead?" Johnnie made a dramatic exit into the schoolhouse, leaving a frustrated, sweaty, and itchy Maggie to find her way home in the dark.

* * *

"The Lord is my shepherd, I lack nothing," Barrymore Tuttle read in a sepulchral tone. It turned out the actor had been ordained online and was a cheap hire, so he'd won the role of officiant at Susannah MacDowell's memorial. The group that gathered in a clearing not far from the schoolhouse was small: the MacDowells, the Crozats, Barrymore, and Emma. Whatever hostility the performer felt about Susannah's iffy psychic abilities had disappeared the moment he was offered the chance to orate. "Even though I walk through the darkest valley . . ." Barrymore paused for effect, then built to a crescendo. "I will fear no evil, for you are with me; your rod and your staff, they comfort me." He delivered the last few words with such force that he dissolved into a fit of coughing, followed by a few gagging sounds and some throat clearing. "Sorry. Allergies. Curse the dust and pollen in this godforsaken Louisiana air." Barrymore punctuated this with a dramatic fist shake at the sky, then closed the Bible he was basically using as a prop since he had his lines—aka the first few verses of Psalm 23—memorized. "Let us pray." He bowed his head, and the others followed suit.

Barrymore slowly lifted his head and gave a slight nod to Doug. The widower, holding an urn, stepped forward. "My late wife Susannah was the kindest, warmest soul who ever lived." Johnnie gave a loud snort, Bonnie tried muffling a giggle, and their father shot them a look. "Her ancestors called this land home. Susannah dreamed of calling it home, too. And today, she will." Doug began pouring an endless stream of ashes onto the ground. "Wow," he said, "that's already a pretty big pile and I'm not half done."

Ninette placed a hand on his arm. "Instead of pouring the rest of them, why not bury the urn? You'll still be making her dream come true—"

"But without the gross mess," Bonnie said.

"Hey!" Doug snapped at his daughter.

"What? I'm not making a joke. It's the truth."

"Bonnie means that, Dad," Johnnie said. "You know she doesn't have a sense of humor."

Bonnie scowled at her twin. "Shut up."

"You shut up."

"Both of you shut up!" Doug barked.

"I'm starting to think Susannah got off easy," Tug muttered.

"Thibault," Gran scolded.

Fearing he'd lost his audience, Barrymore made a stab at reclaiming them. "We shall end with the Lord's Prayer," he announced in a voice so resounding it echoed off the nearby cypress trees. "Our Father, who art in heaven, hallowed be thy name. Thy kingdom come. Thy will be done, on earth as it is in heaven . . ." Barrymore finished the prayer with an "Amen," and the attendees responded in kind.

"If everyone will come back to the manor house, I've fixed a funeral luncheon," Ninette said.

"How appropriate," Gran said. "A mourning meal, just like we're serving our weekend package guests."

"Way to make it sound ghoulish," Maggie muttered.

"Magnolia," Ninette reproached her.

"I wouldn't mind doing a bit of imbibing," Barrymore said. "Leading a service can be hard on the voice.." He coughed again and made a show of clearing his throat.

The mourners left the clearing for the manor house. Maggie found herself keeping step with Emma, who glowered at the ground as they walked. "Are you okay? You look unhappy, and not 'I'm in mourning' unhappy."

"About Susannah?" Emma mimed gagging. "She sucked. Do you know what she did? She talked Doug out of paying for a second round of rehab for Johnnie. He paid for one, but the first time never sticks. For a lot of us, you don't really hit bottom until you fail your first try. Doug was willing to help Johnnie, but Susannah said, 'He's an adult, it's up to him; you're just enabling him.' Helping someone fight a disease isn't 'enabling'; it's the opposite. Susannah just didn't want Doug spending money on anyone but her."

"Johnnie must have done something, because it looks to me like he's in recovery."

"He is, but only because he took out a giant loan to pay for rehab at this great facility in Malibu, California. But his dad will help now that Susannah's gone."

Maggie gave Emma an appraising look. "I'll be honest— I'm surprised you were at her memorial."

"I wanted to make sure she was really dead." Maggie raised her eyebrows. "Sorry, dark humor. I went for Johnnie. I knew he had to go because of his dad, and I wanted to support him. But I'm not going to the luncheon, no offense to your family."

"None taken. I'm not going myself. I have to get to work."

The women reached the family's parking area behind the manor house, where they parted ways. Maggie climbed into her convertible and took off for Doucet. As she drove, she considered what Emma had just told her. Johnnie made it obvious he despised his stepmother in general. Specifically, she'd been an obstacle to his recovery. Had that driven him to kill her?

Once Maggie reached Doucet, she temporarily shelved all murder theories. Since Ione was still short-staffed, she drafted Maggie into providing sales help in the plantation gift shop.

"What's that?" a visitor asked, pointing to an ornament dangling from a broken branch Maggie had spray-painted black and mounted onto a stand to serve as a Halloween tree display.

The ornament in question was a small mirror half covered in black felt. "The Creoles and Cajuns followed the tradition of covering mirrors with black cloth after a death in the household," Maggie said. "People feared that if they saw their reflection after someone in the family died, they would die next."

"Yuck." The woman put the ornament back and took a small doll off the tree. The front of the doll's dress was black, the back lavender. "Why is her dress two different colors?"

"To illustrate two different periods of mourning," Maggie explained. "There were rigid rules regarding mourning apparel. For the first six months, a widow's garments could only be made from a flat black fabric. After six months, the fabric still had to be black, but it could be shiny. After a year, she could wear gray or lavender garments." Maggie took the doll and held it with the black fabric facing front. "Here she is in early mourning attire." She turned the doll around. "And here's what she might wear a year later."

"Very interesting," the woman said. "I'll take it."

Maggie rang up the sale, and the woman departed with her purchase, crossing paths with Ione on her way out. "I can watch the shop for the rest of the afternoon," Ione told Maggie. "You can go back to your real job."

"The job I'll always owe you for," Maggie said.

"None of that, missy. You earned it. What are you working on?"

"The exhibit for this summer. I thought visitors would enjoy seeing portraits of all the Doucet women who've worn the family wedding dress over the last hundred and fifty years. The final display would be the dress itself."

"Wonderful." Ione waved her off. "Go make, my friend."

On her way to her workroom, Maggie ran into Helene Brevelle in the hallway. The voodoo priestess wore a traditional African dress in Mardi Gras colors, with a matching tignon wrap around her head. The women exchanged a hug; then Helene shuddered as if hit by a bolt of lightning. She grabbed Maggie by the arms. "Come with me. *Now.*"

Helene pulled Maggie into the small room she was using to meet with clients and make gris-gris bags. Navy-blue gauze covered the windows. Even though it was late afternoon, the room's light came from a dozen or more spiritual candles in a rainbow of colors, not the sun. "I got a bad feeling when we hugged, Magnolia," the elderly priestess said. "A terrible feeling.

You need protection." Helene pulled a small square of black fabric from a pile. "Black, for protection from negative energy." She pulled various ingredients from jars and placed them inside the square. "St. John's wort, basil, ginseng, yarrow, a garnet." Helene took a piece of black yarn, gathered up the fabric, and tied it together with the yarn, turning it into a small pouch. She closed her eyes and waved a hand over the pouch. "Spirits, I call up you to bless Magnolia Marie Crozat. Banish evil and negativity from her life. Protect her. And make her fertile."

"Excuse me?" Maggie said. "How does *that* fit in?"

"I figured as long as I was doing a spell for you, I'd throw that in." Helene attached a safety pin to the bag and handed it to Maggie. "Wear this under your shirt, close to your heart. Pin it on now." Maggie did so. Helene pulled a tiny bottle out of a box. "This is protection oil. Rose, sandalwood, myrrh, frankincense. Dab it on."

"Frankincense and myrrh? I guess if it was good enough for the Wise Men . . ." Maggie took the bottle and dabbed a drop on each wrist. She recoiled. "Whoa. That's strong stuff."

"You need it." Helene extinguished a black spiritual candle. She handed it to Maggie. "And this, too."

"Helene," Maggie said, unsettled by the priestess's ministrations. "What exactly do you see?"

"It's not what I see, it's what I feel around you. A sense of foreboding. Of danger. But what I've given you will help provide protection."

"O . . . kay." Maggie looked at the candle and bottle of oil in her hands. "Can I pay you for these?"

Helene gave her head a vigorous shake. "Absolutely not. Go and do what you need to do. But with great care until the evil I see is gone."

"It's going to be a little hard to concentrate after all this," Maggie said on her way out the door.

Which it was. She put on an apron and began the delicate task of cleaning a portrait of her three-times-great-aunt Felicity Doucet in her bridal finery, but her heart wasn't in her work. As Maggie used a soft brush to gently remove dust from the old painting, she couldn't shake Helene's dire pronouncements. Where might the danger Helene foresaw be coming from? she wondered. The obvious source was the threat of arrest by VBPD. But was there another threat looming?

Maggie was so absorbed in her brooding that she almost missed hearing Ione announce over the plantation's antiquated PA system that Doucet was closing for the day. She quickly put away her supplies, then placed the candle and potion from Helene in her tote bag. *You're being superstitious*, she chided herself, and took them out. After a beat, she put them back. *Just to be on the safe side*, she thought.

* * *

In the morning, still spooked by Helene's premonitions, Maggie made sure to dab on the protection potion after showering. She pulled on a pair of jeans and a long-sleeved teal T-shirt, then pinned Helene's protection gris-gris bag inside her shirt and left the cottage for the manor house to help Ninette prepare the B and B guests' breakfast. Gran was there, making coffee for everyone. Tug was half hidden as he worked under the sink, fixing the kitchen pipe's chronic leak. Gran wrinkled her nose. "What's that awful smell drowning out the wonderful scent of coffee?" She cast Maggie an accusing glance. "It's coming from your direction."

"I'm trying a new perfume," Maggie lied, embarrassed to admit the truth.

"One that makes you smell like an old-time hippie head shop?" Gran said, not buying Maggie's explanation.

Maggie picked up the coffee carafe Gran had filled and poured herself a cup. Gran stepped back and waved a hand to diffuse the smell. "Being a little extreme, Gran." She took a sip of coffee. "Fine, it's not a perfume. Helene Brevelle got a weird vibe from me and gave me a protection oil."

Tug emerged from under the sink. "That's a whole lotta protection. What's she worried about?"

"She couldn't say. It was a general feeling."

"Maybe we should all dab on that oil," Gran said.

Tug and Ninette voiced agreement with the idea. "I feel a little better," Maggie said. "I thought y'all might think I was being silly. I didn't even tell you about the gris-gris bag Helene made me."

"If you're looking for skeptics about premonitions and the like," Gran said, "you might have to try another state."

"I wish Helene had been less vague, though." Maggie ripped off the heel of a fresh baguette and chewed on it. Ninette used oven mitts to pull a casserole dish out of the oven. "What are you making, Mom?"

"Baked eggs, plus bacon and sausage," Ninette said. "And I thought it would be fun to serve our guests calas," she added, referencing the fried rice balls that had faded into obscurity after being a staple of the nineteenth-century Louisiana diet but were making a comeback. "Help me set up the buffet."

The family carried the breakfast offerings out to the dining room and placed them in chafing dishes. They were about to return to the kitchen when the doorbell screamed. Everyone jumped. "How soon can we switch to a Christmas song for that ring?" Gran asked, her hand on her heart.

"It's probably a guest," Tug said. "Maybe we should all greet whoever it is. Welcome them with a big dose of southern hospitality. Wouldn't hurt to get a few more positive reviews on trippee.com."

Maggie, her parents, and her grandmother trooped through the hallway to the front door. Tug threw it open to reveal a slim man in his midthirties dressed in a suit.

"Hello, welcome to Crozat B and B," Tug said. The others flashed smiles and ad-libbed hellos.

"Wow, nice greeting," the man said. Maggie picked up a mid-Atlantic accent. "And cool doorbell."

"Thanks," Tug said. "Feel free to mention that in any online reviews. Kidding, of course."

"I'm not a guest, although looks like you've got a great place here. I'm Noah Bauman. I'm with Harbor Chemical." Bauman handed Tug his card. "I have a meeting with Doug MacDowell."

The Crozats exchanged a look. "Harbor Chemical," Maggie said. "You built a facility on the other side of the river. Where Laurel Plantation was. Until you bought it."

Bauman nodded. There was an awkward pause. "Is Mr. MacDowell here?"

Tug cast an uneasy glance at Maggie, Ninette, and Grand-mère, then responded to Bauman. "He'd be in our daughter's art studio, the old schoolhouse. Down the side road, then you'll see it through the woods."

"Got it, thanks."

Tug nodded acknowledgment and closed the front door.

"Me, my gris-gris bag, and my protection potion have a bad feeling about this," Maggie said.

"Why would Doug be meeting with Harbor Chemical?" Ninette asked. "You don't think . . ." She trailed off, unable to finish the sentence.

"You only meet with Harbor Chemical for one reason," Maggie said. "To sell them your land."

Chapter 14

Maggie burst out of the manor house's back door, followed by the rest of her family. They hurried through the woods to the schoolhouse. Maggie rapped on the door. After a minute, Doug opened it. "I'm in the middle of a meeting."

"We know." Maggie pushed past him, as did the others.

"Hey," Doug protested. "What the—"

Maggie planted herself between Doug and Noah Bauman. "Are you trying to sell Susannah's land to Harbor Chemical?"

"It's not hers anymore, it's mine. And what I am or am not doing is none of your business."

"Oh, it is." Maggie, furious, crossed her arms in front of her chest. "Remember, part of this place is ours."

"If I could say something here—" Bauman began.

"You can't," Tug shot at him.

"Got it," Bauman said, intimidated.

"This land . . ." Doug made an expansive gesture. "It's full of memories of my time here with Susannah."

"That's a bit hard to imagine, considering you've barely been here three weeks," Gran said.

"Well, it is. Which is why I realized I can't bear staying on it anymore."

"Then go back to Toronto," Maggie said.

"The thing is, I've come to love the area," Doug said. "Us Canadians are snowbirds. We fly south for the winter. Florida is a snore, but here . . . you got warmth, history, atmosphere. And you can't beat the food."

"But—but—" Maggie sputtered. "Dang, I can't argue with any of that."

"I could use the proceeds of a sale to buy a place in Pelican for the winter months—"

"And have plenty left over," Noah chimed in, ignoring Tug's glower.

"Who knows?" Doug continued. "Maybe down the road me and the kids'll become citizens." He launched into "The Star-Spangled Banner." "*O say can you see . . .* and whatever comes next."

Ninette's hands shook from nerves, and she clasped them together. "Doug, we can't have a chemical plant in our backyard. It will ruin our home, as well as our business. No one would ever stay here again. Plus, the cancer rate for people living near these plants is out of control. We'd be risking our lives."

"Not if you sell, too," Bauman said.

Tug stared at him. "Excuse me?"

"I'm sure I could work out a deal for buying both parcels, yours and Mr. MacDowell's. We might even be able to keep the big house for corporate functions, like the gas company up the road did with Bienvenu Plantation."

"It's surrounded by storage tanks," Maggie, outraged, said.

"But it's still there. I can't promise that for your place. But if you're interested in selling the land, let me know. I'll run some numbers and make an offer." Bauman addressed Doug. "Sleep on the figure I gave you. I'll check in tomorrow."

Doug opened the door for the Harbor Chemical executive. Bauman left, and Susannah's widower motioned for the Crozats to leave as well. "Your turn."

"Doug, please don't do this," Maggie pleaded. She flashed on an angle. "You're interested in living here part-time and maybe forever. Everyone in Pelican will hate you if you destroy this land. They're sick of industrial plants. You won't have a friend in town."

Doug shrugged. "I've always been comfortable with my own company. And I think the locals might forgive me once I start throwing around money from the sale." Doug grew thoughtful. He tapped an index finger against his lips. "There is a way out for y'all, as you say around here. You could buy me out."

Tug looked hopeful. "That's a possibility. How much are we talking about?"

Doug handed Tug a sheet of paper. "Harbor's proposal."

Tug pulled reading glasses out of his pocket and perused the page. He blanched. "Wow. That's a lot of money."

"Far as I'm concerned, it's a starting figure. I've got meetings set up with four other companies."

Deflated, Tug handed the proposal back to Doug. "The only way we could come up with this much money is to sell Crozat to Harbor ourselves. Which kinda defeats the purpose."

"I'm giving you options. It's your call what you do with them."

Doug opened the door a little wider. Tug, Ninette, and Gran took the hint and left. Maggie, consumed with fury, lingered. She took a step toward Doug. "This is not going to happen. I will do whatever it takes to stop you from turning this land into a toxic site."

"A threat, huh? Maybe I should mention that to the police. Might make you numero uno on their list of suspects in Susannah's death, if you aren't already."

"You know I had nothing to do with that, Doug."

"Do I?" Doug's demeanor shifted from beleaguered to cunning, colored with a hint of menace. He gestured to the door. "You're letting in mosquitoes. Pretty much the only thing I don't like about Louisiana are those bloodsuckers."

"Takes one to know one," Maggie shot at the man, then walked out of the studio, slamming the door behind her.

Not wanting to give Doug the satisfaction of seeing her cry, Maggie waited until she made it back to the family's parking area before bursting into tears. She didn't see Johnnie and Emma come out of the woods and was startled when they spoke to her. "Maggie, what's wrong?" Emma asked.

Johnnie placed a comforting hand on Maggie's shoulder. "You can tell us. We finished our Zen walk, so we can talk again."

Maggie wiped her eyes. "It's your father. He wants to sell Susannah's land to a chemical company."

She relayed the details of her family's run-in with Doug. Johnnie paced as he listened. "This is what I'm talking about," he said to Emma when Maggie finished. "My greedy, despicable family." His voice was loud and angry. "A chemical plant, Emma. They are willing to *poison* people for money. But are they willing to give a dime to the arts? Noooooo."

"Right now, all I can think about is my family's future," Maggie said, trying to keep the conversation focused on the crisis at hand.

"Of course," Johnnie said. "I'll go talk to my capitalist father. Argh, he infuriates me!"

Johnnie marched off to the schoolhouse. Emma watched him go, a worried look on her face. "He's stressed again. That's bad. He could relapse. I better go with him."

Emma took off after Johnnie. Maggie pulled out her cell phone and speed-dialed Bo. "I'm a terrible person," she sobbed before he could say a word. "Everything is my fault. The MacDowells, and Susannah being murdered, and the chemical plant, and now I made Johnnie go off the wagon."

"Whoa, whoa," Bo said, flummoxed. "That's a whole lotta word salad, chère. You need to calm down. Take deep breaths." Maggie inhaled and exhaled. "Did you take them?"

"Yes."

"Do you feel better?"

"A little."

"Good. Take a few more of them and then meet me at Junie's. But no driving until you calm down. Understand?"

"Understand. I'm sorry. I just lost it."

"No apologizing, sweet girl. If anyone's got reasons to lose it these days, it's you. I'll see you in a few."

Bo signed off. Maggie took enough deep breaths to calm herself. She looked heavenward. "Thank you for bringing that man into my life," she said. "I owe you."

* * *

Maggie confirmed with Ninette and Tug that it would be okay to take the afternoon off, then set out for Junie's. The thought of Cajun comfort food washed down with a bottle— or two, or even three—of Abita Light beer appealed to her. As she drove down the River Road, she noticed Gavin Grody's Tesla, decorated with Rent My Digs decals, parked in front of the old Dupois manor home. Grody was outside his car and appeared to be arguing with Dupois caretaker Walter Breem. Breem took a step forward and yelled something at the techie, who reacted by shoving the old man. Breem lost his balance and fell to the ground. Maggie veered to the side of the road and parked. She jumped out of her car and ran to the caretaker. She helped Breem, who seemed disoriented, to his feet. "Are you okay?" she asked.

"Uh, hello, how about asking if *I'm* okay?" Gavin said, indignant. "There's no cell reception along half this freaking road, so when I finally got some, I pulled over to finish a call and this psycho charged me."

"You're on private property." Breem, who'd shaken off his fall, spat at him.

Gavin pointed to the ground. "*No*, I'm on public land next to private property. I swear, if Pelican wasn't so *charming*"— the hipster heaped as much derision as he could onto the word—"I'd buy property somewhere else."

"Feel free to do that," Maggie said.

"Sorry, you're not getting rid of me that easily. This place is exactly what tourists want. Only an hour from New Orleans. Great food, great setting. It's like time stopped here."

"A Cajun Brigadoon," Maggie murmured.

"I like that," Gavin said. "I'll have to put it on my website." He faced Breem. "I'm gonna make nice and not press charges for you coming at me. But if you try that again, old man, I will be all over you."

The entrepreneur strode to his car, jumped in, and peeled out. "Hate guys like him," Breem said with a sneer. "Thinking they're smarter than the rest of us. They're not."

"Agreed," Maggie said.

"Him with his greed, buying up good homes and sending Pelican in the wrong direction."

"You know about that?"

Breem responded with an annoyed snort. "I may live a life to myself, but I know what all's going on around here. I'd wager I know more'n most people, what with all the distractions taking folks this way and that these days."

The caretaker took a step and winced. "Let me help you get home," Maggie said.

"No need."

He took a few more steps and swayed slightly. Maggie took his arm. "I promise I'll leave as soon as we get you there."

Breen didn't respond, but he let Maggie lead him toward the old house where he lived. They maneuvered their way through the dense brush and forest that had once been Dupois Plantation's acclaimed garden. "Watch out for critters," he warned.

They passed the crumbling remnants of a stone bridge over what had once been a stream. The ruins of a folly still stood atop a small hill carpeted with weeds. "I've never seen any of this up close," Maggie said. "It must have been amazing in its day."

"One of the Dupois family's enslaved people had a way with gardens," the caretaker said. "Designed the whole thing. He fought on the Union side, but after the war he came back and lived with his family where I live now. Kept up the gardens till he died. No one had the heart to keep 'em going after that."

They reached the old man's living quarters, once the plantation overseer's cottage. It was a simple yet dignified building. Four columns supported an overhang to create a front porch. A few wooden steps led up to the porch and a plain wooden front door whose green paint had mostly peeled off. Paint flakes on the building's weathered cypress siding indicated that the cottage had once been white. Maggie helped Breem up the rickety stairs. He opened the front door, which Maggie noted wasn't locked. Still holding the man's arm, she guided him inside. She was taken aback by the cottage's interior.

Unlike the shabby exterior, the main room was pristine and meticulously furnished with lovely antiques. A large Oriental carpet covered most of the well-polished wooden floor. Bookcases covered an entire wall of the room. "Your home is beautiful," Maggie said.

"Surprised?" There was a glint of humor in Walter Breem's eyes.

"No," Maggie quickly responded, Then, a little sheepish, she added, "Maybe."

The caretaker released himself from Maggie's hold. He sat down in an armchair covered with a crisp dark-blue brocade. "Thanks for your help. I don't even know your name."

"Maggie. Maggie Crozat."

This sparked a smile on his worn, weathered face. "A Crozat. That accounts for your manners. Good stock, them."

"My mother's a Doucet," Maggie said, returning his smile. "I'm not bragging, just want to give her any credit that's due."

"Doubly blessed."

"For all the good it does us," Maggie said, feeling gloomy as she flashed on the peril her family and Crozat Plantation faced thanks to interloper Doug MacDowell.

Breem leaned back in his chair. His face contorted as he put his feet up on a Victorian claw-foot mahogany coffee table. "I'd be lying if I said I wasn't feeling my age right now."

"I'll get going and let you rest, but first, let me get you a glass of water or something," Maggie said.

"I'm good."

"You're pale. I'm getting you water." Maggie looked around and saw the doorway leading to the kitchen. Like what she'd seen of the rest of the house, it was neat and comfortable. The cabinets looked recently painted, a bright white that brought light into a house shrouded by trees. Maggie opened a cabinet, found a glass, and filled it with water. She brought it back to the caretaker. "Can I make you something to eat? I'm not the cook my mother is, but I'm sure I can put together something edible."

The old man took a sip of water. "I'm not much of an eater. But I wouldn't mind you getting me the top book over there."

He pointed to a stack of books on a side table whose design matched that of the coffee table. Maggie picked up the book. "I'll check on you later," she said.

The man's taciturn manner returned. "No need."

"Then I'm going to leave my number with you," Maggie persisted. "Do you have a pen and paper?"

"There's a pen on the coffee table. You can write the number in the book. That way I won't be losing it."

"All right."

Maggie picked up the pen and wrote her name and cell number on the first page inside the old book. She handed it to Breem, who turned to a page holding a bookmark. "If you need anything, call me. Day or night, doesn't matter."

He gave a slight nod but didn't look up from the book, so Maggie let herself out.

By the time Maggie reached Junie's, the restaurant was packed with lunch patrons. She saw Bo at a far corner table and started toward him. Kaity Bertrand waved from another table. "Maggie, come here a sec."

Maggie detoured to Kaity. She recognized the girl's tablemates as employees from the other B and Bs participating in the Pelican's Spooky Past weekend packages and greeted them. She picked up a slight chill in their responses. "How are things going with y'all?" she asked. "Any midweek guests?"

"Some, but we would've had more if it wasn't for all the rougarou and ghost bull." This terse response came from Bon Ami's desk clerk.

"All of us have had guests scared by these effed-up sightings," Kaity said. She did a sweep of the table with her hand.

"Everyone here thinks those people staying with you are doing it."

"Why?" Maggie asked, startled by the implied accusation.

"Because the one who died, the one who was your cousin, was wearing a mask like we seen on the others around our places." The Bon Ami desk clerk fixed Maggie with an angry look. "Make 'em stop."

"I've been trying to explain to everyone that it's got nothing to do with you," Kaity said.

"Thanks, Kaity." Maggie appealed to the others. "Trust me, if I see any sign that the MacDowells are behind what's been going on, you have no idea how fast I'll turn them in. But until there's evidence, our B and B is in the same position as you all are. Praying whatever horrible people are doing this get caught *fast*."

Kaity's tablemates looked unconvinced. Maggie gave up and moved on to Bo. He stood and enveloped her in a tight hug, which he followed with a lingering kiss. They broke apart, and Maggie fell into a chair. "And the award for most hated person in town right now goes to . . . drum roll . . . *me*. If I ever have another 'good idea' like the Spooky Past weekend packages, tape my mouth shut before I can share it with the world."

"I wish I could say it's not that bad, but I know it is for you, chère. Maybe these'll perk you up." Bo picked up his cell phone and opened the photos app. "They had a Halloween party at Xander's school today."

He handed the phone to Maggie. She swiped through pictures of Xander, dressed as Captain America, striking poses, playing games, marching proudly with his classmates in a costume parade. "These are beyond wonderful. I love that kids still bob for apples." She swiped to a photo of Xander with an apple in his mouth. "He grabbed one. Awesome. I could never do that." She handed the phone back to Bo. "After looking at these, I'm going to say something I haven't said in years. I can't wait to go trick-or-treating."

"That's my ghoul," Bo said with a grin.

Maggie rolled her eyes. "More jokes like that and I may change my mind." She sipped the bourbon on the rocks Bo had ordered for her and released a breath. "I'm not a day drinker, but I needed this."

"What's going on with the MacDowells? Ever since we talked, I've been trying to figure out how a chemical plant and someone falling off the wagon go together."

"I'll break it down for you." Maggie told Bo about Harbor Chemical's unwelcome visit and Doug's plan to sell Susannah's land to the highest environmentally sketchy bidder.

Bo stared at her, dumbfounded. "That's . . . it's . . ." At a loss, he held up his hands. "I don't know what to say."

"How about, 'Doug, you're under arrest for—fill in the blank.' Whatever might get him deported back to the land of hockey and socialized medicine. Can a DUI do it these days? I'll slip something into his coffee."

"I'll think on it." Bo's tone indicated he wasn't kidding.

"I know Ville Blanc's stonewalling you," Maggie said, "but are there any leads in Susannah's murder? Even teeny tiny ones?"

"Nothing on our end." His face darkened. "And if there are any on theirs, Griffith isn't sharing."

"Doug certainly benefits from her death, and if he does, Bonnie and Johnnie probably do, too." Maggie lowered her voice. "I got a little gossip from Emma. Susannah was an obstacle for the twins in terms of getting their father to part with any money on their behalf. Speaking of Emma, she's become very attached to Johnnie. I don't know if they're having a thing or not."

Bo raised an eyebrow. "I don't think she's his type."

Maggie had to laugh at this. "I feel like an old fart. Everyone's so fluid these days, I can't tell who's anyone's type anymore. Which makes me think of that actress Patria, who's probably everyone's type."

"Not mine."

Maggie squeezed Bo's hand. "You're sweet. Anyway, Patria told me that Barrymore was ticked off at Susannah because he got sucked into her psychic fakery and then couldn't get his money back."

"This is good stuff," Bo said. "Barrymore goes on the list. There's also Walter Breem. He's the obsessive type. All about protecting the Dupois property. He could've run into Susannah in that rougarou costume and been set off by it."

"Funny you should bring him up, I just happened to spend a bit of time with him." Maggie relayed the run-in between Breem and Gavin Grody.

Bo glowered. "That Grody's another one I'd love to have an excuse to arrest."

"You'd be a hero for that," Maggie said. "I think Pelican would throw you a parade. But back to Walter. People around here assume he's 'teched in the head.' He's a loner for sure, but from what I saw today, I think there's a whole other level to him. Which of course doesn't rule him out as a suspect."

"We can't rule out Helene Brevelle either, much as I hate to say it."

"I know. But I can't imagine her killing anyone. She wouldn't even let me use these black pins I found on the voodoo doll she made me."

Bo gave her the side-eye. "You got a voodoo doll? And black pins? 'Have I told you I love you lately?' he asked, trying to stay on her good side."

"Don't worry, cher, you're safe . . ." Maggie spoke in a fake-menacing tone. "For now."

Their conversation was interrupted by JJ delivering their meals: gumbo for Maggie, a catfish po' boy for Bo. "I need to get back to the station," Bo said after they finished eating. "We'll figure out a way around the chemical plant. Get Mayor Banks to throw a few environmental impact studies at it. Go home and relax. Think about something besides murder. Hey, I hear this couple in town is getting married on New Year's Eve."

"Nicely done," Maggie said with a laugh. After they stood up, she wrapped her arms around Bo's waist. "As soon as I get home, I'm getting my wedding gown from the attic and bringing it to the tailor so he has plenty of time to make alterations. My mother was the last Doucet bride to wear the dress. I don't exactly have her waspish waist, so he's got his work cut out for him."

Driving home, Maggie heeded Bo's advice and allowed herself to daydream about her wedding. She imagined herself clad in the gorgeous Doucet gown, walking down the aisle of St. Theresa of Avila, the quaint Pelican church affectionately known to locals as St. Tee's. Parish priest Father Prit would officiate; then a reception at Crozat, open to all, would follow the ceremony. She envisioned friends and neighbors dancing on the B and B's spacious lawn to classic Cajun tunes performed by Gaynell and the Gator Girls. Maggie, who'd never been the kind of girl who longed for a big wedding, found herself growing excited about it. *I may have to wrest some of the planning away from Gran,* she thought as she parked behind the manor house.

She stopped in the B and B office to grab a flashlight and retrieve a key for the new lock her father had installed on the attic door. After heading up the back stairs to the attic's entrance, she inserted the key in the new lock, which promptly fell off the decrepit old door. Useless as the lock might be, Maggie shoved it back in place, hoping it at least gave the illusion of security. Then she scampered up the attic stairs, turned on her flashlight, and gasped. There was an empty space in the middle of the floor where the Doucet bridal gown had been stored.

Maggie's ancestral wedding dress was gone.

Chapter 15

Maggie's heart thumped. *Calm down*, she told herself. *Dad probably moved it.* She scanned the clutter with her flashlight but saw no box. Now panicked, she shoved trunks and old furniture aside, brushing away cobwebs and grime. The air filled with dust. Maggie choked as she inhaled it but continued her search. After combing through the entire attic, she had to accept that the dress wasn't there.

Maggie ran downstairs. She found her parents in the kitchen. "Did you move my wedding gown?"

"No," Tug said. "We'd have told you if we did. Why?"

She didn't stop to answer his question. Maggie ran to the cottage to find her grandmother. Their home was empty. Panting from the run coupled with anxiety, she phoned Gran. "I was about to call you," the octogenarian said. "I'm at a wedding expo, and I found the most darling favor. Alligator-shaped toothpick holders. What do you—"

"Gran, do have my wedding gown?"

"Of course not. Magnolia, what's—"

"I can't talk now."

Maggie ended the call and ran back to the manor house. She burst into the kitchen. "It's gone. My wedding gown. *Our* wedding gown." She pressed her hands against her face. Her voice sounded strangled. "It's been stolen."

Tug opened his mouth, but no words came out. Ninette dropped the empty pot she held, and it clattered to the floor. "No."

Maggie, her face still buried in her hands, nodded. "I searched the attic," she said, fighting back tears. "I called Gran. It's *gone*."

Her father threw down the paper he'd been reading. "I'm calling the police."

Tug jumped up and marched out of the room. Ninette picked up the pot she'd dropped and brandished it above her head. "When I find out who stole that dress, I'm taking this pot to them."

"I'm so lucky you're my mom," Maggie said, relishing an image of her petite mother, who weighed not much more than a feather pillow, beating up a thief with kitchenware.

Ninette put down the pot and took her daughter by the shoulders. "We're gonna find that gown, chère. As God is my witness, you will not be the first Doucet bride to walk down the aisle in a store-bought dress."

"Amen, Mama."

The doorbell screamed, and the women jumped. "Acck! MacMurder, MacDead!" Lovie cawed from the office.

"This place isn't a zoo, it's a madhouse," Ninette said, clutching her chest.

Maggie's phone pinged a text. "Dad said the police arrived. That was quick. He said to meet them round back."

Maggie left the house through the back door. She found her father in the parking area between the manor house and the shotgun cottage, along with detectives Zeke Griffith and Rosalie Broussard, plus two officers wearing polo shirts that read *Law Enforcement* on the back. "I'm glad you're here," Maggie said to Griffith.

"First time I've ever heard anyone say that when I served a search warrant."

The detective handed her a piece of paper. Maggie glanced down at it and saw a jumble of legalese. "Wait, what?"

"It's legit," Tug said, his face grim.

"I thought maybe you were here because my wedding dress was stolen," Maggie said to Griffith. "Along with other items from our attic. It could be tied to Susannah's murder."

"Let's table that until after we conduct our search."

Griffith motioned to his coworkers. The officers snapped on latex gloves and entered Maggie's home. He and Broussard followed them into the cottage. "This is unbelievable," Maggie said, steaming. "Go inside and keep an eye on them, Dad. I'm calling Bo."

She started for the B and B office, then remembered Lovie was ensconced there. Searching for a private spot, she settled on the cast-iron bench in the center of the plantation's beautifully manicured parterre garden. Her call to Bo went straight to voice mail. She left an urgent message and then made another call. Defense attorney Quentin MacIlhoney picked up after one ring. "Magnolia, my dear, you caught me on a run-through break. Rudy Ferrier, the future star playing Jean-Luc Junior, has an AP Chemistry midterm on Monday, so I'm rehearsing his understudy. He doesn't have Rudy's charisma, but the Pelican talent pool is sparse."

"I'm sorry to bother you, but it's an emergency. The detectives from Ville Blanc showed up with a search warrant. They're in my house right now."

The lawyer's usually congenial tone disappeared. "Who signed the warrant?"

Maggie checked the paper. "A Judge Archer."

"They knew Gaudet would never approve it, so they did an end run around him and went to Archer, who never met a search warrant he didn't like. Don't say a word to those bottom feeders. I'm on my way."

After Quentin signed off, Maggie gazed at the cottage, disconsolate. She didn't trust herself to observe the search, afraid she'd either break down or take one of Ninette's pots to Griffith. She slumped back on the cold, hard bench. A squirrel peeked out from a bush. "This is all my fault," Maggie said to him. "You know that expression 'No good deed goes unpunished'? It's true. I thought I was doing something good by bringing our cousin here. Instead she's dead and it doesn't even matter that my wedding dress is gone, because the only aisle I may be walking down is the one that leads to a jail cell. Okay, that's more a hallway than an aisle, but you get the idea." The squirrel chittered and disappeared back into the bushes.

Twenty minutes went by. A custom purple Jaguar sports car with a license plate that read *Lwyr Up* squealed into the parking area. Quentin got out and quickly made his way to Maggie. He wore a bespoke gray suit, crisp white shirt, and a tie in the same shade of purple as his car. Maggie knew the sixty-something attorney well enough to know this wasn't an accident. The look painted him as prosperous, but with a hint of humor. Coupled with the white goatee he'd grown as part of his directorial persona, Quentin gave off the vibe of a good-natured Mephistopheles. "The cops come out yet?"

"No. Dad's in there with them."

"That Griffith's a piece of work. Getting his ducks in a row for a run at office." The attorney eyed Maggie. "Anything interesting they might find?"

"Aside from a necklace made from the ears of my victims? No."

"Save that sparkling wit for people who'll appreciate it. Which won't be this crew."

The cottage front door opened, and Griffith exited with his fellow officers. He was holding what Maggie recognized as an evidence bag. Tug, looking lost, came out last. Maggie jumped up. She and Quentin walked toward the group.

"Well, if it isn't Ville Blanc's boys in blue." Quentin's tone was affable. "What ya got there, my friend?"

"Since you ask . . ." Griffith held up the bag. Inside it was the voodoo doll Helene had made Maggie, along with the container of black pins.

Quentin shook his hands in mock fear. "A voodoo doll? I'm a-scared." He dropped the act. "If that's your best evidence, you might as well arrest half the town and every visitor who bought one of those from Helene Brevelle. I recognize her marvelous workmanship. You know, I was at the bank the other day and she was making a deposit. I'm guessing business has picked up for her now that the competition's been taken care of, so to speak."

Griffith ignored Quentin. "I'll be in touch," he said to Maggie.

He and his team headed for their vehicles. Maggie, Tug, and Quentin watched as the law enforcement officials pulled out of the parking area and drove off. "I'm sorry, chère," Tug said. He dropped his head, unable to make eye contact with his daughter. "I should've done something to stop them. I don't think I've ever felt so helpless in my life."

"Dad, don't blame yourself." Maggie, feeling bad for her father, rubbed his shoulder. "They had a warrant. There was nothing you could do."

Quentin brushed some dust that the patrol cars had kicked up off his jacket. "Operating under the 'It's five o'clock somewhere' rule, I wouldn't say no to a bourbon neat, and I'm guessing you wouldn't either."

"It would be my second drink before sunset today." Maggie turned to the lawyer. "Let's do it."

Maggie, Quentin, and Tug retreated to the office, where they found Ninette. The room smelled like a blend of sugar and spices. A plate of Cajun Pecan Cookie Fingers sat on the coffee table, alongside a Sugar High Pie. "Two desserts?" Maggie knew her mother baked to relieve anxiety. "You must have been super nervous."

"I already had the pie and cookies on hand," Ninette said. "But I've got a bread pudding in the oven. I'm hoping the scent will find its way outdoors and make those officers hungry. Then I'd get to tell them, 'Too bad, you're not getting any.'"

Quentin picked up a cookie. "Punishment by tasty treats. I like it." The lawyer made himself comfortable on the room's antique carved walnut sofa. He took the glass of bourbon Maggie offered him and then bit into his cookie. "Delicious. Too bad these weren't done before Griffith and his cronies showed up. We might have used the cookies to bribe them into not executing that warrant."

Tug took the bottle of bourbon from Maggie and poured himself a double. "Any idea what's gonna happen now, Quentin?"

"Griffith's got a bug up his behind about Magnolia here being a suspect." The lawyer took a swallow of his drink. "He's gonna test the voodoo doll for traces of strychnine to tie it to her, which he won't find."

"Lord, no," Maggie said with vehemence.

"Which means Griffith can't make his case. Even Judge Archer, who'd sign anything except a check for his half of the dinner we were supposed to go Dutch on, wouldn't issue an arrest warrant on such a ridiculous lack of evidence."

"So, we've got some breathing room," Tug said.

"Yes . . ."

Maggie picked up on the hesitation in the defense attorney's voice. "What Quentin doesn't want to say is that I'll still be in Griffith's cross hairs until there are other suspects, or the actual killer is caught."

"I appreciate you not making me have to articulate that, my friend." Quentin knocked back the rest of his drink. "I'd best be going. Vanessa did an interview with Little Earlie for the *Penny Clipper* about her star turn in my production,

ELLEN BYRON

and I promised I'd take glam shots of her for the paper." He handed his empty glass back to Maggie and looked at her with compassion. "They're not gonna get you, Maggie. I won't let them."

Maggie pressed her lips together. She swallowed, then said, "Thanks, Quentin. Just . . . thank you."

Quentin started out of the office, almost colliding with Brianna Poche, Maggie's young helper, on the way out. They danced around each other a minute, then the lawyer left, and Brianna came into the room. The pretty African-American teenager carried full shopping bags in each hand. "Hey, y'all. Maggie, I got awesome stuff for the immortelles."

"Great," Maggie said, welcoming a break from obsessing about her status as a murder suspect. "Let's see what you have."

She moved Ninette's sweets to an end table next to the sofa. Brianna placed her bags on the coffee table. Maggie began pulling out an assortment of leaves, twigs, and flowers. "Nice . . . nice . . ." She held up a branch laden with orange berries. "I haven't seen these before. They're perfect for the immortelles."

"I know," Brianna said. "Don't tell no one, but my friends and me found a way to sneak through the fence into those old gardens at the Dupois place. It's super creepy, but there's so many cool plants and trees and things there."

"Brianna, honey, I appreciate your hard work, but that's trespassing," Maggie said, her tone kind but firm. "From now on, stick to public locations, okay?"

"'Kay, but everyone goes there. I'm the only one look-ing for leaves and stuff. All my friends only go to"—she whispered—"make out."

"Well, I'm glad you're more industrious than your friends," Ninette said, amused. She handed the girl a cookie. "A small reward. I'll make you a bag of them to take home."

"Thank you, ma'am."

"Wait. Let me see that branch." Tug took the branch from Maggie and examined it. He carried it to the computer, where he typed in a search. A photo appeared on the computer screen. "Oh, man. I was afraid of this."

"What's wrong?" Maggie asked.

Tug grimaced and rubbed his forehead. "Remember when I took that horticulture class at Coastal Community? The one that helped me be able to name the plants around here when guests asked about them? There was a section on poisonous plants, and this here was one of them." Tug motioned to the others, who gathered behind him. They peered at the com-puter as he held the branch next to a picture on the screen. The two were an exact match. "See? It's the same berry. And the seeds are poisonous."

"Oh, dear," Ninette said. "What kind of poison?"

Maggie read the description under the photo. Her stom-ach began to roil. "Strychnine."

The family exchanged uneasy glances. No one wanted to say what they were all thinking in front of Brianna.

Strychnine was the poison that had been used to kill Susannah.

Chapter 16

Maggie recovered first. "It's a good thing you identified these before we used them, Dad."

"Am I gonna die?" Brianna asked, wringing her hands.

"No, no, chère, of course not," Ninette said, her voice comforting. "The poison is on the inside, not the outside. But let's wash your hands real well anyway."

Ninette led Brianna from the room. Maggie let go of a breath. "Nice catch, Dad. Thank goodness Brianna didn't find these sooner. We'd have to call all our guests and tell them their immortelles might do the reverse and cut their lives short."

"Now that we know they're from the Dupois property, the police will have to take a closer look at Walter Breem as a possible suspect," Tug said.

"Yes," Maggie said, "except it won't let us off the hook completely. Griffith can claim we knew there was a strychnine tree on the Dupois land. You took a class that covered poisonous plants." Maggie pointed to the computer. "And now there's a search for it on your computer."

"From today. *After* Susannah's death."

Maggie frowned. She twisted a lock of her thick chestnut-brown hair around her finger. "True, but it still makes me nervous."

"We can't withhold potential evidence," Tug said.

"I know," Maggie said with reluctance.

"But . . . that don't mean we have to rush to share it." Tug crooked a corner of his mouth. "I don't know about you, but I got a long to-do list. I think the rest of the day may get away from me."

"And I haven't even had a chance to file a police report about my stolen wedding dress." Maggie was surprised by how emotional she felt saying this out loud.

Tug gave his daughter a sympathetic pat on the hand. "We're gonna get that back, Magnolia. No worries."

Gran breezed into the office. She was dressed in her version of casual, a white silk top tucked into gray slacks buckled with a silver belt. Her silver hair was topped with a crown headband that had the words *Bride-to-Be* emblazoned in hot-pink glitter. She carried a tote bag printed with *Your Big Day!* in a swirly pink font. She greeted her son and granddaughter with kisses on their cheeks. "I finagled a sample of that gator toothpick holder out of the vendor," she said to Maggie. Gran reached into her bag and pulled out a small enameled alligator. His open mouth held toothpicks. "Isn't he adorable?" She handed the favor to Maggie. Noticing the strychnine branch, she picked it up. "I love the color of these berries. Is this for the immortelle workshop? It's perfect."

"It's strychnine."

Gran dropped the branch. "Never mind. Why is it here?"

"Brianna found it when she was gathering flora for this weekend's workshop," Maggie said. "It turns out she's been doing some illegal foraging on the Dupois property. Which is where she came across a strychnine tree."

"'A deciduous tree native to India and southeast Asia," Tug said, reading from his computer screen.

"That makes sense," Gran said. "The Dupois family gathered plants from all over the world. It's what made their garden legendary."

"We need to share this with the police," Tug said, adding with emphasis, "Eventually."

Gran gave a nod. "Got it."

"First, I'm going to Pelican PD to report my missing wedding gown," Maggie said.

Gran put her bag down on the chair. "I'm coming with you. I have a wonderfully vivid image of your mother in that gown. I can provide details, if the police need them." She favored her granddaughter with a compassionate smile. "And provide a bit of moral support as well."

"Thanks, Gran," Maggie said. "I could use it."

* * *

Bo returned Maggie's call while she and Gran were driving to the police station. She put her fiancé on speaker phone and updated him on the VBPD search and her missing wedding gown. "There was a hit-and-run on Airline Highway," he said. "Luckily, no major injuries, but I'll be tied up for the next few hours. When I'm free, I'll call Griffith and rip him a new one. He had a warrant, so he was within his rights, but it'll feel good. After that, I'm all over finding your dress. In the meantime, put whoever's at the station on it."

"We're on our way there now." Maggie debated, then said, "There's something else." She told him about the strychnine branch.

"That's bad news for Walter Breem and good news for you," Bo said, relief in his voice.

"Griffith can still twist it to make me or my family look bad."

"He can try, but it's a reach. No evidence to show you had prior knowledge of the strychnine's presence or any use of it."

"We were going to wait to mention this to VBPD," Maggie said. "But I guess we have to tell them now that I told you. Or you have to tell them."

"Although . . . I got a busy night. There's a good chance I might forget we ever had this conversation. Just in case, maybe you should text me the information sometime tomorrow. Say, late in the day. Real late."

Maggie smiled. "That makes me feel a little better."

"When all this is over, I'm looking forward to making you feel a lot better."

The sexy tone of Bo's voice left no guesswork as to how he planned on doing this. Gran mock-fanned herself. "Oh, my."

"Is that your grandmother?" Bo couldn't have sounded more embarrassed.

"Yes," Maggie said, giggling.

"Um, hello, Mrs. Crozat."

"Hello, Bo. Perhaps we should end this call."

"Yes, ma'am."

Bo instantly signed off, and Gran winked at her granddaughter.

When Maggie and Gran arrived at Pelican PD headquarters, they found Artie Belloise manning the desk. The portly police officer was eating a large order of jambalaya from a Styrofoam container. "Hey there, Crozats. Ru's still out on medical leave and Bo's on a call, so the inmates are running the asylum. Meaning me." He held up the container, which sagged under the jambalaya's weight. "Late-afternoon snack. A little takeout from Junie's. Little in the figurative sense."

"I can see," Maggie said. "But I can't imagine eating anything less than a big portion of Junie's jambalaya."

Artie dabbed his mouth with a paper napkin. "Bo called and gave me the heads-up about your wedding gown. Takes a lotta nerve to steal something so precious."

"Tell me about it," Maggie said. Gran took her hand and gave it a sympathetic squeeze.

Artie reluctantly pushed away his jambalaya and handed Maggie a form. "Here. Let's start the hunt with you filling out this report."

Maggie and Gran took seats on the lobby's aging, hard plastic chairs. Maggie filled out the form with as many details as she could. "We think the thief stole other stuff too, Artie, but we don't know exactly what."

"No worries," the officer said. "When we find your dress, I'm sure we'll find the rest of the loot. That's generally how it works. Usually they store it all in the same place or stick with the same fence to unload the goods."

"Meaning the dress could have been sold already." Maggie couldn't control the quaver in her voice.

"Doubt it," Artie said, his mouth full of the forkful of jambalaya he couldn't resist eating. "A dress like that, all historical and such, requires a real specific buyer. Finding one of those'd take some time, even with the Internet, where a lotta ill-gotten gains end up these days."

"I'm praying you're right," Maggie said.

She finished the form and returned it to Artie. "Thank you, ma'am," he said. "And Maggie . . ." The jocular officer turned serious. "Around here, there's no particular fondness for our brethren over at Ville Blanc. Know that we'll do anything to protect our own citizens. *Anything.*"

"I appreciate that," Maggie said, grateful for the force's support. "But I don't want you doing something that might get you in trouble."

"You know our motto. In Louisiana . . ."

Maggie and Gran chimed in with Artie. "We only follow the rules we like."

The women left Artie to finish what was left of his lunch. It was a beautiful fall day, with a cloudless azure sky and a slight nip in the unusually dry air. "Can I treat you to an early dinner, Gran?"

"Yes, but first . . ." Gran checked her watch. "Good, the bank is still open. Come with me."

The two cut through the verdant town square, setting off the gazebo's band of ghouls as they walked past it. A Frankenstein monster wearing suspenders and a straw boater hat sang, *Halloween, Halloween, this is Halloween, watch for ghouls and ghosties.* An ambulance suddenly zoomed by with its siren blaring, which drowned out the rest of the song.

"Who thought I'd prefer a siren to a song," Gran said. "But when it comes to whatever that 'ghostie' was singing, I do."

"Agreed," Maggie said, "about a bazillion percent."

They stepped into Morrin National Bank, a lofty name for a local institution with a mere three branches in the parish. The bank's interior was a nineteenth-century time capsule, with polished marble columns and ornate brass grates separating the two tellers from customers. Bank president Robert "Bob" Morrin, the seventy-something cadaverous bald descendant of the founding family, greeted Gran like she was a rock star. "Mrs. Crozat, how wonderful to see you. What a delightful end to my day. Come in, come in."

He put a hand under Gran's elbow and guided her into his office. Maggie brought up the rear. Morrin settled Gran into a wingback chair upholstered in navy leather with brass nailhead trim. Since the room lacked a second chair, Maggie stood behind her grandmother. "I assume you know my granddaughter, Magnolia," Gran said.

"I'm afraid not. I don't think she banks with us."

Morrin extended his hand with a smile, but there was enough of a hint of admonishment in his tone to make Maggie feel guilty. "I like to use my phone to make deposits," she said, a little sheepish.

"We just brought my millennial granddaughter into the bank fold, so you can bet she'll have us using an app a-*sapp*," Morrin quipped.

Maggie gave a polite laugh. Gran got down to business. "Robert, I need you to retrieve my safety deposit box."

"Yes, ma'am."

The bank president shot out of the room. Maggie furrowed her brow. "Everything okay, Gran? I know business has been more down than up, but you're not going to cash out anything, are you? We can always cut back on the wedding."

"Never," Gran declared. "No, darling girl, this isn't regarding a financial crisis. At least this week."

Morrin returned with a flat metal box. He placed it on his desk. "Mrs. Crozat, why don't you sit behind my desk? Magnolia can take your seat. I'll keep watch from outside the office."

He unlocked the box and stepped out of the room. Grandmère extracted a flat black velvet case from the strongbox. She handed it to Maggie. "For you, chère. From my side of the family, the Bringiers."

Maggie opened the case and gasped. Resting on a bed of satin was the most beautiful piece of jewelry she'd ever seen. She gently removed the heirloom, a white-gold filigree necklace with vines and blossoms shaped from diamonds and pearls. "Oh, Gran . . ."

"I was going to surprise you with it on our wedding day," her grandmother said. "But I decided not to wait. No matter what gown you walk down the aisle in, you'll be wearing something rife with beauty, history, and sentiment."

Maggie held the necklace up to the light. The diamonds sparkled and cast tiny rainbows. "You're getting married, too. Don't you want to wear it?"

"I'd much rather watch those gems reflect the glow of my beautiful granddaughter."

Maggie threw her arms around her grandmother. She held Grand-mère tightly, then said, "I love you so much."

"I love you more," Gran said, a slight tremor in her voice.

"Impossible," Maggie said. She grinned and wiped her eyes. A few bars of a Trombone Shorty song announced an incoming cell phone call. Maggie checked the ID, and her good mood evaporated. "It's Ville Blanc PD."

Gran's face darkened. "Ignore it."

"I am." Maggie let the call go to voice mail. A text popped up on her phone screen. "It's Detective Griffith. He wants me to come down to the station so we can go over my statement. I've watched enough police TV shows to know a trap when I see one." Maggie took a screenshot of the text. "I'm sending this to Bo and Quentin." She did so and received two quick responses. "Bo said, *I'm on it.* I'm guessing that means he's going to share the info about the strychnine tree on the Dupois property."

"What did Quentin say?"

"One word: *Stall.*" Maggie held up her cell. "I'm turning off my phone."

Gran took out her cell phone. "Me too."

The women powered down. "We're off the grid," Gran said. "What a freeing feeling. Let's celebrate with dinner at LeBlanc's."

"Not Junie's?"

"I feel like dining someplace where the floor is a little less sticky." Gran stood up. "Robert," she called over shoulder.

The bank president bounded in. "Yes, Mrs. Crozat? And it's Bob to my family, close friends, and favorite customers."

"You can lock up my safety deposit box, Bob. I won't access it again until right before our wedding."

"Yes, of course. We heard that was happening. Many congratulations from myself and Mrs. Morrin." The banker adopted his best professional demeanor, which didn't succeed in masking his hurt feelings.

"The invitations haven't gone out yet," Grand-mère said. "We're waiting until the six-week mark. I hope you and Mary will be able to make it, but I know you often visit the grand-children over the holidays."

"No, no, Mary and I will be there." Morrin beamed. "You can count on us."

"Isn't your fourth grandchild due around then?" Gran asked, slightly dubious. "In Atlanta?"

Morrin dismissed this with the wave of a hand. "We were there for the first three; we'll be there for number five. And number four won't know the difference. Where are you registered?"

After assuring Morrin that gifts weren't necessary, Maggie and Gran divested themselves of Morrin's attention and headed for LeBlanc's, Pelican's upscale eating establishment. As they entered, they almost collided with a woman around Gran's age who was leaving the restaurant with a real estate agent Maggie recognized from her ads on Pelican bus benches. Cookie Hampton had co-opted the Pelican town motto—*Yes, We Peli-CAN!*—and turned it into her sales slogan: *Yes, we Peli-CAN sell your home!*

Gran and the older woman exclaimed greetings and exchanged air kisses. "Phyllida, I haven't seen you in forever," Gran said. "We have to get together and catch up."

"We better do it soon, because I just sold my house," Phyllida said. "I'm moving to Mobile to be closer to my daughter and her family."

"Well, Pelican's loss is Mobile's gain," Gran said. "Who's the lucky new owner of your charming home?"

"Not that obnoxious man who's eating up all the local real estate for his application," Phyllida said with a sniff. "I sold my home to a very nice young woman. She's Canadian."

This got Maggie's attention. "Canadian? By any chance would her name be Bonnie MacDowell?"

"Yes," Phyllida said. "She'll be a great addition to our little community. She already has friends here. Like you."

Cookie checked her watch. "Nice to see you all," she said, subtly maneuvering her client toward the door. "We better get going, Phyllida, honey. That paperwork won't sign itself."

The real estate agent hustled Phyllida off, and Gran and Maggie took their seats. "I wonder where young Bonnie got the money to put down on Phyl's house," Gran mused. "I don't see her father handing over a bucket of cash."

Angry, Maggie snapped open her napkin. "This has Gavin Grody's stink all over it. Notice how your friend thought she was avoiding selling to him. But Cookie knows exactly what's going on. That's why she rushed Phyllida away from us. If people are refusing to sell to Grody, he has to find a way around them. I'm sure he funneled the down payment for Phyllida's house through Bonnie. What better way to do that than manipulate some girl who's got the hots for him into being a front for his operation?"

"You sound like a 1950s gumshoe," Gran said. "But I think you're right." She picked up her menu. "Let's put aside all the aggravation of the day and have a lovely meal. With dessert. Maybe two, fitting into whatever wedding dress I end up in be darned."

Maggie perused her menu. "The special today is Coquilles St. Jacque. That sounds—"

The restaurant door flew open. Tug burst in. He glanced around, saw his daughter and mother, and made a beeline to them. "Y'all have your phones off. If we didn't have that app that lets us find each other, I'd be running all over town looking for you."

"Dad, what's wrong?" Maggie was surprised to see him and disturbed by his distraught appearance. "Why are you here?" Her heart raced. "Is it Mom?" Maggie lived in fear of Ninette suffering a relapse of the Hodgkin's lymphoma she'd triumphed over in her twenties.

"Your mother's fine. But Doug MacDowell isn't. He's dead."

Chapter 17

Maggie stared at her father, mouth agape. "Please tell me it was natural causes."

Tug, grim, shook his head. "He was shot."

Gran clutched her hands together. "Oh my Lord."

"That's awful," Maggie said. She closed her eyes, trying to process the tragic development. "Why? Where?"

"Can't answer the first, but apparently he took the bullet while he was marking off the dividing line between our property."

Maggie sucked in a breath, then released it. "Not to sound self-involved, but it's a good thing I don't own a gun. Griffith would be arresting and dragging me out of here right now."

"My guns are in the gun locker," Tug said. "I can't remember when I opened it last."

"Lee has my pistol," Gran said. "He's cleaning it for me."

Maggie faced her grandmother. "You have a gun? How can I not know this?"

"I lived alone in that cottage for years while you were gone in New York, chère," Gran said. "Have I mentioned that I also took a self-defense class and know exactly where to kick an intruder?"

Tug ran a hand through his thinning head of hair, where white was fast outstripping his original ginger color. "At least we all have alibis this time. I heard the gun go off when I was checking in a guest. Your mama came running out of the kitchen, where she was. And y'all were here. Still, we need to get home. I'm sure the police will want to talk to us."

Maggie, trying to process the fact that another murder had taken place on or adjacent to Crozat property, rubbed her temples. "We have to focus. A man died. A man with children. They may be adults, but this will be a horrible shock for them."

"Unless one of them did it," Grand-mère said.

"*Gran.*"

"Don't sound so horrified, Magnolia," her grandmother said. "You know it's a possibility. These people are practically strangers to us. How long have we known them? A month, maybe? We have no idea about the family dynamics that preceded their visit."

"For now," Tug said, "let's assume Johnnie and Bonnie'll be grieving the loss of their father." A pained expression crossed his lined face. "Back to it being all about us. That guest I was checking in when we heard the gunshot—he checked right out as soon as he saw the coroner's van pull up. Here's hoping the weekend guests are less squeamish."

Maggie, Gran, and Tug returned to the B and B as quickly as possible. All was quiet in the immediate area around the plantation. The police action was restricted to the property line, which extended deep into the woods, not far from the old schoolhouse. Maggie traipsed through the woods to where yellow tape marked the crime scene. She was ashamed to feel relieved that Doug's body had already been removed. Bo and his underling, newly minted Detective Brady Rogert, were conferring with the crime scene photographer. Artie Belloise noticed Maggie and approached. "Hey there, Maggie. We meet again. Lucky for all of us there's no Ville Blanc sticking their nose in this case. It's only in our jurisdiction."

"Yay," Maggie said, her tone mordant.

"We're gonna need all the guns y'all own for testing so's we can eliminate them as evidence."

"Not a problem. My dad'll get them for you."

Artie trudged off. Maggie caught Bo's eye, and he came to her. "Another day, another murder," he said, his tone as sardonic as Maggie's.

"This one hits close to home." Maggie pointed to a marking flag delineating the property line that Doug had managed to plant before his death.

Bo was about to respond, but he and Maggie were distracted by the sound of a woman giggling. Bonnie emerged from the woods, talking into her earbud. She wore ripped, belted jeans and a white crop top under a black leather jacket. The young woman kept her eyes on the ground as she tottered over the uneven surface in high-heeled, open-toed booties. "You are so lame," she said into her earbud in a flirty voice. Bonnie bumped into the crime scene tape and looked up. "Gavin, I gotta go. I'll call you later." She ended the call, placed a fist on her hip, and fixed Bo and Maggie with a sour look. "Now what? Seriously, this place is, like, a permanent crime scene. I don't know why you don't want to sell it."

"Bonnie, we need to talk," Bo said as gently as possible. "Let's go inside."

The sour look disappeared, replaced by panic. "No. What happened? Tell me now."

"It's your father, Bonnie. He was shot. And didn't make it."

Bonnie's shock was palpable. She screamed and fell to her knees. Maggie dropped down beside her, but the young woman pushed her away. "Get away!" she screamed. "You killed my stepmother and now you killed my father!"

"I haven't killed anyone, I swear," Maggie protested.

Bo helped Bonnie to her feet. "The Crozats have alibis. We're searching the woods and already found possible clues to the suspect. Prints from a man's boots. Detective Rogert is gonna take you inside. He'll get you some water and go over a few things."

Bonnie, still in shock, nodded. There was a rustling in the woods. Johnnie MacDowell pushed aside branches and came into the small clearing. His sister ran to him. "Johnnie, the most horrible thing—"

Johnnie held up his hand. He scribbled in his ever-present journal, ripped out the page, and held it up. It read *Zen Walk*. His sister grabbed the page and crumpled it up. "Dad is dead. Someone shot him."

Her twin dropped his journal. He swayed, then fell against a tree. "I need a meeting."

Bo took his arm. "We'll get you to one, but first I have to ask you a few questions."

"I'll go find Emma," Maggie told the stricken man. Johnnie tried to speak but couldn't find his voice. He nodded, a sick expression on his face.

Bo and Rogert led the siblings to the schoolhouse while Maggie ran through the woods back to the B and B, where Emma was pulling into the graveled parking lot. "I'm so glad I found you," Maggie said.

"I was in Baton Rouge," Emma said. She parked and got out of the vehicle. "I had to replace some props. Those actors don't just chew the scenery, they chew through the props. What's up?" Maggie shared the news about Doug's death. Emma stared at her, wide-eyed. "I don't believe it. You're making it up."

"No, I'd never do that. He's gone, Emma. Shot to death."

Emma made a small sound. Her body crumpled, and she covered her face with her hands. Maggie felt for the distraught woman, who lacked the exposure to violent death that Maggie had experienced, albeit unwillingly. "It's awful," Maggie said with compassion. "I have no idea if Johnnie and his dad were close. To be honest, I mostly saw them arguing. But I know Johnnie's fragile, and something as shocking as this could be dangerous for his mental health."

Emma straightened up. She used a sleeve of her hoodie to wipe tears from her cheeks. "Yes, right. I'll go to him. Thank you."

Emma took off for the schoolhouse. Maggie turned toward the cottage, but the flutter of a curtain covering a second-floor window in the manor house caught her attention. She looked up and glimpsed Barrymore. She realized he had been watching her and Emma. Something about the look on his face gave Maggie the chills. Her instincts, which sometimes approached a clairvoyant level, kicked in. *He may not be the buffoon I thought he was*, she thought to herself.

*   *   *

Maggie stayed up as late as she could, in case Johnnie or Bonnie needed anything from the Crozats. Around four AM, she passed out on the sofa in the front parlor of the manor house. She slept for an hour, then woke up and stumbled back to the cottage before guests could see her bedraggled self. She crawled into bed and managed to catch a few more hours' sleep, which was followed by a bracing cold shower. Maggie filled a travel mug with coffee, yawning as she evaluated the mug's size. She poured the coffee from the mug into a carafe four times bigger, filling it to the brim before departing for Doucet.

She arrived a half hour before the historic plantation opened to the public. Ione and Helene Brevelle were already in the employee lounge, which was housed in the overseer's house. Helene aimlessly shuffled a deck of tarot cards. "Are you okay?" Ione asked Maggie. The plantation manager stepped into a hoop skirt and yanked it up to her waist. "I heard someone died at your place. I was gonna call, but I figured you didn't need the distraction."

"It wasn't exactly *at* our place," Maggie said. She detailed what she knew about Doug's death. "That protection oil and gris-gris bag you gave me don't seem to be doing their job, Helene."

"Oft times dark forces are much stronger than good," Helene said. "What Crozat needs is a good cleansing."

Something thumped onto the outside doorstep. Ione pulled open the door and retrieved a bound stack of *Pelican Penny Clippers*. She glanced at the headline. "We don't need these," she said. "Our visitors could care less about the *Clipper*. They're headed straight to the recycle bin."

"Hold up," Maggie said. "Let me see." Ione hesitated. "I know you're trying to protect me from something. I need to know what it is."

"Fine. Here."

Ione reluctantly handed the bundle to Maggie. The *Clipper* cover was a collection of sensational tabloid headlines and articles, all revolving around her family's home. "'Crozat Plantation's Spooky Past Has Nothing on Its Scary Present,'" Maggie read. She threw down the bundle.

"The recycling bin is too good for that rag," Ione, ever supportive, said. "It belongs at the bottom of a birdcage. No, I take that back. I'm insulting birds."

Maggie gave the stack a kick. "You were right the first time. I can tell you what our guest parrot Lovie's going to be pooping on tonight. Wait, let me check something." She pulled her cell phone out of her leather tote bag and typed in a search. Doleful, she dropped into a chair. "We could line every birdcage in Louisiana and it wouldn't stop people from seeing these stories. Little Earlie posted them all over social media. Helene, we may take you up on that offer of a cleansing."

Helene snorted. "Wouldn't worry about Little Earlie's social media accounts. I bet his following is in the tens of people."

Maggie spent the rest of the day trying to forget what she'd read in the *Clipper*. She managed to convince herself that Ione was right; the only thing visitors wanted out of the freebie paper was the coupons for Pelican attractions. As for the locals, the *Clipper*'s articles were mostly a rehash of past events that wouldn't tell them anything they didn't already know. *Still, if I had Helene's voodoo doll and those black pins, Little Earlie would find himself in a passel of pain*, she thought to herself, giving the paintbrush she was cleaning a furious shake.

"I'm glad I'm not that paintbrush," a familiar voice said.

Maggie's anger melted away. She ran into Bo's arms. They kissed, and then she rested her head against his chest. "It's that stupid Little Earlie," she said, her voice muffled.

"I know. I saw the *Clipper*. The bundle we got delivered is making itself useful soaking up the oil dripping from under one of our patrol cars."

"A rag being used as rags. Perfect." Maggie disengaged from Bo's arms. She examined her fiancé. His coal-black eyes were shadowed. Under his chiseled cheekbones, Bo's handsome face was gaunt. She brushed back a lock of hair that had fallen over his forehead. "You look exhausted, cher. Did you get any sleep last night?"

"Couple of hours, maybe." Bo blinked and rubbed his eyes. "I don't know when I'll be off the clock. I'm sneaking in a trip to the Halloween store to pick up Xander's costume and thought I'd get in a little time with you, too."

"Did Xander finally land on a costume?"

"Yup. He's going old-school, as Frankenstein's monster. He wants all three of us to dress like that."

"I can be the Bride of."

"Great idea," Bo said. He checked the time on his phone. "I better take off. If I see a Bride of Frankenstein costume, should I pick it up for you?"

Maggie stuck her arms out in front of her and grunted. "That's a yes. I'm getting into character."

Bo chuckled. "That had more of a zombie thing to it. You might want to get a few tips from the cast of Quentin's play."

Maggie faked a pout. "Ouch. Just for that, no goodbye kiss for you. Oh, who am I kidding?"

She grabbed Bo and pulled him toward her. They embraced, then separated. Bo left, and Maggie returned to cleaning the brushes she was using to restore a centuries-old painting from Doucet's collection. Her mind wandered to the image of Barrymore staring down at her from the manor house second-floor window. The look on his face had disturbed her. She dried off her hands and tapped Quentin's telephone number into her cell. "Hello there, mademoiselle-soon-to-be-madame," he cheerfully greeted her. "I assume you're calling about the latest death by murder at Crozat."

"*Near* Crozat, not *at*," Maggie felt compelled to clarify.

"Po-tay-to, po-tay-to. I did a little nosing, and our non-friend Detective Griffith of VBPD is really hoping to tie you to the MacDowell killing and make a double-murder collar."

Maggie felt bile rise from her stomach into her mouth. "You're gonna make me upchuck, Quentin."

"Not necessary. You didn't do this, and Griffith's bone-headed line of thinking provides us with a great stall. While he's trying to build a case he can't build, Pelican PD and your mister can scope out the real killer of the masseuse and her husband and make both cases go away."

"I'll work on finding that reassuring. But it's not why I called. What do you know about Barrymore Tuttle?"

Quentin made a noise that sounded like a verbal raising of the eyebrows. "You intrigue me. Why do you ask?"

"Just a feeling."

"This is Louisiana, chère; there's no such thing as 'just' a feeling. I'd venture a good portion of the state is flat-out psychic. But to answer your question, I only know what I needed to know about him as an actor. He isn't terrible and knows how to project, which has proved invaluable in that sound abyss of a cemetery."

"Okay. If you think of anything else, let me know."

Maggie ended the call. She took off the apron she wore to protect her clothes from errant paint spills and hung it on a hook by the studio door. Then she pondered her next step. *Emma*, she mused. *She has a real attitude toward Barrymore. Maybe there's more to it than finding him generally obnoxious.* Hopefully Emma had recovered from the news of Doug's death, which had produced a surprisingly emotional reaction from the stage manager. *I am so over theatre people*, Maggie thought as she locked up the studio. *I need a break from the drama.*

On her way home, she decided to treat Vince, her beloved Falcon convertible, to a bath. Lee Bertrand, her future

187

step-grandfather, had added carwash facilities to his service station, and he insisted on doing the job himself. By the time he was done waxing and polishing, the vintage auto's chrome exterior and leather interior gleamed. "Only payment required is a hug," Lee told her.

"Here you go," Maggie said, hugging him. "And here's your tip." She hugged him again.

Maggie put the convertible's top down and took the River Road to Crozat, rejuvenated by the rush of cold wind as she drove. She parked in the family's back lot, but rather than go to the shotgun cottage, Maggie decided to check on the MacDowell twins. Gopher, who'd greeted her in the parking lot, tagged along as she detoured through the woods to the schoolhouse. Bonnie answered the door, looking as if she'd slept in her clothes—if she'd slept at all. Her eyes were bloodshot, and a cigarette dangled from her mouth. "I'm so sorry about your dad," Maggie said. "I wanted to see if you needed anything."

Bonnie held up an empty cigarette box. "More ciggies."

She crumpled the box and tossed it on the floor, where it joined a small pile of discarded empty cigarette boxes. Maggie grimaced as she followed Bonnie inside. The room smelled like a combination of stale cigarette smoke, rotting food, dirty laundry, and mildew. *If I ever get this place back, I'll have to fumigate it*, Maggie thought, resisting the urge to hold her nose.

Bonnie collapsed onto the couch. "Johnnie's not here. He's at one of his useless meetings. Gavin was supposed to come over and be with me, but he texted that something came up. He's busy like that."

The mention of the entrepreneur's name recalled the house Bonnie had purchased from Gran's friend Phyllida. Maggie considered the lifestyle blogger's current emotional state and tabled the thought of bringing that up to her. "I can make a run to the Park 'n Shop if you really need cigarettes."

"Thanks, but I'll text Johnnie to pick some up on his way home and have him make a wine run for me."

"Given Johnnie's . . ." Maggie searched for the best way to express her concern. "Given his . . . situation, and the trauma of your dad's death, maybe a wine run isn't the best idea for him. I'm happy to make a run for you."

Bonnie flicked her hand dismissively, sending ash from her cigarette wafting into the air. Maggie's art studio had already survived one fire, an arson attempt on the part of a murder suspect. She prayed an errant ash from Bonnie's cigarette didn't start another conflagration. "Johnnie'll be fine," his sister said. "It'll be a good test of his sobriety. Thanks for stopping by. If we need anything, I'll let you know."

Maggie took the hint. "We're here if you need us."

She left Bonnie texting away on her cell phone and hiked through the woods toward home. *That is one toxic sibling relationship*, she thought to herself. Bonnie's poor twin might be the definition of a hot mess, but Maggie was Team Johnnie all the way. She could almost sympathize with the tortured young man if he'd killed his father to inherit money that would enable him to escape his dysfunctional family.

Maggie called to Gopher, who was relieving himself on a tree. He finished his business and ambled over to her. Maggie bent down to pet him. Suddenly, a scream came from the woods. Maggie's heart did a backflip. *Now what?* she thought. She was about to grab the basset hound, hefty as he was, and take off running when Cindy, the guest from the Paranormals group, staggered out of the dense brush. "I saw one," she gasped. "A rougarou."

Maggie silently cursed whomever was bedeviling the town B and Bs with the beast sightings. "I'm so sorry. We're trying to figure out who's responsible for—"

"I went for a walk because I figured that dusk would be when they come out." Cindy's face lit up. "And I was right! I can't wait to tell the others. They'll be so jealous."

Cindy darted off to the manor house. "Gopher, buddy," Maggie said to the dog as they headed out of the woods. "I'm bewildered by some of our guests. But right now, also relieved that someone's actually happy to see a rougarou."

Gopher woofed a response, then meandered off to troll for snacks. Maggie reached the small auxiliary graveled lot that lay between the back of the manor house and the shotgun cottage. The manor house back door opened and Barrymore emerged, lugging a large suitcase. She watched as he popped the trunk and deposited the bag inside. "Checking out, Barrymore?"

"Agh!" Startled, he turned and saw her. He quickly recovered and plastered on a smile. "Hello there, Maggie. Nope, not going anywhere. What kind of actor would I be if I cut out before my theatrical run was over? I'm meeting friends for a bite. And, uh, putting my props in the trunk for safekeeping. You know us thespians."

Barrymore retreated to the driver's side and got into the car. He gave Maggie a jovial wave as he drove off, which she returned. Then, as soon as he was out of view, Maggie pulled her car keys out of her back pocket, jumped into the Falcon, and began to follow him.

Chapter 18

Maggie, aware that her vintage convertible was not exactly a subtle vehicle, hung back a few cars behind Barrymore. She trailed him onto I-10. While she drove, she used her Bluetooth to connect with Pelican PD. Officer Cal Vichet took the call, and she shared her suspicions about Barrymore. "He's driving a maroon four-door sedan. It's an older-model car. He told me once that he rented it on the cheap from Homely Haul, the place in Ville Blanc that rents used cars. The first three license plate numbers are six, four, nine. I can't see the rest and don't know the number offhand."

"No worries. I can get it from Homely Haul and pass it on to Baton Rouge PD. Any idea what's in the suitcase?"

Maggie frowned. "No. I'm sorry. I know this isn't much to go on, if anything. Oh, he's getting off. I'll let you know where he ends up."

She ended the call and took the same exit as the actor. Night had fallen, which helped disguise her car but made it harder to track Barrymore's dark sedan as he traversed local streets. But a determined Maggie managed to keep up. He finally stopped in front of a Creole cottage on a quiet street in the city's historic district. Maggie slowed down slightly to read the wooden sign dangling over the front door, which identified the cottage as Baton Rouge Antiques. *I knew it*, Maggie thought. She drove past Barrymore, who was focused on extricating the heavy suitcase from the trunk of his car. Maggie made a left and parked. She got out of her car and traversed the sidewalk to the corner, where she hid behind a Tudor-style home. She peered around the home's edge and saw Barrymore drag the suitcase up the cottage steps and into the antique store. Maggie scurried down the sidewalk to the store. She hunched over to create a low profile and crept up the stairs, then dropped to her knees to sneak a peek through a large front window. All she could see was the top of Barrymore's head. The rest of him was blocked by the shop's jumble of large antique furniture. Maggie decided on another tack. She hurried down the steps and around the side of the shop to the back of the building. The handle on the back door was of about the same vintage as the one on the attic door at Crozat, and just as sturdy. *As in not sturdy at all*, Maggie thought.

She opened the door with ease and slipped into the shop's office, where she instantly spotted a familiar brass candlestick—the stolen mate to the one still at Crozat B and B. Maggie glanced around the room and noticed a bundle of what appeared to be ivory silk fabric. She tiptoed over, gently unfolded it, and managed not to gasp when the bundle revealed itself to be her wedding gown. Maggie tamped down the urge to grab the gown and run with it. *No*, she told herself. *I want Barrymore to get caught and pay for what he did.* Instead

ELLEN BYRON

she tapped a message to Cal Vichet on her silenced cell phone, alerting him to her discovery and location. He sent back a thumbs-up emoji and a promise to alert Baton Rouge PD.

Maggie drew closer to the curtain separating the office from the main room. She squatted low to hide herself and listened to see what she could pick up of the conversation between Barrymore and another man. "A great piece of kitchenware," he was saying. She heard the sound of knuckles rapping on metal. "Solid copper." The mystery man's response was muffled. "Stop yanking my chain," Barrymore said, annoyed. "You know this is a beauty."

"I said no," the man, equally annoyed, said in a louder voice. "Millennials don't want copper pots. They barely want any of that other stuff you keep pushing on me. The best thing you brought in is that wedding dress. I can make a nice profit selling it to a museum."

Maggie somehow restrained herself from yelling, "No!" Anxious, she wondered, *Where is BRPD?*

"All righty," Barrymore said in a more genial tone. "No copper pots, select bric-a-brac only, more antique clothing. I'll see what I can do."

The conversation seemed to be wrapping up and there was still no sign of the police. The men exchanged goodbyes. Unable to wait a minute longer, Maggie darted out of the office and ran to the front of the house, arriving just as the actor-slash-thief was leaving with a copper saucepot she recognized from Crozat's attic stash. Maggie dashed up the stairs and, not knowing what else to do, held up a hand. "Stop in the name of the law! I'm making a citizen's arrest."

There was a sudden wail of sirens, which grew louder as the police finally found their way to the antique shop. Barrymore froze. Then he took the pot, whacked Maggie on the head with it, and took off running down the street. Maggie, seeing stars, staggered backward and tumbled down the shop's steps as a patrol car screeched to a halt in front of the shop. Two officers leapt out. One gave chase to Barrymore and the other dropped to his knees next to Maggie, whose fall had ended with her splayed out on the shop's small patch of grass. "Forget me," she told the officer, her voice a whisper. "I wanna see that thieving SOB go *down*."

* * *

"How badly does it hurt?" Bo asked as he drove Maggie down the interstate toward home. He had retrieved his fiancée from the hospital where the police brought her to be checked out after her head met up with the heavy copper pot. Luckily, she'd managed not to have a concussion, but a gash on her forehead had required a half-dozen stitches.

"A lot." Maggie touched the stitches and winced. "At least now I'll actually look like the monster's bride. Did you find out if they caught Barrymore?"

"Yup. He's in custody, facing charges of burglary, assault, and evading arrest."

"*Yes*." Maggie did a fist pump, then winced again. "Ow, that hurt."

"Best if you avoid sudden movements, chère. By the way, it turns out his name isn't really Barrymore Tuttle."

"What a surprise," Maggie said dryly. "What is it?"

"Marvin Crapser."

"Wow."

"Yup. I gotta say, if that were my name, I'd change it too. What made you suspect him, anyway?"

"I have to chalk it up to that famous instinct we Doucet-Crozat women seem to have, which was set off by a look on his face I hadn't seen before. Kind of malevolent. Then I started thinking about how he was coughing during Susannah's memorial. I remembered having the same cough myself—after spending time in the attic before I thought to wear a mask."

Bo took his eyes off the road briefly to favor Maggie with an affectionate glance. "Here's hoping young Detective Rogert develops your instincts."

Maggie touched her temple, which throbbed. "What about my wedding dress? Is it evidence?"

Bo nodded. "But you'll get it back real soon. I doubt Tuttle will want to go to trial. He'll take a plea deal that'll mean doing time but with a reduced sentence."

"They're not gonna need it to bring a case against the antique dealer?" Maggie asked.

"The guy swears he had no idea that Tuttle was a thief. He says Tuttle passed himself off as a plantation owner who fell on hard times."

"I can believe that." Maggie stared out the window. They were coming up on the Dupois cemetery. "They're doing a run-through of the play. You mind stopping here for a minute? I need to break the news to Quentin that he'll have to find a quick replacement for Barrymore."

"You got it."

Bo pulled to the side of the road next to the cemetery, and Maggie got out of his SUV. Quentin saw her and waved, as did Vanessa. "Maggie, chère, you okay?" her frenemy asked with genuine concern. "We heard about your run-in with a copper pot."

Maggie pointed to her stitches. "Aside from my boo-boo, I'm okay. But Quentin, I have bad news about your male star."

"I know all about that. Our costumer is dating that new detective, Rogert. We just finished a run-through with Tuttle's understudy."

"Who did you cast?"

Quentin grinned and pointed to himself with both index fingers. "Me. It was a gimme. I know all the lines, seeing as how I wrote the play."

"And he's wonderful in the role." Patria, who was packing up what looked like a very pricey purse, added her two cents to the conversation. She gestured to Quentin and Vanessa. "They got awesome chemistry."

"They should," Maggie said, bemused. "They're married."

Patria slapped her forehead. "Duh. Right."

The flighty actress giggled as she walked away, earning an eye roll from Vanessa. "And people think *I'm* a dumb blonde. That girl's got miles on me."

Bo got out of the SUV and joined them. "Don't mean to break up the fun, but I'd like to get my girl home so she can rest. It's been a—"

He was interrupted by a blast of police sirens. Moments later, a half dozen Ville Blanc patrol cars barreled down the

River Road. They made a left turn and tore down the dirt road that ran alongside the cemetery to the Dupois caretaker's house.

"What the what?" Vanessa said as they saw officers, including Zeke Griffith, pour out of the cars. They were clad in protective vests and approached the house with guns drawn.

"Quentin, clear your people from the area," Bo said, his brow taut. "I gotta see what's going on."

Bo ran toward the emerging crime scene while Quentin ushered Vanessa and a few curious performers to their cars. Maggie stayed beyond, taking refuge behind a tomb as a precaution. Someone shouted something she couldn't make out from inside the caretaker's cottage, which precipitated a shift in the action. The officers holstered their guns. Griffith strode out of the cottage and reached through the window of the nearest patrol car. He pulled a portable radio out of the car and barked an order into it. Maggie saw Bo confer with an officer. Then he started toward her. She emerged from her hiding place. "What is it? What's going on?"

"It's Walter Breem," Bo said. "VBPD got a complaint from a parent. Breem caught her son cutting through the Dupois property and threatened to eighty-six him with strychnine. Putting that together with Susannah's murder was enough for Griffith to get an arrest warrant from a Ville Blanc judge."

A police officer grabbed a first aid kit from his car and ran into the house. The scene in front of Maggie confused her. "Are they arresting Walter or not?"

"Not," Bo said. "At least not right now. They found him lying on the floor with a knife in his back."

Chapter 19

An ambulance rushed the critically injured caretaker to the hospital. Bo dropped Maggie at home, then took off for the hospital for an update on Breem's condition. After checking in with her worried parents and grandmother, Maggie, depressed and head aching from her copper pot injury, crawled into bed. It was both hard and not hard to envision Walter Breem as a murderer. He presented a disturbing, even scary, façade to the world. But she had seen another side to him, one that made her wonder if what everyone else saw was an act. A way to protect himself from being encroached on by a society he had no interest in joining.

In the morning, she called Bo as soon as she woke up. "Breem's stable but still in critical condition," he told her. "VBPD searched his house but didn't find a gun or strychnine, so his arrest is on hold. He's still a suspect in Susannah and Doug's deaths, though."

"Even though he's a victim himself now?"

"Don't look under that rock, chère. Not to be callous, but you want him to be a suspect. It means Ville Blanc is backing off you and your family. I gotta go. I'll call you later."

Whether Breem was under suspicion or not, Maggie vowed to stop by the hospital and see him when he was well enough to receive visitors. She showered and slipped on jeans and a V-neck T-shirt featuring the stylized rendering of the Crozat manor house that decorated her line of local souvenirs. Then she headed over to the house itself, where she helped her mother serve breakfast to their Paranormal guests before they embarked on a Pelican's Haunted History tour led by the ever-industrious Helene Brevelle, who would also be giving the excited participants spiritual readings. But Maggie sensed an undercurrent of tension. Word of Breem's stabbing had reached the group, engendering a debate about suspects and motives. "I can't help thinking that my sighting of the rougarou was a harbinger of this tragedy," Cindy said, unable to hide the humblebrag in her tone.

"Oh, will you stop with that," Jerome, another member of the group, snapped at her. Others loudly seconded this.

"I was just making a point," Cindy said, affronted.

"A point you keep making over and over again," Jerome said. "You saw a rougarou. We get it. You don't have to keep throwing it in our faces."

"*What?*" Cindy huffed. "Like it's my fault I did the work you were too lazy to do."

"Hey, wait a minute—"

Maggie was about to step in when DruCilla appointed herself peacemaker. "Would y'all like to hear Lovie sing?"

MURDER IN THE BAYOU BONEYARD

"Yes," chorused everyone except Cindy, who responded with a disgruntled "No."

Lovie, who'd spent breakfast perched on DruCilla's shoulder, entertained the guests with a song about worms going in and out of a body. Maggie remembered it from childhood, and it made her lose her appetite. But the others, with the exception of Cindy, seemed to enjoy the bird's lusty rendition, and that's what mattered.

Maggie volunteered to take on cleanup detail after breakfast. First she called Kaity Bertrand to report that Crozat, like the other B and Bs, was still being plagued by a rougarou. Kaity promised to share this with the rest of the B and B reps, which Maggie hoped would dissipate their hostility toward her family's hostelry. Then she focused on mindless tasks that allowed her mind to wander, which in the past had led to unexpected insights into some of the murders bedeviling Crozat. *Who would want to try and kill Walter?* she wondered as she scraped scraps off a plate into a compost container. *Was it revenge? Did someone think he murdered Susannah and Doug? Did they have evidence? If so, what was it?* An hour later, the kitchen and dining room were sparkling clean and Maggie had a long list of questions. Unfortunately, she didn't have an answer to a single one of them.

She walked through the wide hallway that ran the length of the manor house, allowing for breezes to ventilate the home on warm days. Maggie stepped outside onto the veranda. Rain had fallen during the night, and drops still clung to the large lawn that fronted Crozat. The air was redolent with the scent of fresh-cut grass. Maggie heard the repetitive squeak of the porch swing and looked over to see Emma rocking back and forth, a vacant look on her face. The stage manager clutched an unlit cigarette between the index and middle fingers of her left hand. She lifted the cigarette to her mouth, then seeming to remember it wasn't lit, dropped her hand. Maggie approached her. "Emma? Are you all right?"

"I haven't slept in . . . I don't know . . . thirty-six hours?" Emma spoke in a dull, almost robotic tone. "Life never goes according to plan, does it? You do your best, and then . . ." She lifted the cigarette and dropped her hand again. "Doug was such a nice man. He put up with so much from that beeyotch Susannah. He was finally free of her. And that psycho crazy guy from the cemetery had to go kill him."

Maggie sat down next to Emma. "We don't know for sure that Walter Breem is the one who killed Doug."

"Oh, please." Emma's voice was heavy with scorn. "The strychnine was growing on the guy's property, so he obviously used it to kill Susannah. Doug must have figured this out, so then he had to go, too."

"But why would Walter kill Susannah? I don't think he even knew her."

Emma shrugged. "Who knows? Maybe she looked at him wrong. I told you, he's crazy." She held up the cigarette. "I really need to light this. But I know I'm not supposed to smoke here."

"No, not at any of these old wooden places. They're all a fire waiting to happen. But why smoke? What happened to chewing gum?"

"I ran out," Emma said. Her lower lip trembled. Then she began to weep.

Maggie put an arm around the young woman. "Let's get you some gum. Come on."

"O-o-kay," Emma stuttered through her shuddering sobs.

Maggie led Emma to the Falcon and helped her get in. "Great, I knocked my purse over," Emma said. "A bunch of stuff fell out." She bent down and picked up a few items from the car floor with shaky hands. "I'm such a mess. I'm sorry."

"Don't be," Maggie said. "It's traumatic when someone you know is murd—" She stopped herself and chose a gentler path. "Dies unexpectedly."

They drove to the nearest Park 'n Shop. Maggie insisted that Emma rest in the car while she bought the gum. She returned with it to profuse thanks from the stage manager, who immediately stuffed a few pieces in her mouth.

When the women got back to the B and B, they found Ninette waiting on the veranda. "There you are. I'm glad I found both of you."

Maggie noted the look of concern on her mother's face. "What's going on, Mom?"

Ninette wrinkled her brow, deepening the fine lines of aging on her forehead. "I went over to the schoolhouse. The coroner released Doug's body." Maggie heard Emma whimper. "Bonnie and Johnnie are supposed to take him back to Canada tomorrow. Bonnie seems to be managing her grief, but Johnnie looks terrible. Worse than that . . . I think he's drinking again."

"He is." Emma spit her wad of gum into a wrapper and balled it up. She took a new stick out of her purse, then shoved it back and pulled out a cigarette instead.

Maggie and her mother glanced at each other. "Oh, dear," Ninette said. "I'm so sorry to hear that about Johnnie. Is there anything we can do?"

Emma shook her head. "His bottom wasn't rock bottom. He needs to hit that. Until he does, there's nothing anyone can do. Trust me, I know." She gave a strangled, mirthless laugh. "Because, guess what? Turns out my bottom may not have been rock bottom either."

Maggie and her mother watched the young woman slump off with her head down and shoulders sagging. "Is it my imagination, or is she taking Doug's death unusually hard?" Ninette asked.

"It's definitely not your imagination," Maggie said. "Her reaction is pretty extreme for someone who barely knew the guy. Or so we think."

Ninette's cell pinged a text. She pulled the phone from her apron pocket. "Bonnie. She wants to know if we have any packing tape. I like hearing the word *packing*." Ninette's tone was hopeful.

"Unfortunately, she doesn't appear to be heading back to Toronto."

"Oh," Ninette said, deflated.

"It's a long story. I'll tell you later. I have packing tape. I'll bring it to her."

"Thanks, chère. I need to make a batch of ghost cookies for the guests checking in this afternoon. A small group from the riverboat picked us as their weekend excursion."

"Bless those nonrefundable add-on trips," Maggie said.

"Oh yes," Ninette said with a vigorous nod. "They're keeping what's left of the old roof on this place over our heads."

Maggie left her mother for the shotgun cottage, where she dug up a roll of packing tape that she then carried to the schoolhouse. Bags of trash were parked next to the building's door, which was open, helping to dissipate the room's rancid smell. Bonnie, clad in tight jeans and a clingy top, her strawberry-blonde hair pulled into a high ponytail, appeared much more functional than she had the day before. "Hi," she greeted Maggie. She waved her inside. "I'm purging, and, for a change, I'm not talking about my last meal." She noticed the awkward expression on Maggie's face. "That's a joke."

"Oh." Maggie relaxed. "To be honest, I wasn't sure."

Bonnie took the roll of tape Maggie offered her. "I mean, it's not like I *don't* purge. I just didn't today. Which is why it's a joke."

"Ah." Maggie faked a laugh.

Bonnie gestured to a couple of open boxes on the couch. "My dad's stuff. I'm donating it. Is it okay if I leave it here?"

"Sure. I can bring it to the church. They sometimes give away clothes at the food pantry."

Maggie watched while Bonnie ran tape over the top of the box. "Emma's taking your dad's death really hard."

"We all are."

"Yes. I mean, of course you and Johnnie are; he was your father. With Emma, though . . . I was under the impression she barely knew him. But maybe she knew him better than I thought?"

Bonnie slammed down the tape and glared at Maggie. "Can I please mourn my father without you turning this into an investigation?"

"Your father was murdered," Maggie felt compelled to point out. "That actually requires an investigation."

"By detectives, not some B and B waitress."

Maggie managed not to snap back at Bonnie. She wasn't done trying to mine intel from the blogger. "I'm sorry your trip here had to end in such a horrible way." Bonnie had no way of knowing Maggie was privy to her purchase of Phyllida's home, so she decided to lob this fact at the young woman and throw her off-balance. "I guess you'll be back for the closing."

"Huh?" Bonnie said, confused.

"For the house you bought." *Gotcha.* Feeling smug, Maggie waited for Bonnie's reaction.

"Oh. I thought you were talking about the land and the chemical companies."

The conversation had taken a turn that threw Maggie, not Bonnie, off-balance. "Wha-wha—" she stuttered. "Are you saying you're still going to sell the land?"

"Yeah." She tossed a couple of men's shirts into an empty box. "Why wouldn't we? Once we bury Dad, I'm coming back to close the deal on a house I bought so I don't have to keep living in this dump—"

Maggie gritted her teeth to keep from shouting, *It wasn't a dump until you moved in!*

"—and I'll meet with different companies who are interested in the property." Bonnie stopped packing and attempted to fix a sympathetic gaze on Maggie. "I know this is hard on your family."

"A *little*." This time Maggie didn't squelch the anger in her response.

"But I want you to know that I'm not gonna go back on my Dad's offer to combine our properties for a better sale."

"That is *so* generous of you." Bonnie either didn't notice or chose to ignore the sarcasm in Maggie's tone. "You know, you keep saying *I*, not *we*. I assume Johnnie's got as much say in this as you do."

Bonnie picked up a can of shaving cream and tossed it into a nearby trash can. "We're twins. *I* means *we* with us."

We'll see what Johnnie has to say about that. "I need to get going," Maggie said. She headed toward the front door. "Have a safe flight."

"Uh-huh." Bonnie, distracted by an incoming text, eagerly checked her phone. Her face fell.

"No Gavin?" Maggie couldn't resist saying.

"He's super busy," Bonnie said, her tone defensive. "And so am I."

Bonnie slammed the door so hard it almost propelled Maggie down the schoolhouse path.

* * *

"We have to talk them out of it," Tug said. The family was on the veranda waiting for the group from the riverboat. Maggie had broken the news about Bonnie's determination to sell the MacDowell property. "We can't run a vacation business next to a chemical plant or oil storage tanks. Or live next to one. I hate saying this, but if it was worst-case scenario and we couldn't stop the sale, we'd have to sell too. We could put in a proviso that the company had to keep and maintain this house." Tug gestured to the manor home. "Like Shell did with Ashland-Belle Helene. But that's the best case in a worst-case scenario."

The family lapsed into a glum silence. Even the scent of sugary goodness emanating from Ninette's tray of ghost cookies didn't lift their spirits. "I'll tell you one thing," Gran finally said. "Family or not, I am *so* not inviting those evil twins to our wedding."

A minivan made a right turn off the River Road and rumbled down the plantation's long driveway. "Game faces, everyone," Tug said, and the family plastered on big smiles.

"I still think Johnnie's the answer to stopping the sale," Maggie said, as she grinned and waved at the tourists disembarking from the van. "I just have to track him down and talk to him."

The new guests, a small group of retired teachers from Germany on their first visit to the States, proved clueless about Pelican's recent misadventures, much to the Crozats' relief. They chattered enthusiastically in heavily accented English during Maggie's tour of the plantation and its outbuildings. She ended the tour at the spa, where the visitors lined up to book spa treatments with Mo. "I am wanting the Voodoo You package," a spritely woman in her late seventies told Mo.

"That's a wonderful choice," the skin care maven enthused. "It's part Swedish and part hot-stone massage, with stones blessed by our local voodoo priestess. You won't find a treatment like it anywhere else on the planet, and you can quote me on that." The other women oohed and aahed and clamored for their own appointments, much to Maggie's delight. It reinforced her belief that ceding control of the spa to Mo Heedles was the best decision she could have made.

With the new visitors in Mo's capable hands, Maggie set out on a hunt for Johnnie MacDowell. She'd sent a text to him hours earlier, but he'd never responded. Maggie followed his usual Zen walk path but didn't run into him. She was about to give up when she heard someone retching in the woods. She pushed aside brush and ducked branches, hurrying toward the sound. She found Johnnie, covered with sweat, leaning against a tree at the edge of the bayou. "Oh, hi," he said, slurring the two short words. "I've got a wee bit of a stomach thing going on." He giggled. "Okay, that's not true. I'm kind of a lot drunk. I don't blame myself; I blame *you*." He pointed at Maggie with a coquettish gesture. "But I shouldn't be blaming you when I should be thanking you." He held up an almost empty bottle of bourbon. "I'm not familiar with this brand—it must be a Southern thing—but it's *delicious*. What a thoughtful gift."

"That's not from me, Johnnie," Maggie said. "I know you're in recovery. I would never give you liquor."

Johnnie wagged at finger at her. "The card had your name on it, missy, so stop being modest."

He stepped away from the tree, staggered, and fell to his knees, still holding the bottle. Maggie bent down and helped him to his feet. She held him around his waist and put one of his arms around her neck. "Let's get you where you can lie down."

They started walking, Maggie half dragging Johnnie. "Sorry," he said with genuine embarrassment. "I'm not usually such an ugly drunk. Not sure what's happening."

"Maybe the liquor is hitting you harder because you've been sober for a while."

"Yeah, maybe. I feel really dizzy. Like I could faint."

Johnnie's speech was thick and his eyes drooped. Maggie, anxious to reach the manor house before he passed out in her arms, tried moving faster, but he was close to being dead weight. They finally reached the back door. Maggie freed a hand and gave the door a hard rap. "Coming," Tug called. He appeared a few seconds later. "What the—"

"Just open the door, Dad. We'll put him on the day bed in the office."

Tug opened the door and relieved Maggie of her charge. She followed the two men into the office. Tug deposited Johnnie on the antique walnut day bed and the poet quickly passed out, releasing his grip on the bourbon bottle, which fell onto the room's Oriental rug. "Poor guy," Tug said, as he and Maggie watched Johnnie's chest rise and fall with shallow breaths. "Your mama was right. He did fall off the wagon."

"I think it's more than that. I think he was drugged."

Maggie used the corner of her T-shirt to remove the bourbon bottle from Johnnie's tight grip. "Drugged?" her father asked. He scrunched his face, perplexed. "Why? And what are you doing?"

"This is evidence," she said, referencing the bottle. "I think it's spiked. Johnnie didn't fall off the wagon. He was pushed. And someone tried to frame me for it."

Chapter 20

An ambulance arrived within minutes of Maggie dialing 911. "You're on a roll," Cody Pugh told Maggie as he helped load the sick man into the emergency vehicle. "Counting Rufus, that's two that didn't leave Crozat in a body bag for a change."

"Yay, us," Maggie said, her tone dry.

Once Johnnie was on his way to the hospital, Maggie led her father through the woods to the Crozat schoolhouse. Several large garbage bags sat next to the building's door. Maggie peeked through a window. "Good, no Bonnie. We won't have to explain what we're doing."

"What a stench," Tug grumbled. "Too bad we didn't bring the masks we use in the attic."

"I'm hoping we won't be at this too long," Maggie said. "If Johnnie received the bourbon as recently as I think he did, the card that came with it should be on top of the garbage."

She opened a bag, holding her breath, and rummaged through it. Tug did the same. They repeated this with another round of bags. "Aha." Tug triumphantly held up a note card. "Found it."

"Let me see." Maggie took the card from her father and read aloud. "'Johnnie: sending love and sympathy on your father's death, and a little something to ease the pain. Maggie.' It's printed, not handwritten. I'm guessing whoever did this ordered from the liquor store in Ville Blanc. I doubt there are any clues on it. But the store might be able to describe who bought it." She placed the card in the back pocket of her jeans. "I'm bringing the note and bottle over to Pelican PD. Let's tie up the bags we opened and get out of here."

On the drive to the police station, Maggie homed in on Bonnie as the chief suspect in the bourbon debacle. Maggie had announced to the blogger that she was going to ask Johnnie to fight the sale of the MacDowell land. Incapacitating her brother and pointing a finger at Maggie would take them both out of the picture and free up Bonnie to move forward on a deal with one of the local oil or chemical companies.

Maggie parked in an angled spot outside the police station and scurried up the station steps into the lobby. Artie was once again manning the front desk while eating. This time, his meal of choice was a bowl of gumbo. "Late lunch?" she asked.

"Nope," Artie said. "Pre-gaming for lunch. Congrats on tracking down your wedding dress. That Barrymore character won't be playing a part for a change. He's gonna be a real live convict. Ooh, that's a nice chunk a crab right there." He slurped a big spoonful of gumbo.

"I know Bo's not around today, so I need to see Rufus. I heard he's out of the hospital. Is he here today?"

"In his office. I'll buzz you through."

Artie pressed a button and a door flew open. Maggie thanked the officer and headed to the police chief's office. Ru's door was open. The chief sat with his feet up on his desk. Like Artie, he was eating, but his snack consisted of chocolate cake with white fondant icing. "Glad to see you're up and about, Ru," Maggie said. "You look a hundred times better."

"And I feel the same." He held up the paper plate holding his cake slice. "Want a bite? I got an extra fork."

"No thanks, but it does look good. Is that from Fais Dough Dough?"

"Nope. Bridal expo in Baton Rouge. We saw your grand-mère there. Everyone knew her. One of the vendors told me she's a regular."

"Bridal expo?" Maggie side-eyed Rufus. "Is there something you're not telling me?"

"I'm getting hitched." Rufus ingested a large forkful of cake. "Sandy proposed."

Maggie plopped into a chair. "*She* proposed to *you*?"

"Yeah." Rufus grinned. A piece of chocolate cake blacked out one of his bicuspids. "We're all modern like that. My surgery put a scare into her, and she just blurted it out when I came to. I couldn't see any reason to say no, so here we are."

"This is wonderful news, Ru. Congratulations."

"Thanks. One thing I love about Sandy, she won't care that I told you. She's not about turning every little thing into a giant event, like the other one was."

"You mean Vanessa, your ex, and the mother of your child."

"Right, her." He finished the cake, licked the fork, then deposited plate and fork in a trash can under his desk. "So, what brings you here today?"

Maggie pulled the bourbon bottle and the note card, both encased in plastic, out of her tote. "These."

Rufus listened as Maggie explained about Johnnie's relapse and the attempt to paint her as the culprit. "I'll get Artie and Cal to track down where the bottle came from and see what we can dig up on who bought it."

"Thanks, Ru. Can you keep it on the down-low? I don't want Detective Griffith thinking he's got new evidence against me."

"I wouldn't worry about that," Ru said. "Pelican PD took a turn searching Breem's place, and one of our boys noticed a loose floorboard. He pulled it up and whaddya know, he found a gun. Just like in an old-timey movie." A malicious grin spread across Ru's face. "Boy-o-boy, did it feel nice one-upping VBPD."

"The gun was under a floorboard." Maggie was dubious. "That does seem like out of a movie. Maybe it wasn't there when VBPD searched. The real killer could have snuck it in after that."

Ru's face morphed into a sour expression. "Way to take all the fun out of it, Magnolia. Anyhoo, ballistics is checking the gun against the bullet that killed MacDowell. But there is a bit of a twist here. Turns out the gun's not registered to Breem."

"It was hidden in his house, but it's not his." Maggie said, trying to wrap her head around this new development. "Then who's is it?"

"Thanks to Canada's stringent gun registry laws, we got that answer toot suite. The gun belongs to Douglas MacDowell."

Maggie gaped at Rufus. "Doug was killed by his own gun?" Rufus nodded. "Could he have . . . killed himself?"

"Not according to the coroner, based on the bullet's trajectory. Bullet went through his side into his heart. He'd have to be some kind of contortionist to pull that off. My money's still on Breem."

"But why would he do it?" Maggie wondered. "He doesn't have a history of overt violence, or any connection to the MacDowells."

Rufus shrugged. "Maybe he doesn't like Canadians." He took his feet off the desk and planted them on the floor. "Breem is known for yelling at people to get off the property. We don't know his mental state. He's an old dude. He could have some form of dementia that made him cross the line from ornery to violent."

"That could be," Maggie conceded. "But he certainly didn't stick a knife into his own back." She pushed the bottle and letter toward the police chief. "Someone tried to kill Walter Breem. Even if he murdered Susannah and Doug, there's still the question of who attacked him. And maybe the same person tried to put Johnnie MacDowell out of commission."

Rufus groaned. "Argh, my head's like to explode from all this. I'm starting to wish I could turn the whole thing over to VBPD. Griffith does seem to get off on drilling down into investigations. I'm more of an open-and-shut-case kinda guy."

After leaving the police station, instead of heading home, Maggie drove to the St. Pierre Parish Medical Center. "You're Mr. Breem's first visitor," the volunteer at the information desk told her. "Aside from law enforcement officials. He's in ICU. Only family is supposed to visit, but I'll put you down as his niece." The woman winked at Maggie and handed her a pass.

Maggie took an elevator to the fourth floor and the caretaker's room. The old man, his eyes closed, lay on a hospital bed under a sea of tubes and wires connecting him to a panoply of beeping machines. A nurse checked the readings on one machine and made notes on a clipboard. "How is he?" Maggie asked.

The nurse motioned for Maggie to follow her out of the room. "It doesn't look good. I heard he's a suspect in a murder. He's under guard, but they're pretty loose about it." She gazed at Breem through the ICU room's glass window. "It's not like he's going anywhere."

Maggie, due back home to chauffeur the riverboat guests to Quentin's play, left the hospital. When she got home, she checked in with her father for updates. "I texted Bonnie about Johnnie's condition, and she came right over," said Tug, who was at the computer responding to reservation inquiries. "She seemed real upset."

"It could have been an act."

"I don't think so, chère. She burst into tears the minute I told her. Your mom came in, and Bonnie cried in her arms. We were concerned about her driving, so Mom took her to the hospital to see him."

"I was just there myself." Maggie told her father about her visit to Rufus and subsequent stop to check on Walter Breem.

"It'd certainly make things easier if he was the killer," Tug said.

"That's Ru's line of thinking. But why? What would Walter get out of killing the MacDowells?"

"That's a question for the detectives." Tug rubbed his chin. "There was one thing. Bonnie's instant reaction was something we didn't expect. The first thing she said was, 'Gavin.' Like she blamed him for planting the bottle of booze that took down Johnnie. I pressed her for more, but she backed off. All she said was, 'Nothing, never mind.' Still, blurting his name seemed like a gut response."

"I think Grody is soulless and ruthless," Maggie said. "With Susannah and Doug gone, Johnnie's the only obstacle to Bonnie inheriting the property here. I'm assuming that's why Mr. Rent My Digs keeps stringing her along. Rich as he is, I never met an 'entrepreneur' like him who didn't need more money."

Tug sucked in a breath and blew it out as a whistle. "That's basically saying he'd kill for it."

"I know. Ugh, I've got to get out of murder head." Maggie shook her hands vigorously. "I'm shaking it off."

"Shake it off, acck!" Lovie squawked, startling her. "Shake it off!"

"Lovie. I forgot you were there." Maggie, who alternated between being amused and aggravated by the parrot, addressed her father. "When are Lovie and DruCilla checking out?"

Tug checked the schedule. "Not until Monday."

"Oh, goody," she said with an eye roll.

"Goody goody," Lovie sang, launching into the old Johnny Mercer tune.

"Hello? Crozats?" Bo called out from down the hall. "Anyone besides singing birds home?"

"We're in the office," Maggie called back to him.

Bo came into the room, his arms laden with clothes in plastic bags. He greeted Tug and kissed Maggie. Lovie let out a squawk. "Kiss me, acck! Kiss me!"

Lovie made kissing sounds. Bo looked stricken. "Is that something I have to do?"

"Absolutely not. Let's go into the front parlor."

Maggie put a hand under Bo's elbow and steered him out of the office to the parlor, which was blessedly empty of feathered creatures. "What's all that?" she asked, referencing the bundles in Bo's arms.

He set the packages on the sofa. "Our costumes for trick-or-treating. Here's mine." He held up a ragged monster costume replete with a rubber Frankenstein mask. "Here's yours." Bo handed Maggie a bag containing a distressed wedding dress and a wig.

"I won't need the mask. I already have the perfect scar." Maggie pointed to her stitches. "Is that Xander's costume? It looks like a doctor's medical jacket."

"It is. When I explained that Frankenstein wasn't the name of the monster but of the doctor who created him, Xander decided to be the doctor. That way he gets to order us around. He's already told me I have to practice my grunts."

Bo grunted a few times. Maggie laughed. "Yeah, those could use some work."

"He'll get what he gets, and he won't be upset." Bo pushed aside the costumes and sat on the couch. He pulled Maggie down next to him. "This visit's not just for fun. Rufus updated me on the episode with the bourbon bottle. Artie tracked down the sale, and you were right. It was purchased at Ville Blanc Beverages."

"Did he get a description of the buyer?"

"Not a good one. Hoodie, hat, sunglasses. The salesclerk couldn't even say whether it was a man or woman. Artie got the feeling the clerk had been sampling the merchandise, so he wasn't much of a witness."

"So, the only thing keeping me from being in Griffith's cross hairs again is Walter Breem."

"Pretty much," Bo acknowledged. "As soon as he's conscious, he'll be arrested and charged with Susannah and Doug's deaths."

Maggie pursed her lips. "There's still something wrong here. I feel it in my bones."

"I'm with you on that," Bo said. "I can't stand explanations like 'He's just crazy.' Even crazy people have a motive for murder. Something that when you look at it, you go, 'I get it now.' I won't be convinced Breem's the killer until I know his motive."

Maggie turned to face Bo. She took his hands in his. "When was the last time I told you how proud I am to be your fiancée?"

Bo quirked his mouth. "I can never hear that enough. And right back at ya, chère." They kissed, and then Bo rose. "I better get to the station. VBPD may not care about the Johnnie incident and you being framed, but I do."

Maggie followed his lead and stood up. "And I better corral the group I'm taking to the play tonight. Let me know if you get a toxicology report back on the bottle. I'm sure the bourbon was doctored."

"We won't get any results back until next week," Bo said, "but I'll let you know as soon as they come in." He motioned to the costumes. "Give me a heads-up if the costume doesn't fit. It should. It looks pretty much like two sheets sewn together, and that's about it."

Maggie took the bag holding her costume. She opened it and pulled out a tall, puffy black-and-gray wig. "Wow. Well, at least I'll look how I feel. A little bit dead inside."

Crozat's Haunted Happy Hour and a pre-theatre meal of Ninette's Ghoulish Cajun Goulash followed by Pecan Cookie Fingers provided a welcome respite from murder investigations. The German teachers were either fascinated by the members of the Paranormal group or humoring them as they told their tales of spectral phenomenon. Maggie couldn't tell which, but since everyone seemed happy, she didn't care. She loaded all the visitors into the B and B minivan and shuttled them over to the Dupois cemetery, where the aging aboveground tombs became the backdrop to a plethora of selfies. Quentin made an impressive if showy debut as Jean-Luc Dupois Senior and treated himself to several encore bows.

"*Autogramme*," one of the German teachers said to Maggie as she was herding the group together.

"*Autogramme?*" Maggie repeated. "I'm sorry, I don't understand."

"*Autogramme.*" The woman mimed signing her program.

"Oh, you want autographs," Maggie said. "I can't see any of these hambones saying no to that. Come with me."

The woman chattered excitedly to her fellow tourists, and they marched with Maggie as a group to the grassy area behind the cemetery where the cast was receiving guests. "Quentin, these are some of our guests, and they'd love to have the cast sign their programs."

Quentin's face, splotchy with fake tears and running stage makeup, lit up. He gleefully threw his hands in the air. "A star is born," he announced to the air. He placed an arm around the oldest teacher's shoulder, and she tittered. "Madame, you're looking at the lead actor, playwright, and director of this shindig. A triple threat, as they say in the business. I'll introduce y'all to the cast. No worries if you don't have pens." Quentin reached into a jacket pocket and pulled out a handful of purple pens emblazoned with his attorney logo in gold. "I've got plenty."

While Quentin steered the besotted women toward Vanessa and a few other performers, Maggie, thirsty from the goulash, hunted for a bottle of water. She found a tub of them by the company's makeshift concession stand. She helped herself to one and went to wait for her group by the B and B van, which was parked by the edge of the Dupois woods. As she downed the water, she felt a slight vibration under her feet. She glanced around and saw Gavin Grody's gray Tesla rocking back and forth. *Bonnie must be working out her grief with Gavin*, Maggie thought. *If the Tesla's rockin', don't come a-knockin'*.

The rocking stopped. After a few minutes, the passenger's side back door on the car opened. A woman got out of the car. She straightened her top, pulled a brush out of her expensive-looking purse, and brushed her hair with a self-satisfied smile.

The woman wasn't Bonnie MacDowell. It was *Resurrection of the Spirit* ingenue Patria Heloise.

Chapter 21

Maggie slunk back into the shadows so that Patria wouldn't notice her. The fact that Grody was two-timing Bonnie didn't come as a shock. Maggie had seen enough of him in action to know he was what Grand-mère would politely term a cad and she herself would define in much harsher terms. But Patria's canny expression was a revelation. Either she, like Barrymore, wasn't what she seemed, or she was street-smart enough to cash in on the benefits of boffing a tech entrepreneur. *Actors confuse me*, Maggie thought, frustrated. She pulled out her cell phone and texted, *Bo, can you check out Patria Heloise? Thanx.*

He responded, *Okay but why??*

Maggie tapped out a quick explanation of Patria and Grody's hookup and got a thumbs-up emoji in response.

A Babel-like chatter of English and German alerted Maggie to her guests' approach. She bused all the B and B guests home, making sure to scope out the woods near the van parking spot for any errant rougarou. A group text from her fellow hoteliers had warned of guests being frightened by new sightings at Bon Amie and Belle Vista. The Crozat woods were quiet, to Maggie's relief, but she walked all the guests to their rooms before retreating to her own bed and a well-earned sleep.

Halloween dawned crisp and cool, just as it was meant to be. The leaves on the few deciduous trees in the region had obliged by turning shades of yellow and light red, completing the illusion of a New England fall day. Gopher and Jolie, both in costume, traded tushy sniffs with two Chihuahuas who had checked in with a family from Metairie, a suburb of New Orleans. Each small dog wore a Halloween-themed sweater. "We couldn't resist the pet parade," the mother said to Maggie.

"I can see that," Maggie said, offering a dog biscuit to a Chihuahua dressed in a sweater with a mummy bandages pattern. The other Chihuahua, whose sweater boasted a witch on a broomstick, barked a treat request, and Maggie obliged.

Since it was the last weekend of the Pelican's Spooky Past package, the Crozats offered their guests a chance to decorate a batch of Ninette's sugar cookies after they finished making immortelles. Maggie and Ninette covered the long dining room table with butcher paper and set out a variety of frostings and decorations. Dogs ran around the room snacking on fallen cookie pieces while Lovie sang the *Addams Family* theme song. Unfortunately, the parrot knew only the first line, so she sang "They're creepy and they're kooky" ad infinitum until a gentle admonishment from pet mom DruCilla quieted her. Maggie gave Bo a call, inviting him and Xander to join the cookie fun. "We can't," Bo said. "Xander's got two parties and he's decided to wear different costumes to each of them. He's got more costume changes to make today than a pop star at a Madison Square Garden concert. But we'll be by at five to pick you up for trick-or-treating."

It was late afternoon when the guests cleared out, immortelles and cookies in hand. Some returned to their rooms to relax or nap and others made their way to the spa for treatments, but most headed to Bon Ami for the pet parade. Maggie helped herself to a couple of broken cookies while she and Gran cleaned up the dining room. "Did you know they make black wedding gowns?" Gran said. She used a Dustbuster to clear the table of sprinkles and crumbs. "I suppose it would work for a Halloween wedding. Otherwise it's a bit funereal for my tastes."

"Have you found an outfit yet?" Maggie asked.

"No," Gran said with a pout. "Everything around here is either too youthful or too matronly. Can I interest you in a shopping expedition to New Orleans after all the drama around here has settled?"

"You can always interest me in a trip to New Orleans." Maggie crumpled up a long stretch of butcher paper and stuffed it in a trash bag. "We'll bring Mom with us. Make it a girls' day out."

"Wonderful idea. I'll make a lunch reservation at Galatoire's for next—"

Gran stopped midsentence. She stared at the archway separating the parlor from the main hall. Maggie followed her gaze. Johnnie MacDowell stood there, gripping the side of the archway's polished walnut frame. His freckled skin had a sickly grayish pallor, and Maggie got the sense that if he let go of the wood, he'd collapse to the floor. "My goodness," Gran said. "Did the hospital release you already?"

"It's America, not Canada," Johnnie said, his voice barely above a whisper. "They kick you to the curb as soon as they can. Doesn't matter; we're leaving here anyway. I'm looking for Bonnie. We have a late flight from NOLA tonight, and I haven't seen her in a couple of hours." He licked his dry lips and took a deep breath, as if getting out those few sentences had been an effort for him.

"I haven't seen her," Gran said. "Have you, Maggie?"

Maggie shook her head. "I can look for her if you want."

"That's okay," Johnnie said. "Her car's not here. She's probably saying goodbye to that ignoramus Gavin. I'll wait at the schoolhouse."

He let go of his grip and turned to go but pitched forward. Gran and Maggie ran to him. They each grabbed one of his arms, managing to break his fall. "You poor boy," Gran said. "You're not going anywhere but onto this sofa."

The women led him to the couch and helped him lie down. "I'm sorry," he gasped. "I've never had alcohol poisoning before. I know that's hard to believe with my history, but it's true. It's more than a hangover. It's like I'm coming off something. Like I was drugged."

"That's because I'm pretty sure you were," Maggie said.

Johnnie stared at her, glassy-eyed. "What? No. Why?"

Maggie wet a paper towel and dabbed the man's forehead, which was sticky with sweat. "That's what the police are trying to figure out. That bourbon didn't come from me, but someone wanted to make it look like it did. And you seemed way more than drunk. By what you're describing, you feel that way, too. The police are having the contents of the bottle tested. I'm guessing someone loaded it up with a sedative."

"It did taste strange," Johnnie said, "but I figured that's because I hadn't had a drink in a while." He struggled to sit up and took a sip of water that Gran offered him. "Was someone trying to kill me, too?"

"I'm not sure if they wanted to kill you or incapacitate you," Maggie said. "But they definitely wanted me blamed for whatever happened."

Johnnie winced. "I'm sorry."

"Don't be," Maggie said. "It's certainly not your fault."

Johnnie scrunched up his face. Maggie thought he might cry. "Why did we ever come to this despicable, horrible portal to hell? No offense."

"It's okay. I get why it's not your favorite place."

Johnnie held up his hand, declining another offer of water, and fell back against the couch. "If you're wondering if I have a clue why anyone would do something like this, I have zero idea."

"You disagreed with your family about selling the Mac-Dowell land," Maggie said. "It could have something to do with that."

What Maggie was hinting at dawned on him. "You think Bonnie did this? That's nuts. We fight all the time, we don't have anything in common or even like each other that much, but no. We're still family. She would never."

Gran cast a doubtful look at Maggie. "If you say so, dear."

"Maybe her motivation came from another source," Maggie said. "Like her boyfriend."

"Gavin Grody? Ha." Johnnie scoffed. "He's slutting around on Bonnie with a dippy actress from that cemetery freak show. I told her, but she refused to believe me."

"Could she have done this to get back at you?" Gran asked. "You know, a 'kill the messenger' sort of thing?"

He pondered this. "I dunno. Maybe. She's pretty into him. But the only thing that male skank's into is money or hot bodies, and Bonnie doesn't have either. She's cute, but . . ." Johnnie's voice faded. He closed his eyes. "Sorry. I got really tired."

Gran patted his hand. "That's all right. We'll keep an eye out for your sister. You rest."

Johnnie nodded, then drifted off to sleep. "I'll see if I can find her," Maggie said to Gran in a low voice.

"I'll let your parents know to be on the lookout as well," Gran said. She glanced down at Johnnie, passed out on the sofa. "But I'll tell you one thing. That boy is not getting on an airplane tonight."

"I'll text Bonnie. I don't know why she's not getting back to Johnnie, but hopefully she'll get back to me."

"I'll look after Johnnie until someone tracks her down."

"Thanks, Gran." Maggie checked the time on her cell phone. "Now I have to get ready for some serious trick-or-treating."

*   *   *

While Maggie got into costume, she pondered the extreme nature of Johnnie's condition. The MacDowell twin was nothing if not dramatic. She flashed on a glib comment John-nie had made at his stepmother's quasi-funeral: "It's Susan-nah. She was a horror. Who *didn't* want her dead?" Was the comment flippant or telling? Johnnie was an unemployed poet frustrated by his parent and stepparent's rigid control of the MacDowell purse strings. Their deaths removed this obstacle to the family funds. Another thought occurred to Maggie. Could Johnny have staged his own relapse? *Stop it, you're being as dramatic as he is*, she scolded herself. But this new concern gnawed at her. And then another thought struck Maggie. What if Johnnie and Bonnie were coconspirators in the murders? As far as she knew, they benefited equally from Susannah and Doug's deaths. *Could greed have propelled them into patricide and whatever 'cide' you call killing a stepparent?* she wondered.

Her phone flashed a text announcing that Bo had parked and would be there in a minute, so Maggie shelved her mur-der musings and focused on adding the finishing touches to her outfit. *It's a good thing I'm not going for the Sexy Bride of Frankenstein look*, Maggie thought as she studied her reflec-tion in the mirror. The polyester gown was as shapeless out of the bag as it was in it. The fanny pack Maggie strapped on to hold her essentials didn't help, creating an unflattering bunching around her waist. She wore a white makeup base and black lipstick. In addition to her real scar, she'd used a grease stick to draw one on her check and another on her neck. The foot-high frizzy gray-and-black wig that came with the dress completed Maggie's stuck-a-finger-in-a-socket look.

"We're here," Bo called from outside.

"Coming." Maggie stepped out of the cottage onto the front steps. She grunted and clumped down the steps with her arms outstretched. Bo laughed while Xander jumped up and down with glee.

"Madame," Bo said, offering her his arm. He wore a ripped distressed jacket and pants, and his black hair was flattened to his forehead. He'd skipped the Frankenstein mask, instead opting for green makeup, grease paint scars, and blacked-out teeth for added effect.

"No talking, just grunting," Xander scolded, shaking a finger at his father. He wore a white doctor's coat and sported a stethoscope around his neck. The eight-year-old had recently been prescribed eyeglasses, and his costume, coupled with the new black plastic frames, gave him the look of a pint-sized medical professional. He held up his phone. "Selfie."

The three mugged as Xander snapped a shot, and then they walked to Bo's SUV. "We're going to the village first," Bo explained as they loaded into it. "Then we'll hit a few neighborhoods."

The quaint shops that ringed Pelican's town square were prepared for the onslaught of trick-or-treaters. Children received large handfuls of candy at some locations, small toys at others. Maggie, Bo, and Xander passed Vanessa and Quentin, who were pushing Charli, Vanessa's eighteen-month-old by former fiancé Rufus, in a stroller. Charli, dressed as a sparkly unicorn, gabbled and chewed on a stuffed unicorn she held tight with her tiny hands. Vanessa was clad in her heavily embellished wedding gown and Quentin wore the morning suit he'd worn at their wedding, her first and his third or fourth, Maggie wasn't sure which. "You like our costumes?" Van said, striking a pose. "We figured our wedding gear was so nice, why just wear it once? Might as well get a little more mileage outa these duds, especially for what they cost."

"Amen to that," Quentin seconded in a jovial tone.

Vanessa cast a critical eye at Maggie's costume. "No offense, Maggie, but I think I make a way prettier bride than you."

Maggie gestured to her and Bo. "You do know we're not getting married in these outfits?"

"I heard your wedding dress went missing and I wasn't sure. Oh, you'll def wanna stop by Fais Dough," Vanessa said. "The Poche kids are running it so me and Quentin could have the night off."

"Lia told me they were going to put out a bowl of candy at their place, then turn off the lights and hunker down," Maggie said. "They don't want doorbells setting off the triplets."

"*I'll* say an amen to that," Vanessa said. She gestured to Charli. "Soon as this one starts fussing, it's lights out for us too."

"You're not stopping by Bon Ami's costume party?"

Vanessa shook her head. "These Spooky Past weekends were a great idea, but I'm ready for a break. It was fun doing the play, but I'm glad all you B and Bs scheduled a party tonight instead of a performance. Oh, that reminds me, when you see Emma, tell her we have her last check. She was supposed to come by and get it today. I guess she forgot." Van began pushing the stroller. "We need to move on. We gotta hit at least a few more shops before Charli fades."

Maggie eyed Charli's candy bucket, which was also shaped like a unicorn. "Isn't she a little young for all that candy?"

"Oh, she totally is." Vanessa pulled a fun-size chocolate bar out of the bucket, unwrapped it, and popped it in her mouth. "But I ain't."

Maggie's trio moved on to Fais Dough Dough, where a ninja who revealed himself to be Clinton Poche, Brianna's older brother, handed them each a cake pop dripping with red frosting "blood." Brianna, who was manning Bon Bon Sweets, gifted them with ghost-shaped handmade marshmallows.

"Now, onto the Bayou Oaks neighborhood," Bo said through a mouthful of marshmallow.

"Uh-huh," Maggie said, distracted. "Bonnie still hasn't gotten back to me."

"Check your phone. Maybe you didn't hear the text come through."

Maggie pulled out her phone. "Nothing. And it just occurred to me I haven't seen Emma all day."

"Is that unusual for a guest?"

"No," Maggie admitted. "But no Bonnie. Now no Emma."

"Those Crozat instincts sending up flares?" Bo said with affection. He added, more seriously, "I have to drive, but text Rufus. I think it's time for Pelican PD to try tracking down Bonnie."

The three climbed into Bo's SUV. Maggie tapped a message to Rufus and got an instant response. *Already on it. Your Gran was concerned. No sign of Bonnie. Or her car.*

"Now my cop instincts are sending up flares." Bo's tone was grim. Xander chuckled and he glanced back at his son, who was focused on his cell phone. "You good, buddy?"

"Uh-huh. Friend stuff. Lotsa likes for my picture."

Xander held up his phone, where his photo of the Frankenstein trio now sported hearts and likes. Then he put in earbuds and zoned out in the back seat. "Tonight's about him," Bo said, keeping his voice low. "I'm gonna let Ru handle police business, at least until I bring Xander back to Whitney and Zach. They're doing his candy count with him."

"Of course," Maggie said. "We can't do anything to spoil tonight. Xan's having such a great time. And so am I. Thank you for making Halloween fun again."

Bo grinned. "Don't thank me, thank Dr. Frankenstein."

The Bayou Oaks neighborhood proved disappointing, with many homes either dark or housing visitors. Maggie fumed at the number of Rent My Digs stickers affixed to house windows. "That app is like a tech termite, eating up all the local housing," she griped to Bo as they drove to a more promising neighborhood. Xander filled his bucket within a half hour, and the threesome headed for Bon Ami's costume party. Blow-up spiders and ghosts decorated the roof of the plantation's Creole-style raised-cottage "big house," which was painted in the traditional plantation colors of green and yellow that Creole settlers had favored because they hid the mold and mildew that came with Louisiana's sultry climate. Music and loud chatter emanated from the tent Bon Ami had erected in their parking lot. Costumed animals who'd lingered with their parents following the pet parade barked, tweeted, meowed, mooed, brayed, and made whatever sound a lizard dressed as a cowboy might make.

Xander ran off to find his friends while Maggie and Bo separated to circulate. She greeted guests, pleased to see how much fun they were having. "I'm Frida Kahlo," DruCilla announced, modeling her Mexican peasant outfit, which featured Lovie perched on her shoulder.

"Down to the unibrow," Maggie said, and laughed. She saw Gavin Grody hanging out with actors from *Resurrection of the Spirit*. He had his arm around Patria's waist. "Excuse me," Maggie said.

Lovie made a farting sound. "Pee-yew! You're excused."

Maggie negotiated her way through throngs of costumed partygoers until she reached the techie. "Having fun?" she asked him.

Grody crooked his mouth in a half smile that reeked of superiority. "Sure. What is it they say around here? Cajun Country knows how to pass a good time."

Maggie motioned to the party's zydeco band, which had struck up an infectious tune. The dance floor quickly became a sea of two-stepping guests. "People aren't gonna find this at one of your rentals."

The entrepreneur gave an insolent shrug. "My 'people' are way younger than yours. They don't need cheesy stuff like this."

Patria pouted and held out her glass. She spoke in baby talk. "*Waaa*, my wine-y's all gone."

Grody took her glass. "I'll get us refills."

He started for the bar, Maggie on his heels. She got perverse pleasure from seeing how much this annoyed him. "Bonnie MacDowell's not going to be too happy to hear that you're only using her as a front to buy houses from people who think they're not selling them to you."

"A Chardonnay and a whiskey neat," Grody said to the bartender. He got the drinks and started back to Patria. "Bonnie and I were never in a monogamous relationship. It's the sharing economy, bruh. And what she's sharing is me."

"She's gone missing."

For once, Grody's arrogance failed him. He stopped so short Maggie almost bumped into him. Wine slopped out of Patria's drink. "What? What do you mean, missing?"

"I mean, she's missing. No one's seen her all day. She's supposed to catch a flight to Toronto tonight. The police are looking for her. They'll probably want to talk to you."

"Me?" Now the hipster looked scared. "Why? I don't know anything about it."

"I'm sure all they'll want to know is when you last spoke to her or saw her. That kind of thing."

Grody fought to regain his insouciance. "Yeah well, my guess is she caught an early flight to T-town to get away from that head case of a brother of hers." He used his whiskey glass to point in the opposite direction. "Your boyfriend wants you."

Maggie turned and saw Bo trying to get her attention. Grody grabbed the chance to escape her company. She threaded her way through the crowd of revelers to her fiancé. "I just broke it to Grody that one of his girlfriends is missing."

Bo raised an eyebrow. "How did he take it?"

"I wish I could say he acted guilty," Maggie said, "but he didn't. He seemed genuinely thrown by the news." She clenched her fists. "I *so* want the killer to be him. Is it wrong that I don't care if that makes me a bad person?"

Bo couldn't help smiling. He patted Maggie on the shoulder. "Don't give up hope. There's still a chance he could be our guy. You ready to go? It's time for me to tear Xander away from his posse."

"I'm ready. With what all's going on, I'm not in a party mood."

The couple retrieved Xander, whose lab coat pockets were so stuffed with Bon Ami's free candy that he shed small chocolate bars as he walked. Bo dropped Maggie off at home. On her way to the cottage, she crossed paths with a clutch of members of the Paranormal group returning from the Bon Ami party. "Great costume," a woman called out.

"Thanks," Maggie said.

"Oh, I meant the guy behind you," the woman said, "It's so realistic. But I like yours too."

Maggie turned to see Pelican PD officer Cal Vichet emerge from the manor house. "Cal, hi. What's going on?"

Ninette appeared in the back doorway. She smiled at the guests, who sauntered off to their accommodations in the carriage house, then dropped the smile and waved Maggie over. "Bonnie never came back. No one has any idea where she is. She isn't responding to texts or calls."

"We're putting together a search team," Cal explained.

"I'll help," Maggie said. Her mother seconded this. "How's Johnnie?" Maggie asked Ninette.

"When he woke up, he insisted he felt better and disappeared on one of his Zen walks, if you can believe it. Seems like a real odd time for it."

The news sent a frisson through Maggie. She wondered if this verified her instinct about the MacDowell twin faking his drugging and relapse. Then again, the Zen walks seemed to give the unhappy man his only sense of peace. Was Johnnie dangerous? Or in danger?

"Since we can't reach Bonnie," Ninette continued, "I texted Emma to update her about Johnnie's condition, but she hasn't gotten back to me."

"Artie's on his way, along with Rufus," Cal said. "And Bo. He's gonna drop off Xander and head back. Thanks for the offer of help, Mrs. Crozat, but we don't want to alarm your guests by getting you involved. Plus, if the young lady's disappearance is the result of a crime, we don't wanna send an alert to whoever's responsible. They could cut and run. But Maggie, you got that good artist's eye where you sometimes spot stuff we miss, so you're welcome to join us. Find yourself a flashlight."

"I keep one in my glove compartment," Maggie said. She started toward her car.

"And you might wanna change outa that costume."

"Right," Maggie said, embarrassed.

She detoured to the cottage, where she stripped off her Bride of Frankenstein garb, washed off the monster makeup, and slipped on jeans and a long-sleeved shirt. She grabbed a hoodie, then hurried to her car, where she opened the glove compartment and retrieved a flashlight. She was closing the glove compartment when the glint of something on the passenger's side floor mat caught her eye. Maggie pressed a button on her flashlight, illuminating the object, which turned out to be a pen she didn't recognize. She stooped down to pick up the pen, and an orange berry about an inch in diameter rolled out from under the car seat. Maggie caught her breath. The pen might not look familiar, but given the events of the last few weeks, she knew a strychnine berry when she saw one. Only one person had been in the passenger seat since Maggie had gotten the Falcon washed: Emma Fine. Whose purse had fallen and emptied onto the car floor.

Leaving behind a pen . . . and strychnine.

Chapter 22

Maggie stared at the berry, so nondescript and yet so lethal. As a stage manager, Emma was the conduit between Walter Breem and the *Resurrection of the Spirit* production. Had Walter warned her to watch out for the poisonous plant? Had this put her in a mind to murder? Maggie recalled Doug's guilty admission after Susannah death's that he'd done things he felt bad about. She aligned the comment with Emma's extreme reaction to his own death and came to a conclusion: the unlikely duo had been having an affair. *Emma's a damaged soul who's fighting her inner demons twenty-four/seven*, Maggie thought to herself. *She must have seen Doug as a lifeline to a sense of security, both emotional and financial, once Susannah was gone and a sale of the MacDowell property was on the horizon.*

Maggie straightened up. She pulled her cell from her back pocket and placed a call. "Hey," Vanessa said through a mouthful of what Maggie assumed was Charli's candy. "What's up?"

"Did Emma ever come by for her check?"

"No." Vanessa sounded aggravated. "She's also supposed to pick up a bunch of props we brought back to the house. She hasn't returned any of my calls or texts. She's not at your place?"

"She doesn't seem to be. I'll double check."

Maggie ended the call and raced to the main house, where she found her mother in the kitchen. "I don't know what to do with myself, so I'm baking cookies for the police officers," Ninette said. "Have they found anything?"

"Not that I know of. When was the last time you saw Emma?"

Ninette wrinkled her brow. "This morning. Early. I saw her go off into the woods. I figured she was doing one of Johnnie's Zen walks on her own. Why?" she asked, alarmed.

Maggie, not wanting to share her discovery of the strychnine berry with anyone before she told Pelican PD, said, "I only want to make sure she's okay since we haven't seen her in a while either. I'm going to check her room."

She left the kitchen for the back-parlor office, where she grabbed the spare key to Emma's room. Maggie took the stairs to the second floor two at her time. Heart racing, she knocked on the room's door. No one responded. She inserted an old skeleton key into the keyhole. Unsure what she'd find in the room, she opened the door slowly and waited. Again, there was no response, so she stepped inside. The room looked like the room of any guest who was out for the day and expected to return. A laptop sat on the desk, surrounded by papers; clothes hung over a wingback chair; the bed was unmade. Maggie looked out the window to the guests' parking area below. She saw Emma's nondescript sedan parked in its usual spot. *Emma Fine, where are you?* Maggie, filled with anxiety, wondered.

Her cell rang. She saw the caller was Bo and accepted the call. "I'm on my way," he said, "but the River Road's closed at Pass Pierre and I gotta take the back way. Some jokers set off smoke bombs that started a brush fire. I checked in with Cal. They haven't found anything yet."

"I have." Maggie filled Bo in on finding the strychnine berry and her theory about Emma's illicit relationship with Doug. "I'm in her room right now. It looks perfectly normal. But no one has any idea where she is."

"So we have two missing women, not one." Bo's tone was terse. "I'll have Rufus put together a second search team. I'll keep you posted."

"What should I do with the strychnine berry?"

"Leave it and the pen where you found them. Just make sure your car is locked up."

Bo signed off. Maggie took another look around Emma's room, then closed and locked the door. She hurried out of the house to the family's parking area, where she confirmed the Falcon's doors were locked. Maggie's cell phone rang, distracting her. She eyed the screen. "More spam," she muttered, annoyed. Then she suddenly felt something push against her back.

"Drop the cell," a woman's voice commanded her. "I have a gun." Maggie dropped her phone. "Don't turn around."

"I don't need to," Maggie said. "I recognize your voice, Bonnie."

"Whatevs," the blogger said, impatient. "Now get in the car. On the driver's side. And don't think about running away. I know how to shoot. My dad loved to hunt."

Maggie followed her captor's instructions and got behind the wheel of the car. Bonnie, keeping the gun trained on Maggie, jumped into the passenger's seat. She deposited a sack at her feet, and the strychnine berry from Emma's purse rolled under the seat. "The police are looking for you," Maggie said.

"I ride-shared back here after phoning in an anonymous tip that Bonnie MacDowell's rental car was spotted in the Bayou Oaks neighborhood at one of Gavin Grody's Rent My Digs properties." She held up her hand, exposing an ugly slash on her palm. "There's evidence of blood all over the car."

"Making Grody a suspect in your disappearance. Payback for cheating on you with Patria."

"You know it." Bonnie gestured to her with the gun. "Start driving."

Maggie started the engine. "In what direction?"

"Toward the Dupois creep show."

Maggie pulled out of the parking area. She made a right onto the plantation's side road, then another right onto the River Road. "We may have a problem," she said as she drove. "I heard the road's cut off by a brush fire."

"From the north," Bonnie said with an impish grin. "The direction your sad little police force has to take and can't now, thanks to a couple of smoke bombs and some matches and lighter fluid. But we'll be okay getting to the Dupois place. To be sure, though"—Bonnie held the gun to Maggie's ribs—"floor it."

Maggie reluctantly gunned the Falcon's engine, and the women drove down the empty road. "You know," Maggie said, "if your plan is to steal my car and use it to get away, it won't work. Everyone around here knows me and knows it's my car. They'll see I'm not the one driving."

"Or are you?" Bonnie reached into the sack at her feet and pulled out Maggie's Bride of Frankenstein wig. "Thanks for leaving this right on your couch. It's almost touching how people in Pelican think they don't have to lock their front doors because they live in a cutesy small town." She put on the wig. "Since everyone around here knows you, they'll know what costume you wore tonight. It's nighttime and there's a storm blowing in, so there's no light coming from the moon or stars. Anyone I drive by will see this car, see the wig, and think, 'Hey look, it's Maggie. Hi, Maggie!'" Bonnie mimed a wave, then took off the wig and stuffed it back in the sack.

They reached the edge of the abandoned Dupois gardens. "Pull over," Bonnie ordered. Maggie pulled to the side of the road. Bonnie got out first, making sure to keep her gun trained on Maggie. "Now you."

Maggie exited the car. Usually she loved the silence of a sleepy Pelican evening. Tonight, she longed for any sound that would indicate the chance of being rescued. But aside from the chirp of crickets and croak of frogs, the night was maddeningly quiet. "Now what?" Tired of her own fear, the question came out as an angry bark.

"Whoa, somebody needs an attitude adjustment." Bonnie faked shock, then dropped it. "Move. That way."

The women hiked through the jungle of weeds and out-of-control plants for what felt like forever to Maggie. They passed the crumbled stone bridge, then the ruin of the folly. "Stop," Bonnie ordered.

They were at the edge of an old cistern, around six feet wide and six feet deep, that once doubled as a pond in the garden. "Help!" someone cried out from inside, the word muffled by the cistern's mossy stone walls. Maggie looked down and saw Emma at the bottom. "Help!" Emma screamed again. "Get me out of here!"

"Yeah, she won't be doing that," Bonnie called down to Emma. "She's gonna be joining you instead." She pointed her gun at Maggie. "Jump in." Maggie hesitated. Bonnie cocked the gun. "*Now.*"

Maggie jumped, landing in a heap next to Emma. "Agh," Maggie grimaced. "My ankle. I think I sprained it."

"Okay you two, I gotta bounce," Bonnie said. "I have a car to junk and a plane to catch. FYI, Maggie, I made a deal with Harbor Chemical for our land. They wanted it so bad they didn't question me when I said my brother was mentally unfit and I was in charge of the family finances. I got a nice advance from them. Enough to book a private plane out of New Orleans. I'm looking forward to making a habit out of traveling that way."

"We were supposed to split that money, you . . ." Emma spewed a stream of invectives at Bonnie.

"What can I say?" Bonnie shrugged. "I came up with an idea I liked better." Growing thoughtful, she tapped her gun against her chin. "It's interesting. Everyone always thought I was some shallow lightweight. My dad, my stupid stepmom, my brother. That snake Gavin. I guess I proved that old saying right. You know, the one about still waters running deep." She started off, then turned back. "Oh, and speaking of still waters, there's a storm coming, and probably more to follow. There's a chance you'll drown before you starve to death, which might be a better way to go. Bye-yee."

Bonnie disappeared into the woods. Maggie pulled herself to standing, ignoring her throbbing ankle. Emma began shaking and whimpering. "I need gum. I need cigarettes. I need a *drink*."

"Shut up," Maggie said sharply. She'd entered survival mode and refused to let Emma drag her down. She scrutinized their prison from top to bottom and formulated a plan. "I have an idea that could get us out of here."

"Oh, thank God." Tears streamed down Emma's face.

Maggie crossed her arms in front of her chest. "But I'm not sharing it until you tell me exactly what went down with you and Bonnie. Leave out a detail and you and I die here together. No joke. I'm that serious."

"Okay, fine, whatever." Emma began blabbering. "Bonnie hated Susannah. Like, *hated* her. She didn't think Susannah loved her father and just wanted someone she could control, plus Susannah didn't like her or Johnnie. I mean, the whole situation was beyond toxic. It was like a superfund site."

Emma paused to catch her breath. "I'm waiting for you to tell me something I don't know," Maggie said.

Emma sniffled. She wiped her nose with the back of her hand. "Gavin Grody hired some of the actors from our stupid show to dress up as rougarous and scare off tourists at the B and Bs. He figured that would get his Rent My Digs more business. Susannah decided that if she pretended to be a rougarou, she could pick up some extra money *and* make trouble for your B and B by freaking out guests and messing up the Spooky Past weekends."

"And the more trouble we were in," Maggie, furious, said through gritted teeth, "the more we'd be inclined to sell our land along with hers to a chemical or oil company, which would make for a bigger package and more money. That's what Susannah wanted all along."

"Exactly. Gavin hired her and she did the rougarou thing at your place, then brought her act to Belle Vista. That's why she was there the night she died."

"You mean the night you killed her because you were having an affair with Doug and you wanted her out of the way."

"I didn't kill her," Emma protested. "I only gave Bonnie the berries. The caretaker guy told me the seeds could kill someone if they were crushed and inhaled and said I should warn the cast to be careful around them."

"Which you never did because you were coming up with a plot to get rid of your competition."

"It was Bonnie's idea to put the stuff in Susannah's mask," was Emma's lame defense. "All I did was tell her about it."

"You do know that makes you an accessory to murder?"

Emma opened her mouth to respond, then snapped it shut. A loud clap of thunder startled both women. The skies opened and rain poured down on them. "Bonnie's right, we're going to drown here. Agh, something's crawling on me!" She screamed and jumped up and down, shaking her whole body. "Get us out of here, please." She wept and pointed to the top of the cistern. "I'll tell you anything else you want to know up there."

"All right." Maggie, soaked by the storm, neglected to mention she was also more than ready to get out of the dank, claustrophobic space. "Bonnie thought she was trapping both of us, but what she missed is that we can help each other out of here. You're what, five eight or nine? I'm five four. Between us, we're taller than the cistern. I'm going to get on your shoulders and latch on to the top of it to pull myself over. Then I'll pull you up. The stones of the walls are uneven. You can use them like the rocks on a climbing wall."

"It's a great plan, but you hurt your ankle," Emma pointed out. "Maybe we should reverse this. I'll climb on your shoulders, then help *you* out."

Emma's offer was so ludicrous Maggie burst out laughing. "Yeah, right. Like I'm gonna trust you to help me. That won't be happening. It's the original plan or none."

"Fine, fine," Emma said. "Let's do it already." She sneezed. "If I don't drown or starve to death, I'm gonna die of pneumonia."

Emma crouched down, and Maggie climbed on her shoulders. Ignoring the excruciating pain in her ankle, she grabbed onto stones to bring herself to a standing position and found herself at waist height with the top of the cistern. She grabbed onto the edge. "Let go and push me," she told Emma, who did so. Maggie tried to propel herself over the old well's edge and failed. She tried again.

"It's not going to work," Emma said, close to hysteria.

"Yes. It. *Is*."

Maggie grunted, summoned all her energy, and hurled herself over the edge and onto the ground. Emma screamed with joy and applauded. "My turn, my turn!"

Maggie shoved her sopping-wet hair out of her face and bent down into the cistern. She extended her hands to Emma, who grabbed them. "Be careful, the rocks are slippery," Maggie warned. "Focus and don't rush."

Emma's feet slipped several times, but she managed to find enough stone outcroppings to climb three-quarters of the way up the wall. When she was waist-high with the edge, Maggie reached down, grabbed Emma's hands, and helped pull her over it. "We did it," Emma gasped as she lay flat on her stomach.

She staggered to her feet. Then Emma threw a sucker punch at Maggie. But Maggie was prepared for this and fought her off with a large broken branch. Emma grabbed a rock and threw it at Maggie, who swatted it away with the branch. "Nice way to repay me for saving your life," Maggie spit at the treacherous woman.

"You can fight me, but good luck trying to catch up to me." Emma threw another rock that Maggie batted away. Then she made a run for it. "No way am I going to jail," she yelled, her voice fading with each step of distance she put between them. "Trick-or-treat, loser!"

A couple of stitches from the gash on Maggie's forehead broke open and blood dripped down her face. She used her shirt sleeve to wipe it off, then leaned against a tree and sucked in a deep breath to summon up her last ounce of energy. Drenched by the relentless rain and catching herself as she slipped on wet leaves carpeting the ground, Maggie half hopped and half dragged her injured body toward the River Road.

"Happy damn Halloween," she muttered.

Chapter 23

Maggie's eyelids fluttered open. Groggy, she yawned and glanced around. She was on a massage table in Mo' Better Beauty and Day Spa. A diffuser released the scent of orange blossoms into the air. The low, soothing sound of wind chimes came from a speaker. Mo stood in a corner of the small, darkened room, folding a large towel. "What happened?" Maggie asked, her voice thick. She hadn't completely woken up. "Did I fall asleep during my massage?"

"You did indeed," Mo said. "I told your masseuse, Nicole, not to wake you. I figured you needed sleep more than hot stones and deep tissue."

"Thanks, Mo." Maggie stretched, then sat up and swung her feet over the side of the table, keeping a sheet wrapped around her.

"How's your foot feel?"

Maggie gave her left ankle, encased in a boot, a small flex. "Better. It's a hairline fracture, so it'll take at least a few weeks to heal completely. But I think resting my foot and taking a cat nap helped the pain."

"I'm just glad you're all in one piece. Get dressed, then come out to the lounge and tell me everything."

Mo left the room, giving her friend a hug on the way out. Maggie hopped off the table onto her good leg. She pulled on a large T-shirt and a pair of drawstring cotton pants and joined Mo in the spa lounge.

"I've only heard bits and pieces about what happened out at the old Dupois place," Mo said. She handed Maggie a glass of iced cucumber water. "Mostly gossip, and the story's grown to where you had a sword fight with that Emma."

Maggie laughed. "Hardly. I had a branch and she had rocks, so it was more like a violent game of stickball." She sipped on the water. "Bonnie MacDowell was right about one thing. We all underestimated her. She saw a hearts-and-flowers text from Emma on her father's phone, read the thread, and realized they were having an affair."

Mo looked skeptical. "The man didn't exactly look like a playboy."

"Emma wasn't looking for that. She wanted security and a way out of a place and life she'd come to hate. Financially, Doug's income was average at best, but he was looking at a big payday if Susannah sold her property here. And he also represented a chance not just to get out of the state but out of the country."

"If Susannah wasn't around anymore."

"Exactly. That's what I put together when I found the strychnine berry that rolled out of Emma's purse onto the floor of my car. It sealed her status as a prime suspect. But it turned out that was only half of the story. The other half was Bonnie."

Mo shook her head ruefully. "I wrote her off as one of those annoying 'influencers.' And not a very good one."

"We all did. I'm guessing that aggravated Bonnie until she got the idea to use it to her advantage. No one would suspect such a shallow whiner would be capable of killing someone."

"Why, though?"

"Love and money. She was totally into Gavin Grody, but he was a hard guy to coax into a relationship. She let him use her as a front to buy a home here, but figured if she had her own money, he'd find her a lot more desirable. Doug was much looser with the debit card than her stepmother Susannah, who Bonnie couldn't stand in any way, shape, or form. So, given an opportunity to get rid of her, she did."

Mo shuddered. "Cold."

Maggie took another sip of water. Her ankle started to throb, so she lifted her leg and placed it on an upholstered ottoman. "You want cold? When Bonnie found out Gavin Grody was having a thing with this actress Patria, it set her off. Her plan was to frame him for my and Emma's deaths."

Her friend raised an eyebrow. "She couldn't have keyed his car like a normal person?"

"There's nothing normal about her. She cut herself and dripped blood in Grody's car so the police would assume they had a fight, he killed her, and then dumped her body in the bayou for the gators. Emma told the police that Bonnie thought once Grody was arrested for her murder, they'd assume he also killed us because we saw him unload her body. Not the most well-thought-out plan, but I think she was running out of nefarious ideas by then."

Mo released a long sigh. "I don't even know what to say except thank the Lord those two evil women were caught."

Maggie gave a fervent nod. "Emma was never going to get away from Pelican PD on foot. And the storm that could have drowned us doomed Bonnie's plan. The private plane she hired couldn't take off. NOLA PD picked her up and took her in." The thought of how Bonnie paid for the plane depressed Maggie. The Crozats had no idea whether her status as a murder suspect would negate the deal she had struck with Harbor Chemical. Their only hope lay with Johnnie, who was resting at the manor house but hadn't fully recovered from the booze his sister admitted to doctoring—to incapacitate, not kill him, Bonnie had insisted to the NOLA detectives who interviewed her, according to Bo.

DruCilla came into the spa. "Lovie's sleeping, so I thought I'd sneak in a facial before heading home," she said. "If you have an opening."

Mo stood up. "Your timing is perfect. I do have an opening, *and* it's the last day of our special Halloween treatment, the Supernatural All-Natural Pumpkin Peel." She held up a jar with an orange-and-black label. "And I have one last jar left if you like it enough to buy it."

Maggie left Mo to her sales magic and returned to the cottage, hoping to finish the nap she'd started at the spa. She was waylaid by her grandmother. "I know we talked about taking a shopping trip to New Orleans," Gran said. "But I was in Baton Rouge testing a few wedding cakes—"

"Again?" Maggie said, amused. "This cake testing is starting to sound like a scam. You better hope the local bakers don't get together and compare notes."

"When I was done with the tasting, I popped into Panache Boutique," Gran continued, ignoring Maggie's dig. "And I found my bridal outfit."

Gran pulled out a garment bag adorned with the Panache Boutique logo from the front closet. She unzipped the bag and removed an elegant yet simple ivory silk shantung pantsuit. The fitted jacket tied at the waist and doubled as a top. A row of pearl buttons decorated each sleeve. "It's stunning," Maggie said. "But I thought you were going with a more traditional bridal look. You know, like a big dress."

"I thought about that." She zipped up the bag and hung it back in the closet. "It's been fun playing bridezilla. But at the end of the day, this is my second rodeo. The focus should be on the stunning bride who is my granddaughter."

"Oh, Gran," Maggie said, touched. "You don't have to give up being a bridezilla for me."

"To be completely honest, I tried on a couple of those poufy Cinderella dresses, and I looked ridiculous in them. This suits me much better, no pun intended. Although I will have to cut back on the cake testing if I still want to fit into it by January."

Maggie embraced her grandmother. "I love you. And we'll still do a shopping trip to New Orleans, but for our honeymoon trips."

"Agreed. Oh, there's one more thing I want to show you." Gran disappeared into her bedroom. She returned with a large box. "Open it."

Maggie did so, and gasped. Inside, neatly folded, lay her wedding gown. "My dress," she said, choking up. "You got it back from the police."

"I did indeed retrieve it from our law enforcement friends," Gran said. She gave her smooth silver hair a self-satisfied pat. "We'll take it to the tailor tomorrow."

"Definitely." Maggie gently laid a hand on the soft satin fabric. "I'm putting it away. I don't want to start crying and drip tears on it."

"The box is rather large for your tiny room. Let's bring it over to the manor house. We can store it there."

Maggie's phone pinged. "This better not be spam. I had to block one already today." She checked it. "Oh, it's a text from Bo. He's in the kitchen. Mom saw him parking and lured him in for lunch. Dad and Johnnie are there, too."

Grand-mère helped her carry the large box to the manor house, where they placed it in the office parlor closet. Then they joined the others in the kitchen, which smelled like an intoxicating blend of onions, herbs, and broth. "Now that the Spooky Past weekends are over, I'm not trapped into making Halloween-themed meals anymore," Ninette said. She distributed chicken from a large pot into bowls, then ladled a vegetable-and-broth mixture over them. "Holy Trinity Chicken."

Her family chorused their delight. "Holy Trinity?" Johnnie said. His voice was shaky, and he hadn't regained his color. "Is it religious?"

Ninette chuckled and favored him with a warm smile. "No, cher. I named it after the holy trinity of Cajun Cooking: onions, green pepper, and celery. They're all in there, along with a lot else that's good for you. You're not getting on a plane for home until I see color back in those handsome cheeks of yours."

Johnnie's eyes misted. "Yes, ma'am."

Maggie passed out the bowls, and they dug in. "I've got some updates," Bo said. He hesitated. "Johnnie? You okay if I talk about it?"

Johnnie, who was inhaling his bowl of Holy Trinity Chicken, gave his free hand a wave. "Go ahead. If what doesn't kill you makes you stronger, I'm freaking Hercules by now."

Bo, who'd emptied his bowl at warp speed, helped himself to seconds. "When it came to landing on who tried to take out Walter Breem, there was a lot of 'She did it,' 'No, she did it' between Bonnie and Emma. But Cal took another look-see around the old man's place and found a footprint that matched a pair of Emma's shoes. Our theory is that she became nervous Breem might tell the police how he warned her about the strychnine. This would have made her the prime suspect in Susannah's death, especially if our investigation uncovered her and Doug's affair. So, she tried to remove Breem from the equation."

"Bonnie and Emma's mini killing spree divides straight down the middle," Bo continued. "We have Emma on attempted murder and accessory to murder. And one of the actors in the play witnessed Bonnie messing around with Susannah's rougarou costume, so we have her on murder. The guy was earning a little money himself dressing up to scare visitors. He didn't know the costume was Susannah's and figured Bonnie was doing the same as him."

"Do you know which one of the deadly duo killed my father? My loving sister or my Pelican bestie?"

Johnnie's attempt at sarcasm didn't disguise the hurt in his voice. Maggie felt for the fragile twentysomething. She could tell Bo did too. When he answered Johnnie's question, his voice was laced with compassion. "Neither. Ballistics matched the bullet to your father's gun, which the police found at Walter Breem's house. He's still in ICU, so we haven't been able to interview him about a motive. But he'll be charged with your dad's murder, and if he makes it out of the hospital, I can pretty much guarantee he'll go away for life."

"I guess that's something," Johnnie said. His hand trembled as he lifted a spoonful of broth to his mouth.

"Knock, knock," a voice sang out. Eula Banks appeared in the doorway. She used her cane to wave hello.

"Hey, Eula," Tug greeted her. "We're just having lunch. Come join us. It's Ninette's famous Holy Trinity Chicken."

"You're not gonna hear me say no to that." The others made room for Eula at the large trestle table, and Maggie fixed her a bowl of the chicken dish. "Thanks, darlin'," Eula said. "I dropped by because I have some interesting news for you." She addressed Johnnie. "It's about what I assume is now yours and your jailbird sister's property, since your stepmother willed it to your father."

Johnnie put down his spoon. "I'm listening."

"These people are important to our town," the mayor said, motioning to the Crozats. "Their ancestors helped found it. So, when it came to land being taken from them and their home and business being threatened, I wasn't gonna let that happen without a fight. But it turns out we won't need to go that far."

"I'm confused," Johnnie said.

"Me too," Maggie said. Her family nodded agreement.

"I did a little digging into the Pelican real estate records. Years ago, what I'm gonna call Johnnie's land was put into a trust. Then a big chunk was taken out of the trust—probably to borrow against for whatever reason."

"Maybe gambling debts," Tug surmised. "I remember my great-granddad saying how it was a problem with his side of the family."

"That part of the land—and it's a big part—never got put back in the trust. It's like the family forgot all about it, and so did the past town accessors. Susannah's family only paid taxes on the small spit of land still in the trust. Which means there's a big old tax bill dating back more'n a hundred years on the rest of the land."

"How big?" Johnnie asked. Eula named a figure that earned a gasp from the entire room. "I don't have that kind of money."

"Then I'm afraid the town of Pelican will have to put a lien on the property. Of course, that means no one else will be able to buy it."

"Including Harbor Chemical," Tug murmured. Ninette clutched his hand.

"What about the land still in the trust?" Maggie asked. "Could that be sold?"

"Yes," Eula said. "All one tiny acre of it."

Maggie managed to refrain from shouting, "Woo-hoo!" She cast a surreptitious glance at her family members and saw they were restraining themselves as well.

"I might have the tax money if I sold Dad's printing business," Johnnie mused. Maggie couldn't contain her anxiety. She bit on the knuckle of her index finger. "But I was thinking, since we're already a printing company and I'm the only one left to run it, I might expand into publishing. Of poetry and underrepresented communities."

The Crozats responded with a chorus of "Great idea!" "Go for it!" and "What a wonderful plan!"

Johnnie leaned back and gave them the side-eye. "You're just saying that because you don't want me to sell the property to the chemical company."

"Yes," Maggie admitted, then added, "But I genuinely think it's a fantastic plan. You showed me poems you wrote on our Zen walks. They're beautiful. I think you have a lot to say. And giving others a voice may be your calling."

"Thank you," Johnnie said. "It's the first thing I've ever been excited about. As soon as I feel a hundred percent better, I'm going home. To Toronto."

"You'll always be welcome back here," Ninette said. "You're family."

"Technically, I'm not. Susannah was your blood relative."

"It's not about that, cher." Ninette put one hand on her heart and the other on Johnnie's. "It's about this. Now, finish every last drop of that broth so we can get you on a plane and off to your new life."

Johnnie did as Ninette ordered, then excused himself to return to his room and rest. Ninette, her maternal instincts at work, had insisted he move from the schoolhouse into the manor house so she could nurse him back to health.

Eula lingered. "I've never had a Crozat meal that wasn't followed by dessert."

"And you won't today." Ninette took the lid off a cake plate and cut the mayor a large slice of Sugar High Pie.

"I was wondering," Tug said. "If the town is taking possession of the MacDowell property, what's the plan for it?"

"We're gonna sell it." Eula took a big forkful of pie. "To you."

"We can't afford that bill for back taxes any more than Johnnie can."

"I'm making an executive decision to forgive that. But to make it official, who's got a dollar bill?"

"Me!" Gran reached down into her shirt and pulled out a single. "I always keep a bit of mad money in my brassiere."

Bo's eyes widened. "TMI, ma'am."

Gran handed the dollar bill to Eula, who pocketed it. "I'll write up a receipt for payment when I get back to the office. I'll also have Laurent Guidry, the town assessor, draw up a new deed. This has been an eye-opener for me. I'm gonna sic Laurent on all the recent sales to that Gavin Grody character. I mean to make him sorry he ever bought a house in our fair town."

"Eula, we don't know how to thank you," Maggie said. "You saved our lives and our livelihood."

The mayor lifted a corner of her mouth. "I can think of one way. Make your mama give me the recipe for this pie."

"Done." Ninette grabbed the pie and held it out to Eula. "You can have the rest of the pie, too."

The conversation dissolved into a cacophony of happy chatter. Celebrating the unexpected turn of events almost caused them to miss the ring of the kitchen phone. "I'll get it," Maggie said. She picked up the handheld receiver. The others quieted. "Hello? . . . Yes, speaking." Her expression turned serious as she listened to the person on the other end of the call. "Me? Did he say why? . . . All right. I'll get there as fast as I can." Maggie hung up the phone. "That was Walter Breem's doctor. He regained consciousness."

"I'm glad to hear that," Tug said, "but why did the doctor call you?"

Maggie stared at the phone, trying to process what the doctor had told her. "Because Mr. Breem insisted on talking to me. And no one else."

Chapter 24

Maggie sat by Walter Breem's side, waiting for him to find the strength to share why he had summoned her. Bo stood in the doorway, arms crossed, legs akimbo. The caretaker had agreed to let Maggie's fiancé guard the room but refused to speak to anyone but her. A persistent low beep emanated from one of the machines hooked up to the old man. It was the only sound in the room.

Breem licked his lips and muttered something Maggie couldn't make out. "I'm sorry, I couldn't hear what you said." She took a cup of water off his bedside table. "Do you need a drink?" He nodded, and Maggie held the cup to his dry, parched lips. The water brought a flicker of life to his pale, watery eyes.

"I killed him," Breem said, his voice stronger. "Didn't mean to, but I did."

Maggie heard Bo shift position. She kept her voice calm. "What exactly happened?"

"I heard he was gonna sell to Harbor. Told you I know what all goes on around here." Maggie gave a slight nod but didn't say anything, instead waiting for Breem to find the strength to continue. "Chemicals. Don't need more of 'em on the River Road. Went to try and talk sense into the man. He got mad. Pulled a gun and yelled at me to get off his property. I didn't take to that and yelled back. He went to shoot, I grabbed the gun, bullet ricocheted off a rock and got him in the side."

"So you took the gun and hid it?"

"Coward's way out. I was gonna own up to it. Turn myself in. But then this." Breem winced. He motioned to the cup of water, and Maggie helped him take another rejuvenating sip. "Land. Lifeblood of a town. Preserve it or leave it to nature."

"Like with the Dupois gardens, Mr. Dupois?"

Bo shifted position again. The caretaker stared at her. Then he formed a shaky smile. "You know."

Maggie nodded. "When I was at your house that one time, you asked me to hand you a book. I did. It was in French. From what I heard of the man who claimed to be Walter Dupois, he wasn't much of a reader, if he could read at all. Walter Dupois went off to college and came back a young man. A young man who kept to himself. And I'm guessing who, like his family, wanted to shut away the world. Especially after his one love, his wife, left him." She gestured to Bo. "My fiancé is a detective. He's been looking into the real Walter Breem's past. He was an uneducated day laborer who liked to drink and party with women. And he definitely didn't speak French. But you know who did? Etienne Dupois. Fluently. In fact, he majored in it at Columbia University."

Dupois took in Maggie's revelation. "Always knew you were a smart girl. I'd be working on the land when you and your friends walked by on the way to school. Heard the way you talked. And how kids teased you for being a smarty-pants. And artsy. I could tell it hurt. I felt bad for you."

Exhausted, Dupois closed his eyes and took a few shallow, raspy breaths. Maggie took the old man's hand. It felt like bones and a thin layer of skin. "I wish I had known," she said. "We could have been friends."

"Least we are now."

"Yes." Maggie gave his hand a gentle squeeze. "We are."

Dupois closed eyes again. Each breath he took sounded harder to release. The nurse tending to him came into the room. She was followed by Father Prit, Pelican's beloved local priest, who greeted Maggie with an empathetic nod. The nurse and Father Prit examined the readings on the room's monitors. "It won't be long," the priest said. "I'll stay."

"I will, too," Maggie said.

And she sat by Etienne Dupois's bedside holding the old man's hand until he drew his last breath.

* * *

Pelican laid native son Etienne Dupois to rest on a day darkened by lowering gray and black clouds. With the real Walter Breem's body discreetly reinterred in a nearby cemetery, Etienne Dupois was placed next to the memorial tomb for the fan dancer who'd broken his heart and hastened his descent into living as a recluse. Gran theorized, "Knowing what we do of the Dupois history, I believe that was their natural inclination. It never would have occurred to any of them, including Etienne, that the problem lay within the family and not with the world around them. A strain of depression and pos-sible mental illness passed from one generation to the next."

After a somber ceremony, the Crozats hosted a luncheon for the attendees in the tent housed on the B and B grounds. Being that this was Pelican, word quickly spread, and the lun-cheon transformed into a party, albeit a low-key one. Long folding tables sagged under the weight of casserole dishes and pie plates. Local musicians took to the tent's stage to perform, sticking to ballads like "Jolie Blon."

"How soon before they break into dance songs?" Maggie said in a wry tone to Bo. She, her family, and a few friends had established a bulwark on the manor house veranda, where they were hydrating themselves with pitchers of Pimm's Cups, courtesy of Tug.

"An hour, maybe two," Bo guessed. He pointed to a man dunning a frottoir, the washboard instrument favored by zydeco musicians. "Or any minute. Tuneece Labadie is already in position."

Maggie's cell rang. "Great, another spam call. Ignoring." She pressed the red button to end the call.

"I wonder how Etienne would have felt about all this," Ninette said, surveying the growing crowd. "I'm not sure he would have liked it."

"Probably not," Maggie said. "He was a loner by nature."

"It's still hard to believe no one figured out the switch between him and the real Walter Breem until now," Ione said.

"On the surface maybe, but when you drill down, not really," Maggie said. "The Dupois family kept to themselves. They almost lived like it was still the nineteenth century.

Etienne was the only child and his mother homeschooled him."

"He and I were about the same age, and I can't say I ever laid eyes on him," Grand-mère said.

"Does anyone know what's gonna happen to that old house of his and all his property?" Ione asked. "Not that I'd want it. Lord knows what's going on in that old wreck of a place."

"The caretaker cottage where he lived is in good shape on the inside," Maggie said. "That's one of the reasons I got suspicious about whether or not Walter Breem was for real. The manor house probably needs a ton of work."

"It would be a shame to see it rot away," Tug said. "Pelican needs all the housing it can get."

"At least Eula shut down that Gavin Grody," said Mo, who was taking a break from her busy spa schedule. "No more Rent My Digs and fake rougarous."

"What a relief that is," Ninette said. "Our guests who were looking for paranormal and supernatural activity may have enjoyed those sightings, but no one else did."

"I heard he's buying up property in Ville Blanc now," Lee said, "and they are *not* happy about it."

"Speaking of not happy in Ville Blanc," Bo said, a smug gleam in his eye, "the one friend I got at Ville Blanc PD told me Zeke Griffith got reamed by his superiors for missing pretty much every clue to the real killers because he was so focused on pinning the crimes on y'all."

"Why?" Tug wondered. "What did we ever do to him?"

"It's not about us but what we represent to him," Maggie said. "It's a class thing. He called me an 'upper-cruster.' He's got a chip on his shoulder about people with a lineage like ours thinking we're better than everyone else."

Tug barked a laugh. "Seriously? If I'd known that, I would've shown him the bill I got for roof repair after the last big storm. Too bad our fancy-shmancy 'lineage' can't pay it off."

Tuneece Labadie climbed onto the stage, and the band transitioned into an up-tempo zydeco tune. The dance floor quickly filled up. "So much for the respectful slow songs," Bo said with a grin.

"They're good." Maggie turned to her grandmother. "If Gaynell and the Gator Girls aren't back from their tour, we should hire them for our wedding."

"Noted," Gran said. "Lee and I have made a few other decisions that I hope you'll sign off on. We thought we could have the meal catered by JJ and Junie's, get the cake from Fais Dough Dough, and give truffles from Bon Bon Sweets as favors."

Maggie shook her head, amused. "After running all those wedding expo vendors through hoops, you're going with what I suggested in the first place."

"Those vendors won't suffer. I gave my list of the ones I liked to Sandy, now that she and Rufus will be planning a wedding."

"And Kaity helped me write up nice reviews of the places we visited and put them on the Internet," Lee added. "Thank goodness I got a great-granddaughter who does all that posting stuff."

"I'll be gifting you ladies with a special Here Comes the Beauty package for your big day," Mo said to Maggie and

Gran. "You can build your bachelorette party around it." She pointed first at Bo and then Lee. "I'm also offering Man Up Massages. Ain't no reason why every bachelor party has to end up at a strip club."

Gran's phone sounded an alert. She checked it. "The B and B just got a wonderful reservation for next weekend. Listen to this—'I read a review posted by the Paranormals and saw the video. Can't wait to check out Crozat B and B for myself and for my TV show, *Great Weekend Getaways*. Richard Seideman, Executive Producer.'"

This news was met with high-fives and *woo-hoo!*s from the group. "*Great Weekend Getaways*?" Mo said, thrilled. "That's huge! It's one of Travel TV's most popular shows. I love it."

"It'll be great for business," Tug said, beaming.

"It's fantastic," Maggie said. "But what review? And what video?"

"Hold on," Gran said, head bent over her cell phone. "I'm doing a search. Ah, found the review: 'Our visit exceeded expectations. The Crozat family does everything possible to make their guests' stays a wonderful weekend they'll never forget. If you're lucky, you might even run across a rougarou in the woods."

"That has to be from Cindy," Maggie said, amused.

"It is. But it's signed Cindy and the Paranormals, so she's speaking for all of them. Oh, and here's the video. It's from someone else. Look."

Gran held up her phone, and the others crowded around it. DruCilla appeared on the screen with Lovie on her shoulder.

"Lovie, tell people what you thought about our visit to Crozat B and B."

"Acck!" Lovie squawked. "Lovie loooooved it! Acck!"

"Awesome," Maggie said. "Let's hear it for Crozat's favorite bird."

The others laughed and cheered. They clinked their glasses together, then fell into relaxed chatter. Maggie noticed a middle-aged man dressed in what looked like a Quentin MacIlhoney–pricey suit wandering around the Crozat grounds. He carried a briefcase that also looked expensive. "Does anyone know who that is? I saw him at the funeral. He looks lost." She waved to him and called, "Hello. Can we help you?"

"Yes," the man said, relieved. He clambered up the manor house steps. "I'm looking for Magnolia Marie Crozat."

"That's me," she said, surprised.

"Finally. I tried calling you from two different numbers, but you hung up and blocked both of them."

"I'm sorry. I thought you were a robocall. But you are . . ." she prompted him.

"F. Jackson Stoddard. Jack for short." The man extended his hand, and a mystified Maggie shook it. "I'm the late Etienne Dupois's lawyer. Is there somewhere private we can talk?"

* * *

"Everything?" Maggie said, stunned. "He left everything to me?" She and her family had retreated to the B and B's parlor office, where F. Jackson Stoddard informed her that she was Etienne Dupois's sole heir. "I barely knew him."

"You knew him as well as anybody," Stoddard said.

"The first time I talked to him was, what?" She looked to her family and Bo for help, but they also appeared to be in shock. "Two, maybe three weeks ago?"

"You gave him aid after he was attacked by a Gavin Grody. Mr. Dubois filed suit against him, by the way, and it's pending. After you helped Mr. Dubois out, he called me and said he wanted to draw up a will. He'd never had one before. He found me in a phone book. Can you believe that? In this day and age."

"He never did want much to do with the modern world," Gran said.

The lawyer pulled a file out of his briefcase. "Here's a copy of the will. I recommend that you read it, make notes of any questions you have, and then set up an appointment with me to finalize things. My card is attached to the will. The estate is substantial. But you'll have to decide what to do with that white elephant of a manor house, as well as that abandoned lot of a garden." He glanced at his high-end watch. "I best be going. I'm having dinner with an old friend from law school. Y'all know Quentin MacIlhoney?"

"We do," Tug said.

"He wants to talk to me about joining his practice. Says the murder rate around here could give New Orleans a run for her money. Hard to believe. Seems like a pretty sleepy place. Anyway . . ." He again extended his hand to Maggie. "I look forward to hearing from you."

Stoddard departed. No one spoke. Then Maggie said, "Did that just happen?"

"It did." Tug held up the will, which he'd been perusing. "This is real. And the lawyer wasn't kidding. It is substantial."

He handed the document to Maggie. "Will you look at it with me?" she asked Bo.

"Of course."

"This is all . . . I don't know what it is." Ninette clutched her head in her hands. "Tug, honey, would you mind mixing up another pitcher of Pimm's Cups? I could use one. Or many."

"I was thinking the same thing," her husband responded. "I'll get us fresh glasses."

Tug left for the veranda and Ninette headed to the kitchen. Maggie and Bo sat down at the parlor's antique desk and thumbed through the will. Gran peered over her granddaughter's shoulder. "My oh my. I guess our wedding is on you. I'm joking, of course."

"No joke, it is. And the roof repair, and our honeymoons, and . . . and . . . and . . ."

Bo put a hand on Maggie's shoulder. "Whoa, chère. It's okay. You can slow down. Plenty of time to take a hard look at this and figure out the future. Right now, forget about the money and everything else. You made a difference in a lonely man's life. Take a minute to let that sink in."

"Thank you." Maggie opened the desk's top drawer and placed the will in it. She closed the drawer, then turned to Bo. "I could use a hug."

"I can give you way more than that."

Bo took Maggie in his arms. Gran headed for the door. "As a cartoon character once said, 'Exit, stage left.' I have some calls to make. I need to confab with Lia and Kyle about the flavors of our wedding cake. I think a tasting might be in order."

* * *

It was dark when the funeral luncheon–turned–party finally wound down. Maggie walked Bo to his SUV. "I've been thinking about the Dupois manor house. I read an article on something called co-living. Where people have separate living quarters but share common areas like a kitchen and rec room. Maybe I could hire Chret Bertrand and his crew to fix up the house for that kind of arrangement." Chret was her friend Gaynell's boyfriend and an ex-Marine who now ran a successful construction business staffed solely with fellow veterans. "It would give people who feel like they're being priced out of Pelican a chance to stay here."

"Magnolia Crozat, landlady," Bo said, laughing.

She wrinkled her nose. "I hadn't thought about it that way."

"It's a fantastic idea," he said, kissing her forehead. "Something to talk about when the time is right. But we both need some rest after the last few days. The last few *weeks*."

He pulled Maggie into his arms, and they shared an embrace. Bo reluctantly let go. He climbed into his car and took off for home. Rather than tuck herself in for the night, however, Maggie pulled out her car keys. She got in the Falcon, turned on the engine, and backed out of the parking area.

* * *

Maggie stood in front of Etienne Dupois's tomb. The cemetery was silent but peaceful. Any sense of danger around the Dupois estate had dissipated. The stillness brought to mind a quote from her favorite novel, *Wuthering Heights*: "I lingered round them, under that benign sky; watched the moths fluttering among the heath, and hare-bells; listened to the soft wind breathing through the grass; and wondered how anyone could ever imagine unquiet slumbers, for the sleepers in that quiet earth."

Maggie dropped to her knees. She crossed herself and recited the Lord's Prayer, then placed a hand on the tomb. "*Bonjour*, Etienne. I've thought a lot about what you said to me about the land before you died. Preserve it or leave it to nature. I wanted to let you know that I will preserve your home. But I will let nature reclaim the Dupois gardens. You made me the custodian of your family's heritage, and I will do everything in my power to live up to that honor."

She rose and returned to her car. Maggie drove toward home but stopped across the River Road from Crozat B and B and got out of the car. She hiked up the levee, a full moon and clear night sky lighting her way. At the top, she perched on a log left over from the Crozat Christmas Eve bonfires on the levee and contemplated how much her life had changed in the year plus since she'd retreated to her family's ancestral home in failure mode, thanks to a disastrous relationship and career crisis. Now she had friends. A fiancé. A future. There had been a time when Maggie couldn't imagine living out her life in Pelican. Now she couldn't imagine leaving it.

She gazed at the river below, winding its lazy way past New Orleans to the Gulf of Mexico. Behind her lay the quaint streets of her hometown. Locals might joke that their small village was a Cajun Brigadoon. But unlike Brigadoon, Pelican, magical as it might be, would never disappear into the mists of time. One generation would beget another for time immemorial.

"Yes, we Peli-can." Maggie murmured the town's proud slogan to the wind. "Now and forever."

Recipes

Holy Trinity Chicken

Ingredients

1 whole chicken
Salt and freshly ground pepper to taste
1 tbsp butter
1 onion, chopped
½ green pepper, chopped
2 stalks celery, chopped
3 cups chicken broth mixed with 1 cup water
½ tsp salt
1 tsp minced garlic
1 tsp Creole or Cajun seasoning
2 to 3 carrots, cut into ¼-inch rounds
1 cup frozen peas
4 cups egg noodles

Instructions

1. Remove giblets from chicken and discard. Rinse the chicken well, removing excess fat. Sprinkle with salt and pepper inside and out.

2. In a large, heavy pot (a Dutch oven or cast-iron pot is ideal) melt the butter and sauté the onion, pepper, and celery until wilted. Add the broth and water, ½ tsp salt, garlic, and seasoning. Stir to blend. Add the chicken. Bring to a boil, reduce heat to a simmer, cover, and simmer on low heat for about twenty minutes.

3. Turn the chicken over very carefully and add the carrots and peas to the pot. Cover and simmer for thirty minutes. Turn the chicken over again, increase heat to boiling, and add the noodles, pressing them into the water. Reduce heat again and simmer until the noodles are al dente, about ten minutes. Cut a slice of chicken from the breast to make sure it's cooked through, then remove the pot from the heat. To serve, cut the chicken into pieces, distribute into bowls, then ladle the broth, noodles, and vegetables over each bowl.

Serves 6.

Sugar High Pie

Sometimes one recipe begets another. I was making the Pecan Coconut Pie Bars from the recipe in *A Cajun Christmas Killing*, my fourth Cajun Country Mystery, when inspiration struck. What if I took a frozen pie crust, made the pecan pie base, and threw in a bunch of stuff along with the pecans? Thus Sugar High Pie was born.

The name comes from the fact that in addition to that basic pecan base, the ingredients for this dessert include dark chocolate, milk chocolate, coconut, and raisins. When you think about it, it's like a candy bar inside a pie.

While you're welcome to follow the recipe below and enjoy the ensuing deliciousness, feel free to experiment. Add a half cup of chopped dates or dried cherries. Or both. Just make sure you share the recipe with all of us!

Ingredients

1 unbaked 8- or 9-inch frozen pie crust
1 cup brown sugar
6 tbsp light butter
1 whole egg
3 egg whites
2 tbsp bourbon

½ tsp salt
½ cup light corn syrup
½ cup pecan pieces
½ cup milk chocolate bits
½ cup dark chocolate bits
½ cup golden raisins
½ cup shredded coconut

Instructions

1. Preheat oven to 375 degrees.

2. Cream brown sugar and butter until well blended. Beat in egg and egg whites one at a time. Stir in bourbon, salt, and corn syrup.

3. Add pecans, chocolate, raisins, and coconut one ingredient at a time. Stir to blend well.

4. Pour mixture into pie crust. Bake for 35 to 45 minutes until middle sets or a knife inserted in the pie comes out clean.

Serves 6–8.

Ghoulish Cajun Goulash

Loaded with pasta and cheese, this dish is something the whole family will love—especially the kids.

Ingredients

2 cups elbow macaroni

1 tbsp olive oil

1½ pounds ground beef or ground turkey

1 small white onion, chopped

1 small green bell pepper, seeded, chopped

¼ cup chopped celery

3 garlic cloves, diced

¼ cup beef, chicken, or turkey broth

1 (14.5-ounce) can tomato sauce

1 (14.5-ounce) can diced tomatoes (I found a brand that includes onions, peppers, and celery—the Cajun Holy Trinity! But that was a fluke. Regular diced tomatoes are fine.)

1 tbsp Cajun seasoning

1 tsp Italian seasoning

½ tsp paprika

Salt and pepper to taste (if your Cajun seasoning includes salt, go easy on it here)

1 cup cheddar cheese, shredded

1 cup mozzarella cheese, shredded
¼ cup parsley, chopped
Tabasco sauce to taste

Instructions

1. Cook elbow macaroni according to directions on package. Drain. Set aside.

2. In a large cast-iron or Dutch oven over medium heat, cook olive oil, beef or turkey, onion, pepper, celery, and garlic for 5 to 6 minutes until beef or turkey is browned and vegetables are softened. Add broth, tomato sauce, diced tomatoes, Cajun seasoning, Italian seasoning, paprika, salt, and pepper. Bring the mixture to a boil, then mix in cooked pasta. Cover and reduce to a simmer for 8 to 10 minutes.

3. Just before serving, add the mozzarella and cheddar cheeses to the pot, stirring for 2 to 3 minutes until cheese is melted. Garnish each serving with parsley. Serve immediately, with Tabasco sauce on the side for anyone who wants to add a little heat to their meal.

Serves 8.

Crawtatoes

Crawtatoes can be served as a fun, filling appetizer or as a side dish to a meal. Since crawfish are seasonal, you can easily substitute shrimp for this recipe and make Shrimptatoes instead.

Ingredients

8 cooked small red potatoes, cut in half and trimmed on the bottom so they sit flat

2 cups cooked, chopped crawfish or shrimp

½ cup light mayonnaise

1 tbsp Creole or stone-ground mustard

1 tsp Creole or Cajun seasoning

1 minced garlic clove

¼ cup sweet relish, plus more for garnish

Instructions

1. In a medium bowl, mix the mayonnaise, mustard, seasoning, garlic, and relish together. Add the crawfish or shrimp and stir well to combine. Chill for an hour or more.

2. Gently spoon out a hole in each potato so each one becomes a small bowl. Fill the holes with a small spoonful of the seafood mixture. Top with a dab of sweet relish. Serve immediately.

Makes 16 Crawtatoes.

Cajun Pecan Cookie Fingers

These cookies are similar in texture to Pecan Sandies. They're tasty and not super sweet. Shape them like fingers. You can even skip rolling them in powdered sugar and use ready-made frosting to create "fingernails" by frosting one tip of each cookie.

Ingredients

2¾ cups flour
6 tbsp powdered sugar
¼ tsp salt
1 cup softened butter
4 tsp vanilla
1 tbsp ice water
1 cup finely chopped pecans
Extra powdered sugar in which to roll the cookies

Instructions

1. Preheat the oven to 350 degrees.

2. Combine flour, sugar, and salt in a large mixing bowl. Mix together to blend. Add the other ingredients and work the dough together with your hands. (Yes, your hands. It's like you're making pie crust dough.)

3. Chill the dough for about an hour, unless you feel you can work with it without chilling.

4. Shape the dough into finger-length strips, almost like small cigars. Place on ungreased cookie sheets and bake for about 15 minutes.

5. Remove them from the oven and roll in powdered sugar while they're still hot. They're delicate, so be gentle. And be careful not to burn yourself. Let the cookies cool, then roll them in powdered sugar again.

Yields 24–36, depending on the size of the cookies.

The recipe for jambalaya appears in *Body on the Bayou* as JJ's Jambalaya.

The recipe for Shrimp Remoulade appears in *A Cajun Christmas Killing*.

The recipe for Bourbon Pecan Bread Pudding appears in *Plantation Shudders*.

The recipe for Bananas Foster Coffee Cake appears in *Body on the Bayou*.

The recipe for Spicy Cajun Sugar Cookies appears in *A Cajun Christmas Killing*.

The recipe for gumbo appears in *Mardi Gras Murder*.

Lagniappe

The Dupois plantation and garden is inspired by a massive plantation that once dominated Louisiana's Great River Road, an estate so grand it was nicknamed Le Petite Versailles. Built by Francoise-Gabriel "Valcour" Aime, who was considered the wealthiest man in the South during the early to mid 1800s—and earned himself the nickname "the Louis XIV of Louisiana"—the plantation's twenty-acre garden was particularly legendary, with flora imported from around the world. Exotic fish floated in an artificial lake. Violets covered a manmade hill that featured a Chinese pagoda. Bridges spanned a bucolic stream. Aime also built the iconic Louisiana plantation, Oak Alley, and eventually purchased Felicity and St. Joseph plantations for his daughters.

Aime had one son, Gabriel, who died of yellow fever at the age of twenty-eight. Aime never recovered from the loss, which was exacerbated by the death of his beloved wife Joséphine and his daughter Felicie within the following two years. He became a virtual recluse, passing away in 1867. The once palatial grounds of the plantation fell into disrepair. A fire destroyed the manor house in 1920, and nature eventually reclaimed the garden. All that remains of the legendary place is a marker on the River Road and the family's deteriorating tomb. The former gardens are now private property, but Mary Ann Sternberg, author of the quintessential guidebook *Along the River Road*, details a fascinating tour she got to take of them in another wonderful book, *River Road Rambler*.

* * *

One of my favorite events to attend as an author is the Louisiana Book Festival. A couple of years ago, I decided to stop at St. Joseph Plantation after my festival panel and take its Creole Mourning Tour. The tour, presented as living history with actors playing the roles of doctors, priests, and mourning family members, was a wonderful experience. I learned so much that I was able to incorporate into *Murder in the Bayou Boneyard*. I wrote a blog post about it that I'm thrilled to see is now featured on the St. Joseph website. You can find it, along with photos I took, at https://www.stjosephplantation.com/2017/11/mourning-tour-review.

* * *

The word *rougarou* derives from the French word *loup-garou*. *Loup* is French for *wolf*, while *garou* means *man who transforms into an animal*. The English equivalent for both words is *werewolf*.

The legend of the rougarou dates back to the first Cajun settlers. Like the werewolf, the Cajun monster is described as having a human body with a wolf's head. As this is a Louisiana beast, a vampire element was eventually added to the legend.

A rougarou is under a spell for one hundred and one days, after which it can transfer the curse by drawing a human's blood. Rougarous were rumored to prowl the swamps and woods of Acadia and the greater New Orleans area.

Cajun parents used the beast as a threat, as in, "You'd better behave or the rougarou will get you." Legend also had it that rougarous would hunt down and kill Catholics who weren't following the rules of Lent.

Pop culture has jumped on the rougarou bandwagon. New Orleans's Audubon Zoo has a rougarou exhibit, complete with a scary statue of the feared creature. There's a summer collegiate baseball team named the Baton Rouge Rougarou. And Houma, Louisiana, hosts a yearly Rougarou Fest, featuring a parade, costume contests, live music, and family events. Only in Louisiana can a fearsome mythical beast generate a weekend of nonstop partying!

Acknowledgments

A shout-out as always to my indefatigable agent, Doug Grad, and to the wonderful team at Crooked Lane Books, including Matt Martz, Ashley Di Dio, Chelsey Emmelhainz, Melissa Rechter, and Jenny Chen. I must give a special thank-you to my extraordinarily gifted cover artist, Stephen Gardner, for bringing my cover dreams to life. Eternal gratitude to my fellow chicks at chicksonthecase.com: Lisa Q. Mathews, Kellye Garrett, Mariella Krause, Vickie Fee, Cynthia Kuhn, Leslie Karst, Kathleen Valenti, and Becky Clark. Ladies, I am nothing without your priceless feedback.

Nancy Cole Silverman, our weekly walks have been lifesavers. West Donas Walkers Lisa Libatique, Kelly Goode, Kathy Wood, and Nancy McIlvaney, same goes for our Power Walks! Super thanks to my Louisiana krewe: Jan Gilbert and Kevin McCaffrey, Charlotte Allen, Gaynell Bourgeois Moore, Laurie Smith Becker, Shawn Holahan, Madeline Hedgepeth Feldman, and Jonathan and Debra Jo Burnette. More thanks to Maria Cordero and Joe Coates for their input and advice regarding Louisiana real estate deals and trusts. And a shout-out to my Facebook support team, the Gator Gals, otherwise known as the Dirty (Rice) Dozen. Gals, thanks so much for sharing what you respond to in Halloween-themed mysteries.

Bob and Mary Morrin, thank you for your generosity at the Malice Domestic Convention, and I hope you enjoy being in print.

I'm blessed to belong to Sisters in Crime and Mystery Writers of America, specifically the chapters SinCLA and SoCalMWA. Without the Guppies, a SinC subgroup, I never would have gotten anywhere in the mystery world. A million fin flaps to all of you! Thanks to all the bloggers who let me blather, and friends who've supported me throughout this fabulous journey—I'm talking to you, June Stoddard, Laurie Graff, Nancy Adler, Denise and Stacy Smithers, Karen Fried, Von Rae Wood, Kim Rose, dearest cousin Marie Tenaglia Olasov, and everyone I forgot to name! And infinite thanks to my mom, my bros David and Tony, and especially my husband Jerry and daughter Eliza.

Finally, you'll see the executive producer of *Great Weekend Getaways* is named Richard Seideman. The producer is named after my late father, a fantastic writer in his own right. Dad was a classic Mad Man, the veteran of many well-known Madison Avenue ad agencies. He lived for the written word, and it's no accident that all three of his children became writers.

How I wish Dad had lived to see me published—and to help me with advertising and promoting my books! I think of him all the time, and while I'll always miss him, he'll live in my heart forever.